BRAVE TAILS

—

THE MOON'S PROPHECY

ALSO BY JONATHAN SPARROW

———

Invasion of thē Boars (forthcoming)

BRAVE TAILS

—

THE MOON'S PROPHECY

Jonathan Sparrow

WINGS

BRAVE TAILS: THE MOON'S PROPHECY

Wings
www.wings-books.com

ISBN: 978-1-60701-100-2

For our animal friends,
our pets,
who magnify our humanity
by loving us beyond belief.

Riversplash Mountain

by Jonathan Sparrow

Bracken Knoll

Cloud Forest

Elsewhere Woods

The Holt

The Mere

True friends are rare.

—Aesop

"The Mouse and the Hedgehog"

The Mere

At the bottom of Riversplash Mountain, where the River Rill dumps its annual load of silt, the Mere sprawls: an extensive marsh of quicksand, bulrush bogs, and gloomy groves of shadows. Here dwell the ruder lives of this crater mountain—the mud dwellers and the scavengers existing in a murk of biting flies and mosquitoes. Here, in this ooze at the underside of the world, our story crawls forth . . .

CHAPTER ONE

Invaders

Through brown sunlight wrinkled with marsh gas, boars arrived. A dozen hulking shapes silently crossed the ghostly swamp. Malign and barbarous in spiky armor and horned helmets, they bore lances black with dried blood of recent conquests.

At their lead crept the boar lord, Griml. He was not the largest of the boars, and his tusks were not the most formidable or the sharpest. In fact, one tusk—his right—had long ago broken and lost its tip. Yet, the lumps of scar tissue around his tiny eyes and across his blunt snout attested to his ferocity. The boar lord alone wore bear claws and fangs on his helmet.

Griml paused, and the dozen following boars stopped noiselessly. They stood as unmoving and voiceless as boulders.

Within the scrub trees ahead of the invaders, furtive shadows drifted. Moments later a boar camouflaged in ivy and wearing reed sandals and a head wrap of muddy straw appeared.

"Kungu!" Griml huffed crossly. "Thee was supposed to scout ahead an' meet us at the mountain spur."

"M'lord." Kungu doffed his straw hat and pressed his snout into the bog. He muttered some praise of the boar lord that bubbled

13

incoherently in the muck before he raised his clotted nose. "As thee commanded, I done. Far as the spur, I scouted. But I hurry back to warn thee. In this swamp, there be crofters—sneaky peasant farmers, them. On the high slopes, there be paddies and fields. This mountain—it be a more developed land than we had hoped."

"Bah!" Griml turned his helmeted head slowly, scanning the shadows in the chaos of congested trees and snarled grass. "Ne'er mind. No space for a boar to breathe in this foul quag. We must go up. We must go up from the mud to the sweet roots."

"To the sweet roots!" the waiting boars muttered loudly in agreement.

"Hush!" Griml snapped. His long mouth turned down, distressed. "It ain't right, I tell thee. It ain't right that we lords of the mountains suffer bitin' flies an' stinkin' rot here at the bottom o' the world. But it be worse for us if we be found here wit'out our legions."

"We shoulda brung our legions," a gruff voice spoke up. The largest of the boars budged forward. He stood as massive as a bull, bristles as stiff as quills, tusks as long as sabers, thrusting forth from his massive head. "We coulda marched right up to the sweet roots. We'd be munchin' 'em now if we'd brung the legions."

"Quiet, Ull." Griml faced the giant boar, turning softly—and soft his voice in the brown, still air: "Mountain farmers be tough an' wily. They be fightin' for their very lives, aye? We'd not be the first boar horde crushed marchin' uphill 'gainst war machines rainin' rocks an' spears down on us. Me legions won't suffer that shame. No, Ull. It be good we left 'em behind. None o' ours will be killt an' skinned by these clod busters. Our hides, our tusks—it ain't proper they be cut from us for trophy."

The waiting boars growled agreement.

Ull shifted his lumbering weight uncomfortably as he considered this, and the broad muscles that packed his shoulders twitched under a green cloud of flies. "I don't like the bitin' bugs."

"Aye, but there be no other way, Ull. It were bad to come through the muck an' the bitin' bugs. But on the high rocky pass, them farmers woulda knowed we was about. Now we got the surprise on 'em, Ull. Wit' our clever scout Kungu guidin' us, we be sure to take the measure o' these dirt farmers an' their defenses 'fore they even knowed we be here. And when we take their measure, our legions take this mountain. An' we do our part wit'out losin' any o' our hides. Do thee understand, Ull? Not one—I tell thee, mighty Ull— not one o' ours will die takin' the measure o' this mountain. That be Griml's oath." The boar lord turned back to Kungu. "Tell us wut thee seed."

"As we guessed, m'lord, there be one way and one way only to reach this mountain—along the stony gorge brung us here to this muck." Kungu lifted his muddy head toward the heights of the swamp forest as if his tiny eyes could penetrate the obscuring canopy of the Mere and behold once more the mountain's regal slopes. "Across the high pass where all on this mountain will see 'em, our legions be forced to march. A narrow pass it be, m'lord, as thee learned, having belly-crawled its gutters getting here. To hide or retreat, there be no place for that. If'n the clod busters got war machines, many boars will die."

"You seen war machines?" Ull growled with a deep, angry fear. "You seen tar cauldrons? I don't like boilin' tar."

"Keep thy voice down, Ull." Once more Griml cast a tight look around him. "By the Holy Sow, thee be a turrible loud boar." The warlord twitched the stiff bristles along his jowl to drive off pestering flies. "We ain't crawled this far through that rocky pass an' now this stinkin' bog to be found out an' butchered in the mud. We must take high ground."

"High ground . . . high ground . . . " the squad of boar warriors murmured.

"Them machines could be hidden," Ull whispered. "Big cauldrons o' boilin' tar covered up with ivy, just like you, Kungu."

"I know not," Kungu admitted and turned around, his ivy-draped, mud-slathered body returning the way he had arrived. "Come. I took a prisoner. Perhaps he can tell us."

CHAPTER TWO

An Old Citizen of the Mere

Griml signed for his troops to wait as he and Ull followed Kungu. They waded quietly through thick mire, sinking up to their hocks in silty water. Under a moss-draped cypress, they paused. Rising above marsh reeds and curling ferns, a tall, slim cypress knee held a box turtle, scaly limbs swimming in midair.

The bald, hook-nosed head bobbed with exertion. "Hey-dee!" the terrapin called to the boars. "Hey-dee thar, you big fellas. Get me down off a here."

Griml glared at the loud echoes resounding from the hollows of the swamp.

"Shut up, ol' turkle," Kungu croaked, "or a rock I take to yore shell."

"I didn't do nothin'," the terrapin griped. "You ain't got no cause to put me up here."

Out of the smoky water, Ull lifted a rock as big as a mallet. "Let me squash him."

Griml stopped the giant with a frown. He turned to the captive. "Thee—wut be thy name?"

"Everybody 'round these parts knows me," the box turtle

replied indignantly. "But you boys ain't from 'round here, are ye now?"

Griml snatched the rock from Ull's grasp, sloshed up to the terrapin and rapped his shell so hard the impact sounded like a gunshot. "Thy name, turkle."

The terrapin grimaced in agony. "My name don't matter none. You got me up here for no good. And I reckon ye aim to kill me no matter what all I say. Ain't that right, boys?"

"There be different kinds o' killin', turkle." Griml firmly tapped the rock against the terrapin's shell. "I makes thee an offer. Thee be old an' knows well this land. Tell me true wut I ask, an' I be lettin' thee go."

"That right?" The turtle's dark, wet eyes blinked with sad surmise. "What all ye want to know?"

"Wut be the name o' this land?"

"You fellas must've come a far stretch not to know this here is Riversplash Mountain." He pulled his round head halfway into his shell. "And from the looks of them jim-dandy helmets and spears, you all ain't here to trade for crops."

"Riversplash—" Griml chewed the name contemplatively. From afar, Riversplash had glistened with waterfalls and rainbows. A caldera crowned the large mountain—a giant bowl of snow and ice that melted in the warm season and overflowed into tumultuous cascades and shining streams. As the boars had marched toward it, the high cliffs glowed green. The vision of those fertile crannies and their promise of succulent roots had sustained them on their toilsome trek.

"Riversplash," Griml repeated dreamily. "Aye, that be meet."

"Where be the tar cauldrons?" Ull moaned apprehensively.

The terrapin peeked from his shell. "The what?"

"Be there war machines on Riversplash Mountain?" Griml inquired. "Who be defendin' the farms?"

"I'd be proud to direct you boys out of this danky old swamp," the box turtle replied. "But that's about all the help you'll be gettin' off me. I'm jest an old citizen of the Mere. I don't know nothin' 'bout no war machines."

"By the Sow's Twelve Swollen Teats, thee will tell us!" Griml whacked the rock hard against the terrapin's shell, and the captive's leathery head and webbed claws shot straight out.

"Hey-dee!" The box turtle's limbs flurried frantically and then went limp. "Bust my shell, bust my hade, I cain't tell ye what I don't know."

Griml raised the large rock high and brought it down with all his might. He missed the turtle by an inch, and the force of the blow spouted water into the sunny air. "I'll have thy turkle guts for suspenders!" the boar lord gruffly promised. "But first, thee be dyin' a slow death." He showed his back to the terrapin. "Leave him."

"Wait up now!" the turtle called as the three boars retreated into umber shadows. "Hey-dee, you big pigs! Don't be leavin' me here. Hey! Come back! Ain't right you killin' me for what I don't know. Hey-dee!"

Griml ignored him. "Bring me the mouse maiden."

Kungu slipped silently into the bracken while Ull glanced anxiously back toward the whining terrapin. "Let me squash him."

"No. His cries be our bait. If'n his friends come, we take 'em an' beat 'em. Someone be tellin' us wut we needs to know. Aye? An' if not, then—ah!" His wee eyes crinkled merrily at the sight of Kungu pushing through the reeds with a young female mouse tossed across his shoulder. "If we get no help from the beasts of this stinkin' bog, then we be trustin' our little spy."

CHAPTER THREE

The Mouse Maiden

Kungu lowered the mouse maiden to the ground and yanked the filthy rag blindfolding her. White fur, pink nose, and large blue eyes bright with fear trembled. She held herself erect, though muddy and grass-stained, a proud but shaken figure in a torn dress of green silk.

"Olweena, girl,"—Griml showed the jagged teeth of his smile—"we be needin' thy help now, girl. Thee be prepared to aid us? Aye? Will thee do our biddin' as thee has sworn?"

Olweena stared at the three large boars in their battle gear, and her head spun dizzily. "I—I'm . . . " She swayed where she stood.

Griml scowled at Kungu. "Thee be feedin' an' tendin' our Olweena proper?"

"M'lord, aye!" Kungu grabbed the mouse maiden by the collar and jerked her upright. "Fed an' watered proper."

Olweena steadied herself. "I have been bound these many days . . . blindfolded and forcibly marched . . . "

"Olweena, girl, we must move swift an' silent for to make good our usefulness. 'Tis naught to distress thee." Griml delicately brushed a black trotter against her nose whiskers, his sharp-toothed smile widening. "Thee be our ally—"

"Taken by force."

"Conscripted, aye—that be the nature o' the Boar March. We be takin' wut we need as we go. Even so, thee be our ally—an ally wut agreed to do our biddin'. Nigh time for thee to be keepin' thy word."

Olweena's large pink ears cupped from the air the pitiful cries of the trapped terrapin. "Is that another of your allies, Lord Griml?"

"Talk no sass to our lord!" Kungu snarled and hitched the mouse maiden by her collar so that she stood on the tips of her scuffed brogans, muddy work boots that rubbed her feet sore.

"Easy, Kungu. Olweena be an ally to the boars an' be worthy of our care." Griml pointed with his broken tusk toward the moans of the box turtle. "Wut misery thee hears gives out from one who would not help. But that be no concern for thee. Thee be strong ally to we boars. Aye?"

"My mother—my father—" The mouse maiden's large eyes searched among the scars of the boar lord's long face, probing for the truth. "My parents, they—"

"They be well, Olweena," Griml assured her even as a flick of his tail made an obscene gesture that only the boars noticed and understood. "With thy service to the boars completed, thee shall be reunited with thy beloved ma an' da. That be our plight, aye?"

"Let me see them," Olweena beseeched. "Please, let me know they are all right."

"They be mountains away, girl, back at Blossom Vale."

"Your hordes devoured Blossom Vale," Olweena said, a crease of despair in her voice. "You left our realm a muddy wasteland."

"That be the way o' the March." Griml shared with Kungu and Ull another obscene flick of his tail. "We take wut we need. An' we leave the land *refreshed!* Aye, retrieved from every manner o' congestion. No more walls, fences, roads, to get in thy way. The

March mends all plowed-asunder fields an' each itty garden pockin' this mortal world's wild beauty."

"And how shall my parents and the creatures on Blossom Vale live without their crops?" Olweena's fright had chilled to anger. "You have taken everything from us."

"Not everything, girl." Griml sidled close enough for his hot, acrid breath to flatten the mouse's whiskers. "We left thy parents with their lives."

"So you say—"

"The word of our lord you doubt?" Kungu lifted Olweena off her feet and dangled her before the massive, warty face of Ull. "Her head, Ull—bite it off!"

Ull's mouth widened, a web of sticky drool stretching over his notched teeth.

"Hold!" Griml motioned for Kungu to lower the mouse maiden. "Thee be right to doubt, girl. Boars take no captives. We kill them wut stands against the March. That be well-known. But it be different for thee an' thine an' all wut be *effectual* to the March. Wit' thy genteel upbringin' an' polished ways, thee be most seemly suited for makin' fair appraisal o' this land wit'out inspirin' alarm amongst the wee an' skittish natives. Aye?"

Kungu lowered the mouse to her brogans yet kept his trotter firmly hooked upon her collar.

"What am I to do?"

"Go forth, Olweena!" Griml motioned expansively with his tusks. "Climb Riversplash Mountain. See wut thee sees. An' pay especial good heed to wut thee sees o' soldiers an' machines o' war. Thee grasps my intent, girl?"

"And when I am stopped and questioned, what am I to say?"

"Naught of us, girl. Thee be but a wanderin' mousie. A pilgrim. Or refugee. Whate'er comes to mind. But if thee betray us, thy parents be hanged by their tails o'er a slow fire. By the Holy Sow, they be doomed to a horrible doom, dare thee offend us."

Olweena put a paw to her brow to steady her dizzying fear. "When I discover what you want, how will I inform you?"

From a pocket of his leather armor, Griml withdrew an oval mirror as small as a wren's egg. "Catch the sun with this. Three short flashes, then one long. Where'er thee be upon Riversplash, we will spy thee an' come."

"And my parents?" Olweena accepted the mirror. "You will release them unharmed as you promised?"

"Thee has the word of the boar lord. Now, go. This day an' full three more be thine. Ample time to survey the defenses o' Riversplash. Come dawn o' day five, thy parents be forsook to a miserable death. Now, hurry. Go!"

CHAPTER FOUR

An Encounter in the Mere

Olweena burst away in the direction that the scout Kungu pointed, enormously relieved to flee her captors. Stumbling along in her battered brogans, groping past trees soft in green velour, she shivered uncontrollably: Dread for her parents and her clan clung to her.

Even as she slogged across algae-covered pools and clambered over fallen trees, she recalled again with terror boars battering cottages and farmhouses, trampling screaming crofters and field workers under hooves that chewed the land to muck.

She threw her attention back into the sunlight that lit her way upon the seeping landscape. The Mere rose up to thwart her. Hanging moss, strangler vines, and brambles blocked the way, yet she ran full out. She crashed through walls of ivy and splashed into a creek.

Climbing the far bank, the bedraggled mouse crawled at a furious pace through the shrub. Upon dry ground, she collapsed, heart at the back of her throat, limbs palsied with exhaustion.

"Are you all right?"

Olweena rolled upright, startled. A young mouse, no older than she, stood before her. He wore rope sandals, a frayed brown tunic, and a floppy straw hat. Over his shoulder, he carried a blanket of woven grass tied off to a sack. When he lowered it, a small clatter announced his humble wares.

"Don't be frightened." The mouse took off his oversized hat and revealed a gentle countenance of beige fur and alert yet timid whiskers. "I thought you might be lost. I saw you from up there on the ridge." He motioned to a scene of bunched hills and patched farmland.

She had collapsed at the very edge of the Mere, and when she squinted, she could just discern the foothills of Riversplash Mountain. "You—you—" She hauled in a deep breath, looking at the blurry distance. "You *saw* me—from up there?"

The mouse sighed a small laugh. "Oh, yes, that must seem odd." From a shoulder pocket, he produced a pair of pince-nez spectacles with thick lenses and fit them to his snout so that his eyes magnified to staring gray orbs. "I can see clearly far-off things. But what is near is just a fog to me unless I wear these lenses." His already large eyes widened, observing her closely for the first time. "Oh my, you're beautiful … " With an embarrassed squinch of those enlarged eyes, he caught himself. "I'm sorry." He fumbled with his hat. "My name is Thrym Seedcorn. I—I'm a crofter—from these parts."

The mouse maiden, having caught her breath, ventured to rise. When her weary legs wobbled, Thrym steadied her by her elbow. "Thank you." She nodded gratefully to the odd-looking stranger. "I am Olweena Talkingstone."

Sure that she had her balance, Thrym stepped back. "You're a refugee?" Concern pulled his ears forward and twitched his whiskers. "Are you hurt?"

She indicated not. "Just lost."

Thrym glanced back into the Mere, where windy sunlight gusted through dark corridors. "I can take you to a clinic. The frogs there will provide shelter and food and help you relocate."

"No!" She bit her lip to quiet herself. "No, no thank you, kind Thrym. I have seen enough of this spooky swamp. Please, just get me out of here."

He fit his hat on his head and lifted his noisy sack. "Come with me."

CHAPTER FIVE

A Frightful Beauty

Thrym led Olweena up a brook path. Clasping paws, they climbed slippery slabs of shale alongside a drunken current weaving over and around green rocks. The Mere fell away quickly. "Are you hungry?"

"There was plenty to eat in the swamp."

"Plenty to eat in the Mere?" Thrym flexed his ears back, flabbergasted. "That's hard living down there for mice. You survived Weasel's Pass and the Mere—alone?"

"Not alone," she answered truthfully, then let silence carry her fear. Thrym noted her flattened whiskers and did not press for details.

In open sunlight, Olweena felt her dread begin to dim. Slopes of wildflowers glared like pieces of sky fallen to earth.

Gratefully she sat and gazed back at the way they had come. The Mere lay flat to the horizon, smoking faintly. In its dark depths the boar lord Griml and his warriors skulked, and her tail curled again with fright.

"We must find you shelter," Thrym said, squatting in the grass beside her. "The boars who destroyed your home are headed here."

"You know that?" Olweena asked, surprised.

"You're not the first refugee to reach Riversplash."

"What will you do?" Her ears stretched attentively. "How will Riversplash defend itself?"

"I'm on my way to the Holt to find out." He looked over his shoulder, upslope at distant green cliffs and rainbowlike waterfalls. "All the great landowners live on those heights. My sister, Magdi, and her husband, Squire Cheevie, have an estate there, Bracken Knoll. If any can defend Riversplash, it will be those in the Holt."

"Take me with you."

"Maiden Olweena—" Thrym's cheeks ballooned at the prospect, and he exhaled gustily. "That's a grueling trek even for someone who hasn't been hiking for days. You must be exhausted. We'll find you shelter with the farmers on the River Rill."

"No." Olweena placed an urgent paw on Thrym's arm. "I must go with you to the Holt."

Bewilderment shimmered across Thrym's magnified eyes. "Why? You should rest."

"I dare not rest." Olweena rose to her knees. "When the swine devoured Blossom Vale, I lost everything. My parents—" Her throat constricted, unable to say that they were dead. *They are not dead,* she insisted to herself. *I will save them.*

Thrym interpreted her anguish as mourning and gave a consoling nod. "I would be mad with grief if I'd suffered your loss. You need time, time away from war." He noticed that his heart was racing, his whiskers twitching. The presence of the mouse maiden—the sorry sight of her clothes, her milky scent, the velvet timber of her voice— moved him. "I have a croft not far from here. It's in the Mere, I'm sorry to say. But it's on a remote bluff I cleared from thistle brush. Nobody will bother you. You can stay there. Not much in way of provisions, but there's good shelter of stone and sod and a nearby spring . . ."

The mouse maiden stopped him. "Thrym, the boars *are* coming. They are already . . . " She wanted to say "on Riversplash Mountain" and tell him everything. But the horror of her parents hanging by their tails over a slow fire stayed her, and she said, "The legions are already in sight of this mountain. We can't hide from them." Grim determination steeled her voice. "I want to fight the boars. I want vengeance for the massacre at Blossom Vale. And I am going to the Holt to join with the defenders of this mountain."

Suppressing a pained expression, Thrym removed his eyeglasses. Olweena's beauty filled him with an anxiety he had never experienced before, and he dared not continue gazing at her. Even when the sight of her bleared to a bright shadow, the gentle smell of her still filled him with dismaying ardor.

"Why do you look so worried?" Olweena swished her tail through the grass, annoyed that one of her own kind had less faith in her than did Griml. "I can handle myself. I won't slow you down. Take me with you to Bracken Knoll. Or at least show me the direction."

"I will do neither." Thrym sent his long sight out over the Mere. He focused on distant, twisted trees overgrown with creeping fungi. Even that sorrowful horizon did not diminish the adoration this maiden provoked in him. "You can't come with me."

Her tail stiffened with frustration. "Don't try to protect me."

"I'm not." Thrym stood and tucked his spectacles into the shoulder pocket of his tunic. "I'm trying to protect myself."

Baffled, she stared up at him. "What are you saying?"

"You are too beautiful."

"I don't understand."

"I am going to war, Olweena." He adjusted the hat on his head so that it fit more snugly. "Your beauty distracts me. If you are near, I won't be as alert as I must. And my distraction will doom us both."

"Don't talk nonsense." The pink of her nose flushed with anger.

Here was her best chance to fulfill her mission quickly and free her parents, but this peculiar mouse was impossible. "You're a coward. You're not going to Bracken Knoll or to war, are you? You're running away, and you don't want me to know."

Thrym lowered his sack, stunned by her accusation. "That's not true."

"Of course it is." She paced before him, assessing his humble garments. "Look at you. A dirt-poor mouse with eyeglasses. You're not a fighter."

"I'm a farmer," Thrym said proudly. "And I will fight to defend our mountain, because survival requires struggle—even for a mouse with spectacles."

Olweena paused before this oddly well-spoken farmer, arms crossed, mind racing to find a way to move him to her purpose. "Have you ever seen a boar, Thrym?"

"No."

"They are massive, powerful creatures." She spoke from the blackest memories. "They have tusks that can split a tree and hooves as sharp as axes. But their most devastating weapon is their wicked swine brain. It is a brain of a most evil intelligence that despises all other creatures. You will not defeat them in combat, for destruction is their philosophy. And they delight in it."

Thrym's drooping whiskers perked. "There are other ways to defend ourselves than combat."

"What ways?" Olweena's arms unfolded. "Explain yourself."

CHAPTER SIX

What the Old Moon Said

"I can't explain," Thrym answered honestly. Wonder overwhelmed him. Earlier that day, he had chopped earth with a hoe in the dim Mere. Now, he stood in brash sunlight on the River Rill, breathing in the awesome beauty of this mouse maiden. His heartbeat skipped in fear as he remembered that all this had been predicted for him that very morning—by the moon.

At first light, Thrym had been turning furrows for a root garden. Another of the north winds was swirling about impatiently, full of the scent of pine from the mountain and full of curiosity about a mouse with eyeglasses. This was the third north wind in two days who had asked about Thrym's pince-nez. Each time one of these seasonal stragglers happened by, the lonely mouse had welcomed the company. And each time he had leaned on his hoe to explain a rodent's unhappiness with far sight. "You see, I never could play the nutshell games when I was a mouseling or wager on ant races as I grew older. And now that I'm an adult, I'm hopeless with the mouse maidens. Who would want a suitor that can't whisker-tickle or dance in the glades without bumping snouts?"

This wind listened no more attentively than the others had and soon skipped away. Alone again, the mouse huffed and applied renewed vigor to turning the stiff ground.

"The world is wide," a silver voice spoke up. "And the heart is not something you can hide. Somewhere under the sky's blue is someone just right for you."

Startled, Thrym's big ears pivoted to either side, before he realized who addressed him. "Oh, you." He frowned up at the old moon. "Please don't trouble me with your rhymes. I've work to do, and I've squandered enough time talking to the north wind."

"Dreams are not easy to realize," the moon noted, a smile tucked in his shadowy beard, "because life is so full of surprise."

"I mean it. No games right now." Thrym glared at the pocked face. "No time for poems or prophecy. I've seeds to plant."

"Prophecy?" The moon hummed. "Let me see. Oh, yes. Here's a guess. Before this morning is fully done, your greatest adventure will have begun."

The young mouse gazed hard at the pale-lit face. "Adventure? For me—on this backwoods croft? The empty-headed winds are my only visitors. Three planting seasons, I've done nothing but grow tubers and potatoes. The only adventure for me today will be lancing blisters. What do you say to that?"

But the old moon said nothing. He floated silently in the sky, as pale as glass.

In the distance the metallic rattling of a tinker's wagon called. Thrym reached with his far sight to see the creature harnessed to that heap of clattering tin. The traveler wore a tattered green mantle and hat of plaited fronds. Sunlight flicked off wire-rim lenses, and crimped whiskers twitched on the hedgehog's grizzled face.

"Old Muspul," Thrym muttered aloud, disgruntled. He hadn't expected the itinerant merchant and letter carrier to make his way to this isolated bluff until much later in the season. If Old Muspul brought a letter, it could only be another outraged missive from Magdi, Thrym's robust elder sister. Their parents and siblings had died some years ago during a flood that would have drowned him as well if Magdi hadn't held his puny body abovewater for hours. She remained his sole family—and never ceased to remind him of that melancholy fact. With angry letters, she berated him for leaving the employ of her husband, Squire Cheevie. As if Thrym were an ingrate for not wanting to lick his brother-in-law's boots!

"No more letters, Muspul." Thrym turned his back on the old hedgehog, who had set down the tines of his wagon with a sigh.

Muspul adjusted the lenses on his snout and kneaded a paw against a crick in his bent back. "Squinty, you must question your assumptions more vigorously. Or else you must answer to them!"

Thrym took another whack at the stiff clods with his hoe. He liked not at all the nickname Squinty—however, he accepted it from this visitor. "I've work to do, dominie," he replied, calling the hedgehog by his title—an old-fashioned term for teacher. Muspul had taught Squinty many fancy words.

"I've no letter for you, Thrym." Muspul sat down heavily on a tree stump.

"Hullo! Hullo!" A two-wheeled pushcart laded with winter nuts and bricks of peat clattered into the dried weeds atop the bluff. Down the path scrambled a shrew wearing maroon pantaloons and a sporty green cap, waving both arms. "Ya told him th' big news yet, Muspul?"

"Not yet, Notty." The hedgehog held out a rigid arm to stay the racing shrew. "Not yet."

Notty and Thrym had grown up together on the Mere's impoverished banks, sharing many a childhood lark. They had not seen each other since the mouse began farming this far-off croft, and so the simultaneous arrival of Notty with Muspul signaled something positively frightful. The mouse stood and braced himself for momentous tidings.

"So what ya waitin' for?" Notty asked, huffing as he skidded over loose gravel. "A grand fortune is in our grasp, Thrym! A grand fortune! And glory, too! Throw down that hoe, mousie. Ya ain't a clod buster no more, I tell ya. Now we're soldiers o' fortune!"

The young mouse's lens-swollen eyes looked to Muspul. "What's he ranting about, dominie?"

The hedgehog sighed unhappily.

"Th' swine hordes are marchin' on Riversplash!" Notty stopped bent over to catch his breath at the edge of the garden plot. "Fernholt's all in a panic."

"Forget about *Fernholt.*" Muspul snapped his head back. "The Holt is the domain of privilege. You learned that harsh truth, Squinty, when you worked on your brother-in-law's estate. You did all the dirty work while the squire enjoyed the fruits of your labors, yes? Well, I came to warn you to stay out of this conflict. Let the boars have the Holt's sweet roots. Stay safe on your croft, boy—sustained by your own honest toil."

"But wit'out th' Holt above us, who buys our crops?" the shrew asked sharply. "Ta what'll we aspire wit' Fernholt an' th' finest of our estates gone?"

Muspul closed one eye and looked at the glowering shrew. "How many denizens of the Mere ever earn their way up the hillsides of Riversplash to the Rill, let alone to the exalted altitudes of the Holt? And those few who do, *without fail,* those lucky ones turn haughty and vain—very like your sister, Magdi, eh, Squinty?" The hedgehog gazed at the shaken Thrym. "No, lads. The Holt is a useless dream for creatures of the Mere. Why forsake our lives in defense of those who look down on us? Without the foolish wish of moving up in the world, our fellow creatures here will learn to find happiness at the bottom of the world, among the Mere's scum ponds, mosquitoes and flies."

Tiny eyes wide, Notty looked to Thrym. "Don't listen ta that bitter ol' beetlechewer! We've a chance for glory an' riches, I tell ya! Squire Cheevie an' th' other posh lords o' th' Holt are offering a fortune ta any who'll open th' rock dams an' send down th' avalanches that'll block Weasel's Pass ta keep th' swine away. Let's go bust open those dams!"

CHAPTER SEVEN

When Peril Fires the Heart

Thrym wanted to explain to the beautiful Olweena Talkingstone that she was safe. Riversplash Mountain had rock-slide dams. Or something very like . . .

"They are not dams," Muspul had corrected, one claw upraised. "Dams are barriers, lads. More properly, these constructions are rockfall *weirs*, with moveable gates worked by gears and levers."

And just like that, old Muspul dropped his diatribe against the privileged of the Holt and held forth on rockfall weirs.

"Four enormous bulwarks strategically situated on the high, rocky fields of Riversplash. They each hold back thousands of tons of boulders. Should their gates be opened and those granite monsters sent hurtling down the mountainside, that's it for Weasel's Pass! The one gorge that leads to Riversplash Mountain shall be closed to virtually all wingless creatures forever. No swine will negotiate those steep obstacles, and even the most sure-footed goats would be hard pressed to reach our slopes unbruised."

But Thrym told none of this to Olweena. He had to hurry along, to help open those avalanche weirs, because Muspul was too old and cantankerous to care—and Notty, bold and adventurous Notty, well . . . A prior commitment had unexpectedly required Notty's full attention.

Unise, a stout shrew with a babe in her arms and a young fellow clutching her apron, had fixed Thrym with a stare this morning when she first strode up out of the thickets. "Don't ya say word one, mouse! Don't ya add ta his lie. The hedgehog tinker told me all." She had charged closer, aiming her rage at her husband. "You're runnin' off ta th' Holt ta adventure for those posh squires. I'll not have it, Notty. You've a family ta provide for."

"Ah, but Unise, don't ya see, my curly tail?" Notty had tried to back away, but old Muspul had stood as if prepared to run him down. "I'm doin' this for ya an' for our precious dear ones."

"No more lies, you!" With her free paw, she had grabbed Notty by the ear and dragged him along the gravel path that climbed to where the pushcart waited with its sad load.

"Ow!" Notty had cried louder than the screaming baby.

The little boy clutching his mother's apron glanced back meekly and offered a vague wave.

Thrym lifted a paw.

The reality of the moon's prophecy intensified as he watched Notty hurrying his pushcart downhill, with Unise striding behind. Destiny had denied his friend.

The mouse turned a resigned look to the blue sky, where the old moon dangled. An adventure had begun for Thrym, as promised. *My greatest?* he questioned. *Against boars? Then, surely, my only adventure.* His friend couldn't join him, his teacher had no persuasion to thwart him, and this beautiful maiden he had found along the way would not distract him.

"No time to explain, beautiful Olweena." Thrym swung the clattering sack over his shoulder. "I'm not going to risk you—or myself and the fate of Riversplash. We *cannot* go together. If you'll take refuge at my croft, I can . . . "

"Cat's claw!"

Thrym's ears flattened against his head, and he drew back at the curse words. "That's a foul sound from so lovely a mouth."

"What farmer speaks as well as you?" Olweena clicked her tongue suspiciously. "You dress like an impoverished dirt farmer—but the way you speak tells me you are not what you say."

"Really?" Thrym once again lowered his sack of meager possessions. He hated obscenities—and *cat's claw* was among the worst. He was also not fond of anyone calling him a liar. But with this mouse maiden, he experienced only momentary shock—and in the next instant found himself admiring her.

After all that she has suffered and lost, he reasoned, *she has the right to curse.* He reached for his eyeglasses, and asked, "If I'm not a crofter, who do you think I am?"

"I don't know." Olweena spoke more softly, annoyed at herself for losing her patience. Fear for her parents had overshadowed the cunning she needed to save her family. This male had said she was beautiful, distressed as she was. He was hers for the taking—if she used the right tone. She lowered her voice and said slowly, "You're not what you seem. Let me look at your paws."

Thrym pulled back his sleeves and exposed thick forearms, sinewy wrists, and paws barked with callus.

Olweena's whiskers fanned, impressed. "You're strong." She took his paws in hers. "Perhaps I was wrong about you. In Blossom Vale, farmers don't speak like toffs."

"Toffs?" he asked. In his lens-focused eyes, Olweena appeared as beautiful as he had first thought, and the touch of her paws filled him with a smoldering calm.

"Toffs are swells. The upper class."

"Oh, *toffs!*" Thrym pulled his paws away. Mention of the upper class reminded him of his mission to Bracken Knoll and the inevitable encounter with his family: arrogant Squire Cheevie and snobbish Magdi. His heart hardened with renewed purpose. "I'm not a toff. I'm from the Mere. The way I talk is . . . it's a gift from my teacher." Thrym reached for his sack. "I must go."

"Please," Olweena entreated, "take me with you."

Thrym regarded her warily. "I must go."

Olweena saw the look of love dim in his eyes. He had closed his heart. *All for the best*, she thought. She didn't want to deceive anyone, least of all by pretense of love. Yet, if she had not tried, the desperate fear for her parents would have crushed her.

"Perhaps we will meet again in Bracken Knoll," she said with a weak smile.

"You would do best to accept my offer." Thrym shouldered his belongings. "You'll be safe in my stone hut. You've lost your home and that's a terrible sorrow. But why add to it by seeking revenge?"

She squared her shoulders. "Why would you be in such a hurry to get to Bracken Knoll if there were not some chance of thwarting the swine? Let me help you."

Thrym sighed. "*You* are a toff, aren't you?"

"My family was the largest landowner in Blossom Vale." Her brazen gaze did not waver. "I knew privilege. So?"

"You knew privilege and lost it to the boars." He nodded with sympathy. "But I can't knowingly endanger you, Olweena. If you want to toss your life to the boars, you'll have to do that without my help."

"All right." Olweena offered a kindly smile. "You've made yourself clear. You're a good mouse."

"Yes," Thrym agreed tentatively. "Yes, I am." He pointed his snout toward the Mere. "Will you stay at my croft?"

"You're the mouse with all the answers," she replied cooly. "What do you think?"

He reached into his sack, and surveyed his provisions. Among the small wrapped packets of food, an extra pair of warm socks, and his beloved copy of *The Chaunt of the Dead Riders*, he found what he was looking for. He took out three dented pennies. "I think it's a long, hard climb to the Holt from here. Take these." He pushed the coins into her paw.

CHAPTER EIGHT

Viper Magic

High on Riversplash, in the giant bowl of the dormant volcano, the serpent Vidar roamed. Ice green pools surrounded him. These mirror lakes reflected the cloudless sky and fierce rays of the white sun. Their glare protected Vidar from the hungry gaze of eagles as he slithered over shelves of rock. A slick flow of oil, his snaky length appeared and disappeared among the shadows.

He scanned his terrain for food and enemies and saw neither. The layers of shale once sheltered rock mice, but he had devoured the last of them long ago. Occasionally a rodent from below made the mistake of poaching fish roe in his streams. That was a rare treat for the snake. Usually he had to risk going down the mountain to find prey, exposing himself to enemies.

All that would soon change. Vidar had a plan.

In the time of the great-great-grandfathers, Vidar's ancestors had arrived from a distant jungle, bringing with them knowledge that they had learned from strange and hairless apes of legend now long extinct. Without that magic, Vidar's ancestors could never have survived in this crater land known as the Tarn.

Alas, magic had proved no defense against the ruthless Brave

Tails. Otherwise peaceful creatures—hare, chipmunk, vole, and gerbil—crazed wrathful by atrocities of the Mere—had banded together in a secret society dedicated to exterminating carnivores. Armed with enchanted swords, the Brave Tails had charged out of the Mere more than a century ago and, in one long, terrible killing season, wiped out the large meateaters. Wolves, bobcats, foxes, badgers, weasels, lordly bears—and all of Vidar's clan—murdered.

Vidar had survived only by chance. An adolescent at the time, he had been away at school, learning his clan's magic. When he returned as the last of the vipers on Riversplash Mountain, he came for revenge. And magic was his weapon.

Serpent magic involved slitherholes. Hidden passages. One entered the mountain through a fracture or fault, crossed a short distance of dreamspace, no more than a snake-length, and exited at another point on Riversplash furlongs or even leagues distant. Any animal could travel through a slitherhole—if the creature could find one and was flexible enough to fit those narrow rock clefts. And, of course, those few small beasties who found or accidentally fell through a slitherhole often became unexpected and welcome meals for Vidar.

Apart from providing an occasional free meal, revenge on the Brave Tails had proven far less gratifying than the viper had first expected. In the century since the destruction of his clan, he had successfully raided many burrows and lairs and had eaten himself fat with furry mammals. But he had not been able to do anything to destroy the prosperity that the Brave Tails had won by exterminating their predators—and his family.

For years, he had suffered until lately, when a new strategy had finally focused all his savage thoughts.

Curled around a puddle of ice melt, Vidar contemplated his reflection. It was not vanity motivating him to gaze upon his sleek black coil. Not vanity but trance magic locked his topaz eyes onto their reflections in the water. Deeply he stared, past his image to the dreamspace—to an image of marsh reeds and ferns.

Vidar peered at a scene from the Mere: a terrapin perched atop the kneelike root of a limbless tree, flurrying helplessly, and his beaked head bobbing and calling as he tried to free himself from his ill-fated roost.

Griml has surprised me, Vidar noticed. *He has chosen not to march on Riversplash but to sneak in! He's penetrated the Mere already! But where are his legions?*

Through the magic of dreamspace, Vidar could touch any point in the world with his mind. It was he who had reached out to pollute the boars' dreams by placing images of the Holt's beautiful lands and delectable flora. Lord Griml had no idea that his inspiration to march on Riversplash Mountain had begun inside the wedged skull of a serpent.

But where are the boar legions?

The mirror pool disclosed to Vidar a boar in a camouflage of ivy and grass circling the trapped turtle.

Suddenly the vision in the pool vanished. Vidar saw mirrored in it blue sky cut by outstretched wings.

A giant red-winged eagle shrieked and swooped across the pool. It veered upward, talons empty, its scowling gaze searching for its elusive prey.

But the serpent was nowhere among the rocks of the crater floor.

CHAPTER NINE

Runaway

All morning, Thrym ascended along half-dry creeks, narrow and winding. He avoided roads and cart paths, hoping to cross the river without having to explain himself to anyone. A loner, he preferred to dwell uninterrupted on the impending invasion and decide what he was going to say to his sister and her arrogant husband—and to the beautiful Olweena if they met again.

Crossing through watercress paddies in the Rill, he sensed someone following him. *Olweena?* he wondered with heart-fluttering hope. No, even with the cumbersome burden of his sack thrown over his shoulder, he was moving far too quickly for her to keep up.

Bandits? he worried, knowing that martens and ferrets from other mountains occasionally crawled through Weasel's Pass to poach carp and catfish from the river. If they seized a lone mouse on a hidden trail, he would become lunch.

Looking around at the paddies, Thrym spied sturdy beaver women planting shoots and skimming algae froth with wicker sieves. No bandits would expose themselves to so many witnesses. Within minutes, these farmers would be whistling alarms and slapping their tails noisily upon the water. The famously organized beaver patrols would beat the grass-lined paths. Unlike the choked Mere, the Rill's manicured fields offered few places to hide.

And when beavers caught bandits, punishment was swift and awful: a bruising ride down the Riprap, the Rill's most turbulent rapids. Very few victims of the Riprap's white waters ever appeared again among the living.

Confident that bandits were not shadowing him, Thrym decided to lie in wait for whoever *was* following. He crossed a dike between a reedy canal and a field of barley.

On its other side, a willow bent its blue-green branches over the still water of the canal. Thrym hung his sack from the willow so that it rocked in the breeze, clanging with a rhythm as though it were still walking with him. Then, he ducked into the high grass beside the canal and waited.

A moment later, a young shrew hurried across the dike in scuffed clogs, tattered breeches, torn shirt stained gray. When he spotted the sack dangling from the willow, he gave an angry squeak. Spinning about, he slammed into a sturdy mouse.

"Hold on there, rascal." Thrym held the boy's arm with one paw and with the other tried to fit his spectacles into place. "Unless you'd like to take a swim in the canal, stop pulling. I want to see who you are."

His eyes in focus, Thrym recognized the squirming shrew. "You're Notty's boy!"

The little shrew stopped struggling and with tiny, blinking eyes gazed at the mouse.

"I saw you with your mother at my croft in the Mere." Thrym released the boy's arm. "You ran off, didn't you?"

The shrew wiped his quivering snout on a frazzled sleeve.

"Why are you following me?" Thrym placed his fists on his hips.

"Speak up." The mouse leaned forward inquisitively. "You can talk, can't you?"

The small shrew offered a curt nod.

"All right, then. What's your name?"

"Wili."

"You realize, Wili, your mother right now is sick with worry."

Wili gazed down at the twigs and weeds sticking out of his clogs. "Ma's all wore out lookin' after the wee un an' puttin' up wit' the likes o' me." He extracted a seedcob from his back pocket and gnawed nervously at it.

"So, you just ran off, did you?" Thrym hid a small smile for this juvenile's daring. "Where do you think you're going?"

"Wit' you," Wili replied at once. He brandished the seedcob like a sword. "We goin' pig huntin'!"

Thrym shook his head in dull amazement. "Wherever did you get that idea?"

Wili aimed his moist snout across the paddies to the steamy gray smudge of the Mere far downhill. "I heard that ol' bristleback talkin' to Ma."

"Muspul?"

"He done said they some swine a-comin'. He done said Pa had gone off pig huntin'." The boy's dark eyes widened with expectation. "The rich folk up in the Holt be givin' out guns to any an' all fit to face down a pig. I figure if I'm fit to haul well water three times a day an' chop firewood tall as I can reach, then why cain't I be goin' up the Holt like Pa, gettin' me a gun, an' shootin' pig?" Wili dropped a look to his worn clogs. "But Ma brung Pa home an' told him strictlike he was too old for adventurin'." When he lifted his pointy face, he wore a determined expression. "Well, I ain't too old. But I never yet been out of the Mere. So, I seen you goin' an' I done follered."

"Just like that?"

"Jest like that."

Thrym removed his floppy hat and wiped his brow with his sleeve, while he pondered what to say. "You think you can handle a firearm?"

"Heck! Any idjit can shoot a gun. Even a li'l fella like me. You jest pint an' shoot." He leveled his seedcob on zipping dragonflies and fired several imaginary rounds. "*Weee-oo! Weee-oo! Weee-oo!* That's all they is to it."

"Wili, guns are strictly controlled." Thrym squatted and stared directly into the boy's eyes. "There aren't enough guns to arm everybody. The gentry of the Holt are offering swords and lances for those willing to fight the boars."

"I'd be right proud to take me up a sword an' lance," Wili said with a nod. "That's more than we got in the Mere, where it's jest clubs an' slings."

"Do you have any idea what a boar is?"

"It's a pig! I seed drawins, an' I ain't a-feared o' no pig."

"Well, I am. And you should be, too." Thrym stood up with a sigh. "I can't leave you alone out here, young shrew. So—let's go."

"Go?" Wili narrowed one beady eye. "Where we a-goin'?"

Thrym fit the big hat over his ears. "Back to your ma and pa in the Mere."

"I ain't a-goin' back." The little shrew edged away. "They doan' want me there. Pa ain't gonna be there no how. And Ma'll jest whup me fer runnin' off."

"I'll talk to your pa—and your ma."

"Fergit it. I doan' need you." The young shrew bolted across the dike and disappeared through the willows.

"Hey!" Thrym shouted. "Come back here, you! Hey!" He ran after the fleeing boy, paused for a moment at the willow to retrieve his possessions, thought better of it, and scrambled after the runaway.

CHAPTER TEN

Cave of Secrets

Thrym lunged in time to see the little shrew's tail whip out of sight beneath a granite slab. With exasperation, the mouse called out in an irritated voice, "Wili, if you make me crawl in there after you, I will tie your tail in a knot so tight you'll be using it for a hammer."

"Hey-dee!" Wili's voice echoed forth, dim and distant. "Hey-dee up thar! You be wantin' to see this."

"What?" Thrym stuck his head through the fern-shadowed crevice, where he saw a shimmering glow on the rock walls. Painfully he pressed his shoulders into the harrow space. "What's down there?"

"Sure as I doan' know!"

The ping and splash of water sounded softly from below. The mouse emptied his lungs to squeeze through—and the ground under him disappeared.

Tumbling head over paws Thrym came to an abrupt halt sitting up of the floor of a cavern lit with one shaft of pale sunlight.

"Lookee here!" Wili called from a slender, underground passageway between braided roots. "Where you reckon this goes?"

"Don't you go in there," he warned. "That might be the den of a bear."

"Owl spit!" the little shrew's derisive curse echoed from down the passageway. "They ain't no bears on Riversplash. Them Brave Tails done killt every one."

"Don't be so sure!" Thrym called. "Stay where you are!"

The passage beyond the roots was pitch-black, and the shrew had scampered far ahead. Thrym proceeded with paws outstretched and whiskers fanned wide, feeling the damp walls left, then right. The mouse could just barely hear the clopping of the youngster's clogs down the lightless tunnel.

"Wili! Get back here! I'm not running after you!" he shouted even as he hurried faster through the cramped dark. Straining to hear, his ears caught a muffled roar in the distance.

A terrified shriek stabbed the darkness.

"Wili!" Thrym scurried full speed, slammed into a slimy wall, and careened along a maze of turns and bends. The tunnel ended at a glowing hole, a narrow descending stairwell of stone steps. "Wili! You all right?"

Hearing no response, the worried mouse charged down two steps at a time and rushed into a grotto crammed with squat boulders and deformed rocks. Thrym pulled up short on an embankment that overlooked speeding rapids.

"Wili!" Thrym cried.

"Here I be!" Wili waved from deeper in the grotto, where he stood among red and mottled rocks as bellshaped as toadstools. "Lookee here! Lookee what I found!"

The mouse fumbled with his spectacles, fitting them to his face, as he saw a large white limestone monument adorned with carvings, ablaze in sunlight.

Carved pigs held aloft by feathered wings posed gracefully at each of the eight corners. Across the sides, knots of serpents entangled toad gargoyles beneath umbrella-winged bats.

"Them hognose snakes scared the spit out o' me!" Wili laughed and ran his paws over the polished marble vipers. "But they jest whittlins on the most whoppin' bathtub I ever did see."

"That's not a bathtub, Wili." Thrym approached the limestone structure. The height of it extended well above his ears. "That's a crypt."

"Like fer dead critters?"

"Very special dead critters." Thrym gazed up in awe at the fabulous sculpture. "I've read about this in the old texts."

"You think they's treasure in this ol' crypt?" Wili asked and began climbing up the carved marble. "Famous critters oft got treasure buried wit' em, ain't that right?"

Thrym boosted Wili to the top of the crypt, then clambered up himself. The mouse nearly toppled backward when the young shrew, retreating in fear, banged into him. "Slow down, pal. There's nothing here to hurt you."

"They's monster critters in thar!"

Thrym peeked into the crypt and his tail jerked straight out with astonishment. Four abreast, mummified animals with faces like dried fruit lay together on their backs. Bleached fur clung to the shriveled bodies, and decayed capes of regal crimson draped the carcasses.

"It's the Dead Riders," Thrym whispered, wonderstruck. "This is the tomb of the four Brave Tails raised from the dead by black magic."

"I knowed who the Dead Riders is!" Wili turned about, small bead eyes large with fright. "Let's git!"

Thrym let the shrew crab back down the face of the crypt, but he remained standing, unwilling to move. *Are these truly the Dead Riders of legend?*

The possibility boggled him. He had never doubted that the cunning Brave Tails had driven off the meateaters until they all had abandoned Riversplash Mountain. As for the supernatural adventures of the Dead Riders, he had assumed the infamous zombie warriors existed solely as myth.

Of course, they are myth! he reassured himself, scrutinizing the four shrunken hides. *These were four living animals once—hare, chipmunk, rat, and gerbil. No magic here.*

He glanced around at the grotto's rock formations, some complete as temple pillars, others drooling from domed heights into midair or bulging up from the cavern floor. From his vantage atop the crypt, he could see the grotto's source of light: one whole side opened upon the sky—and the stony banks of a racing river, where rapids flew past.

The Riprap!

The Brave Tails had situated this memorial on a shelf of the mountain alongside the thrashing rapids. Sun rays sparkled through the river's spray and waves, illuminating the white marble crypt in a holy shimmer.

CHAPTER ELEVEN

Thrym Finds Yesterday's Promise

Thrym's excitement hardened to curiosity. He removed his spectacles and surveyed the dripping grotto with farsighted eyes. Behind a boulder frosted in pink and green minerals, he glimpsed a tuft of red fur!

"Hey-dee!" Wili called from behind a cauliflower-shaped dripstone, hiding from the Dead Riders, "what all ye seein' up thar?"

"I'm not sure." Thrym jumped down from the crypt and strode purposefully amid large candy-colored stalagmites. "But I don't think it's anything to be afraid of."

"I ain't skeered o' nothin!" Wili declared loudly and stepped forth. "Don't ye fergit who found this here burial holler."

"Twitch a whisker!" Thrym rounded the frosted boulder and reared back. "This is incredible!"

"That thar a treasure?" Wili ran toward the mouse, casting an anxious look over his shoulder at the white crypt of snakecoils, bat faces, and feathered swine. "Dead critters famous as them Brave Tails ort to be buried wit' treasure."

"It's a kind of treasure," Thrym confirmed and reached out a curious paw. "A priceless treasure."

Wili crept up behind him. "Yeee!" His gray fur fluffed with alarm even before he knew what he was seeing. "Another dead 'un!"

Red fur draped a rectangular stone box. The pelt retained the vague, ruddy shape of a slinky carnivore with long limbs that ended in glove-white paws and sharp black claws.

"I knowed what this be." Wili's wee paw stroked the bushy red tail and its silver tip. "This here be the hide of a fox."

"That's right, Wili." Thrym spoke in a respectful whisper. "But this is not the pelt from one of the common foxes that once stalked this mountain, preying on the likes of you and me." The rapids muffled the mouse's quiet voice, and the shrew had to lean close to hear Thrym's words. "This was the last fox on Riversplash Mountain—the fox, Rumner, whom the Brave Tails befriended."

"Rumner the Swift?" Wili paced the length of the fox hide, running his paw over the lustrous red fur. "Fer sure?"

"Well, that *is* the sepulcher of the Dead Riders over there. And Rumner the Swift was the one who carried them during their escapades. I'll bet that under this pelt we'll find the Dead Riders' equipage."

"Eck-wee—what?"

"Military equipment." Gently Thrym rolled aside the fox's plush hide. "The arms they used to drive out the wolves and the bears. Equipage. Weapons and armor."

"Them Dead Riders didn't wear no armor." Wili shook his head in sad dismay at the mouse's ignorance. "They was awready dead an' couldn't be killt twice."

"Yes, of course—maybe, then, we'll find their riding gear." Thrym unveiled a bin carved of toffee-colored rock, low to the ground and covered with a slab of black slate. "Help me shove this open."

The mouse and the young shrew pushed at the polished lid, and it slid aside with a harsh rasp. "Eeek!" Wili clapped paws over his ears and looked down into the bin. "Skin a cat—lookee that!"

Four swords sheathed in woven-grass scabbards, two fire-hardened lances, and three unstrung bows lay atop a dented shield with a faded insignia. "Look—there's their famous emblem:

"The Open Claw, the icon of the Brave Tails! These are the weapons that brought peace to Riversplash Mountain," Thrym said.

The mouse reached in and fit his paw about the gnarled wood hilt of a sword. The blade pulled free of the decayed grass scabbard. The same chill, humid, mineral-salted air that had preserved Rumner the Swift's lambent pelt had ruined the weapons. The blade's metal had rusted so thoroughly that red and black blotches of corrosion looked like snakeskin.

Wili lifted one of the lances and stared cross-eyed along its length. "Must've been good once upon, but sure ain't nothin' much now." He tossed the crooked shaft back into the bin. "I reckon we oughter at least make off wit' one o' them sorry swords so's folks won't think we're pullin' tails." He slipped a sword free of its rotted sheath and brandished the blade over his head.

"Put it back." Thrym gently returned the sword he had hefted.

"What fer?" Wili wagged the ruined sword at the mouse.

Thrym held a hard stare on the boy shrew. "They're the *Dead* Riders, Wili. This is their sacred memorial."

Wili stopped flourishing the sword and chucked a nervous look toward the crypt. "Oh, yeah. If'n they raise up agin, they'd be meaner'n bobcats to find their stuff missin'." He carefully returned the weapon to its scabbard.

Thrym swallowed the impulse to tell the boy that those bodies would never rise up except in fable. He pulled the slate lid back into place.

The mouse wished these dead heroes could indeed rise and save Riversplash Mountain from the boar hordes already on the march, but he felt foolish entertaining such a fantasy. All that remained of the Brave Tails was yesterday's promise: legend and rust.

Wili tugged at Thrym's sleeve. "Let's git!"

They walked across the grotto toward the rushing water. At the mouth of the cave, they paused and looked back. Sunlight chimed off the limestone sepulcher with ghostly radiance, softly bright, warmed with innumerable dreams.

CHAPTER TWELVE

The Boar Horde's Terrible Religion

Across the Rill, Griml and his heavily armored squad of boars gazed hungrily upon cultivated fields, paddies, and meadows. "I wanna eat," said Ull in his big voice. "I wanna eat sweet roots."

"Aye, mighty Ull, in good time," Griml promised, crouching low in the dense hedges. "We be waitin' on night."

"I wanna eat *now*." Ull rose, and the hedge quaked as in a stiff wind. "By day, boars sleep. By night, boars march and feed. That be the boar way. Yet, you march us by day, Griml."

The boar leader did not stir from where he lay in silky mud, his chipped tusks, armor spikes, and helmet of bear claws and fangs protruding. "In them swamps below, we did march by day to befuddle our enemies, who be expectin' us by night. Now we be crossin' open country an' needs be movin' again by night. So, lay thee down, Ull, take thy rest till dark. Then, we be eatin' our full o' these paddies."

Ull shoved his massive head through the hedge, and his snout quivered to smell the sweetness of tender plants basking in the sun. "We done marched by day climbin' here—now we eat by day."

"Hunger addles thy senses, Ull!" Yet again, Griml rued choosing

Ull for this scouting patrol. The brawn of the giant had seemed good security against unknown defenses, if only that brawn were loyal to other than hunger and fear. "Ain't thee afeared o' traps? Fields surely be hidin' trenches set wit' sticks sharpened to pierce a boar's belly. Best thee stayed put."

That threat gave Ull pause—until a breeze wafted over him with aromas of flowering, seeding, and fruiting. "I wanna eat now!" He barged through the hedge and sloshed into the nearest paddy, long-muzzled face rooting among lily pads. When he raised his giant head, cheeks packed with lily shoots, the other boars grumbled hungrily.

Thou impossible fool! Griml spat a curse into the mud. "Behold brave Ull—aye, by the Great Sow, behold brave an' mighty Ull who has took 'pon hisself grave risk so all us'n may eat!" Griml rose from the mud, and the other boars surfaced around him, twelve grizzled hulks lathered in muck. " 'Tis feedin' time, lads! Put thy tusks into it!"

The boars surged forward with elated grunts, stomping the hedge.

Kungu, attired in dappled ivy, sidled up to Griml. "M'lord—exposin' ourselves by light o' day this high upon the mountain, be that wise?"

"What be wise ain't always wisdom, Kungu." Griml spit out a wad of duckweed chewed to cud. "If'n I be leadin' this patrol, I muss lead. Wut good comes o' havin' the lads watch mighty Ull eatin' his full while we loiter empty-bellied?"

The dozen famished boars plowed their way across half the lily paddy before a sleepy beaver emerged from under a log. He frantically slapped his flat tail hard upon the water and cried out, "Pigs! Stinkin' swine in the paddy! Get ye to arms! We got grunters in the field!"

Ull reared up, shawled in lily pads, and hurled a rock he had wedged in his trotter for just such an eventuality. The missile streaked with lethal velocity across the full diagonal of the paddy. Past the startled faces of the other boars, it blurred—close enough to twitch snout hairs—before it struck the beaver's brow with such force his eyes popped out and bits of his skull skittered across the water like tossed pebbles.

Ull shouted, a triumphant toll and the other boars responded instantly, roiling up out of the water to stand on their hind legs and answer the victory cry. The warriors nearest the fallen beaver fell upon its body and, with splintering crunches, devoured it entire.

Griml watched dispassionately from a corner of the paddy, working up the appetite to make himself eat lily shoots. He glanced around for other beavers about in the day.

"Well beyond yonder willow brake, the nearest lodge be," Kungu reported, emerging from under water lilies to stand beside the boar leader. "At this hour, beavers in their lodge slumber deep. Likely, we be yet undetected."

Griml gave the low staccato call to fall back, and the boars instantly ceased their jubilant, thrashing dance and slid through the cloudy water swift and silent, vanishing from the paddy. "Wut be done, be done. The March be movin' on. Aye. When we gets to them hedgerows higher up the mountain, we stop and rest till night. Ain't none the wiser boars was here."

Kungu surveyed the devastated paddy. "Our tracks the silt erases. But what of this ruin?"

"Raiders from out the Mere," Griml answered confidently. "Have our lads leave behind marsh grass an' ferns we gathered up for camouflage. When them beavers spy that, they be confident sure vile louts o' the swamps below plundered this parcel."

Kungu slid back under the lily floats and crossed the paddy unseen to where the others had gathered upon the trodden hedge.

Griml lingered to thank the luckless spirit of the dead beaver. "Thee done served us well, dead paddle tail. Were not for thee, I'd be munchin' stinkin', weevil-gnawed lily root now. An', by the Sacred Sow's Twelve Swollen Teats, Griml ain't marchin' this far to cud lilies! Nay! Me craw be made to taste them most rare succulents, sweetness o' life, the high mountain orchids' most tender shoots. An' thee, dead bucktoothed web foot, thee hast lost all so that we fearless boars be tastin' of life's honeyed secret ere we too be ripped to pieces in the Holy Sow's hungry jaws."

That was the boars' terrible religion. No pain, no disfigurement, no loss of life within the horde—and no slaughter of other creatures—was too severe a price to pay for the momentary rapture of feeding above the clouds. Griml's long mouth drooled. He hankered to taste again those puffs of mushroom, swaths of blue moss, and sprouts of snow orchids.

There, with the whole world under their trotters and earth's horizons cushioned in clouds, the boar horde would celebrate life's brief moment with gluttonous feasting and revelry. *That* was the only valid reply to the fact of death.

The boar lord sighed with longing and trudged across the watery field. "Life be a dream. Aye. But a dream."

CHAPTER THIRTEEN

Dreamcasting

So, life is but a dream, eh, Lord Griml? The serpent Vidar gazed in a pool of icy water to where trance magic revealed the boars sloshing across a trampled paddy far down Riversplash Mountain.

Yes, yes—believe that life is but a dream, you hungry swine. Haunted by the specter of old age and death, you are forced to live in the moment, here, right now, trapped in the present with your appetites—because that is all there is for you. And my secret remains safe.

The viper slid across mica rocks, leaving behind him the vision of muddy boars fading away within the pool. He rippled over the big, flat stones swiftly, alert for shadows of eagles upon the silver path.

Life is but a dream? he chortled as he wriggled under a plate of blue shale. *No! The dream is life.* The crevice was a slitherhole, and it admitted Vidar into dreamspace.

For a moment, the serpent flew across a speed-blurred night sky. Daylight swept over him, and he found himself on a windswept sand dune near crashing sea waves. He crawled among the blades of beach grass, following with his jittery tongue a tasty scent.

At a sandpiper's nest, he rapidly swallowed all six eggs clustered there. Then, his black length drew a swish in the sand and disappeared again into the fissure that opened upon dreamspace. Stars flew by till he wriggled out beneath a black cliff where cocoa-brown frogs shrieked in the sunny haze, "Eek! Snake!"

Vidar had not come to this fern forest to eat frogs—though he frequently did. He came to writhe across the rim of the cliff, knocking over rocks that had fallen from higher up the mountain. The hefty stones clattered off the edge and pounded tall stalks of bamboo below.

Several rocks split open a giant beehive he had spied on an earlier visit. Teeming honeybees swirled in a spreading cloud of buzzing wrath, looking for the invader.

Before they reassembled, Vidar succeeded in slinking down the cliff and swallowing whole a large comb of black mountain honey. He returned the way he had come and soared once more through dreamspace. Stars whipped past—and a moment later, he scrammed with speed toward the cave of his good friend, Bestla.

This old brown bear had crossed through Weasel's Pass many years ago, nearly forsaking her life on those treacherous goat trails to find her way to fabled Riversplash Mountain, where no other bruins dwelled. She had come for the solitude, and she lived as a hermit, devoting her last years to spiritual practice.

"Bestla!" Vidar glided fleetly into the cave. "They have arrived! My dreamcasting has succeeded."

"Silly snake," a voice chided. From out of darkness, a haggard giant rose. "No good will come." Mangy fur hung loosely on the aged bear, a clownish uniform with badges and medallions of scabs and sores. "No good at all will come of this."

"Nonsense, old lady." Vidar regurgitated the honeycomb and the six sandpiper eggs intact in their shells. "At least, you'll get the good of a free meal."

For several seasons, Vidar had been Bestla's sole provider.

Without his offerings, she would have starved, too intent on her meditations to hunt for herself. And without her counsel, Vidar would no longer exist, his spirit lost to grief for his family, his flesh to the claws of the red eagles.

The viper coiled atop a patch of orange lichen and proudly lifted his head. "My dreamcasting has finally attracted boars to Riversplash Mountain. Soon, they will march on the Holt and devour the root wall—and I shall fulfill my vengeance."

With shrunken shoulders and hollowed flanks, Bestla sat down in soft light. "Vidar—Vidar—the root wall will grow back. Your success offers only a temporary solution."

"All is temporary," the snake replied defensively. "You've said so yourself, many times."

"All created things are swept away by passing time," said the old bear, "no different than paw prints in the river's wet sand."

The serpent's grin widened. "Soon, there shall be great feasting upon the Tarn as the wee creatures flee—right into my jaws!"

"And when the feasting is done?"

"I shall have my revenge," Vidar answered confidently. "I shall savor it."

Bestla pawed the comb of black honey. "And how will you survive when your prey has been devoured and the Holt is gone, washed away by eroding rains?"

"Well then, I will leave this mountain," Vidar replied, "and I will return to the ancient jungle of my ancestors and find a mate. We shall have many young. I will teach them all the secrets of the dreaming."

Bestla licked her sticky lips. "You are counting eggs not yet laid—let alone hatched."

"I'm a viper, Bestla. My kind does not lay eggs. We birth live young. Yet, I take your point, old friend." Vidar spiraled tighter, flat head weighted down with doubt. "I've gotten far ahead of myself. The boars have only just arrived." His voice brightened. "All the same, my dreamcasting has finally borne fruit. The boars *have* come to Riversplash Mountain! I summoned them in their dreams—and today I saw them marching upon the Rill!"

Bestla scooped three eggs into her mouth and mumbled, "Boars are dangerous beasts with whom to conspire."

"Ah, that's the beauty of dreamcasting, Bestla." Vidar's arrowhead skull bobbed higher, jaw hinges loosening around a cold grin. "Those swine have no notion that I have led them here. They don't even know I exist!"

"I remember the boars—I remember them from other mountains I have roamed." Her tiny amber eyes radiated as memories kindled. "They will suffer any indignity or torment to satisfy their appetite for rare delicacies. It is their religion, you see. They live to suffer bravely and to eat well, because they believe life is a dream."

"But we know better, don't we?" With an outsize gesture, Vidar unwound from his tight coil and rose up as taut as a cobra. "So long as other animals believe life is but a dream, they will not grasp the source of the serpent's power: The dream *is* life! And those who master dreaming, as vipers have done, can manipulate the living."

"Why manipulate anything, Vidar?"

Vidar's hooded eyes darkened. "If I hadn't manipulated those eggs and honey, you wouldn't have eaten today."

The old bear shrugged. "You need not bring me food."

"You will die."

"Nothing is forever."

Vidar declared, more stiffly than he intended, "*I* will live as long as I can."

"Why?"

"Oh, let's not have this discussion again." The serpent twirled back, unhappy with the direction of their conversation. "I came to you for encouragement. When I was depressed and ready to give myself to the eagles' claws, you persuaded me to live. You said we must hold life's riddle with our fangs until death tears it away from us."

"Yes. I said that."

"So, now you want to die?"

"No. I am still holding the riddle between my fangs, even though they are the few teeth I have left." She consumed the last of the sandpiper eggs and closed her eyes as if relishing her meal, when actually she was contemplating whether to say anything more.

Out of gratitude for the viper's kindness, she decided to tell him what she knew he would not understand. "I came to Riversplash Mountain to live as a hermit, so I would free myself from the foulness of the world and discover the sublime. But now, at last, I have come to realize that finding the sublime alone is impossible. The world is not only sublime. And the freedom I sought is unavailable without loving the filth of the world—even life's miseries and terrors. One must embrace everything in a mighty bear hug."

Vidar's crimson tongue quivered in his mouth as triumphant as a flame. "Then, I am free to manipulate the world as I please!"

"Who is free?" Bestla asked. "Who is not free? Hold *that* riddle between your fangs, Vidar—until death tears it away."

CHAPTER FOURTEEN

Reaping the Wind

Glittering stars spilled across the clear night all the way to the horizon. By their slim light, Notty strode purposefully across the fields of the Rill. He bounded a dam separating paddies and, preoccupied with the pine nuts he nibbled, nearly tripped over an exhausted mouse propped against the levee.

"Hey!" he shouted, twisting in midleap and—to keep from toppling off the trail into the mud—waving both arms while tossing pine nuts like a wedding guest. "Hey!"

The startled mouse sprang up and, seeing the shrew tottering backward, reached out to steady him. Notty grabbed at the helpful paws, but the gravel under his soles slid away and he collapsed backward tugging the mouse after him. They splashed into a ditch of silt and thrashed about clumsily.

Entangled in weeds, the two small animals flailed noisily before finally hauling their drenched bodies back onto the silt bar. They stood glowering at each other, their soaked garments dripping clots of mud.

"Ya addled mousie!" the shrew blurted, spitting out dirt. "What ya doin' lurkin' outta sight?"

"*Me?*" She trembled involuntarily, scattering a spray of mud. "What are *you* doing pouncing along without looking?"

"Hey!" The angry protest in Notty's lungs withered when he noticed that he confronted no ordinary mouse but a white-furred (albeit muddy) maiden of high station. Even soused in muck, the green silk gown she wore hung gracefully on her and her begrimed brogans displayed craft not common below the Holt. "Hullo! Who are you?"

Before the maiden could reply, a gruff shout pummeled them from above: "That's them! That's them that's runnin' off!"

Atop the dam, several beavers clambered, thumping their large flat tails angrily. They wore traditional beaver garb, males and females alike, carmine cloaks and shawls, woolen boots crusted with mud, and heavy necklaces of bronze amulets.

Notty raised his arms in feeble greeting and offered a grin, hoping to inspire laughter at his soaked and sorry figure.

The beavers glared back irately. "That's two of them varmits for sure!"

"Varmits?" Notty cleared the mud from his brow and blinked without comprehending. "What ya talkin' about? I ain't no varmit. I'm Notty Burrtail, carter from the Mere."

"Y'all heard him!" One of the females thwacked her paddle tail on the dam. "These here are the marauders from the Mere!"

"Marauders?" Notty squawked with alarm. "What ya talkin' 'bout? I doan' know nothin' 'bout this mousie, but I sure ain't no marauder."

"Look at 'em all lathered up in mud!" A male pointed a sturdy walking staff at the soaked animals. "Of course they're marauders. They all grimed and soaked with silt. We done caught these two filthy with guilt!"

"Haul 'em to the Riprap!" the cry went up. "Shoot 'em back to the

Mere all bust up! That'll send a right clear message to them thievin' beasties in the swamp."

"You're mistaken," the mouse maiden spoke up. She lifted her smirched face to the beavers and faced them with placid certainty. "This shrew and I don't know each other."

"So you say." The beaver with the staff hopped down from the dam and stood threateningly over the smaller creatures. "And what all else would a pair of pilferers say?"

"What'd we steal?" Notty asked, edging away. "Look at us. We ain't got nothin' that's yores." As he spoke, he spun on his heels, intending to run. But the beaver's staff snagged him by his vest and lifted him off the ground.

"Git over here, you lyin' scoundrel."

"Hey now!" Notty protested, legs churning in midair. "Ya let me down. Let me down or I'll scratch yore eyes right out o' yore head!"

"There you have it!" the staff-wielding beaver said. "He threatened us. These are two of the marauders for sure." He brusquely removed a sheathed dagger from inside the shrew's muddy vest. "I got his blade. He ain't cuttin' nobody."

"The Riprap!" the cry went up again, and the other beavers swooped down from the dam. Notty howled and beat his limbs violently as the beavers hauled him off. The mouse maiden, thrown over the shoulder of a burly male, offered no protest at all.

The beavers carried the suspects up trails notched into rocky slopes. All the while, Notty shouted threats. As they ascended through stunted evergreens dense with sharp needle smells, the sky opened wider—and the shrew's cries dwindled before the oppressive roar of rushing water.

Atop a gorge wall seamed with mushrooms, the beavers stopped and lowered their captives to the ground. Shrew and mouse wobbled at the verge of a cliff that peered down into the torrent whose violent waters spiraled around black rocks.

"There's the villainy you cutthroat thieves visited on us beavers!" one of the female beavers shouted. She pointed down and across the Rill to a blackened splotch of earth among the otherwise orderly paddies. "You done ripped up everything, made off with our harvest—and then . . . " Her voice broke.

Another female finished for her, "You done killed one of our own! And you hid his body, and we ain't found nothin' more of him but his torn hat and one boot soaked in beaver blood."

"What ya talkin' 'bout?" Notty whined. "We never done nothin' o' the like!"

A beaver gruffly jerked the shrew around to face the plunge into the waters of the Riprap. "You think hard on what your ilk did. You think hard durin' your ride back to the Mere, you murderous rogue."

The farmers shouted in angry agreement, "Into the Riprap!"

Facing his doom, Notty fell silent. Then, the mouse maiden spoke, barely audible above the din of the rapids, "I can prove we had nothing to do with what you've shown us."

The beavers turned their scowling faces toward her. "You can't trick your way out of this fix, mousie."

"Is this a trick?" The maiden turned back from her shoulder the fabric of her gown, revealing a bruise broad as her back. The large contusion bore the outline of two toes and two dewclaws from the trotter that had stamped her into captivity on Blossom Vale.

Before the startled stares of the beavers, she told her story of abduction. "Boars who have already arrived here on Riversplash Mountain. They're the ones who raided your fields and murdered your comrade."

"So you say!" a beaver challenged testily. "We ain't seen no trotter prints in our paddies."

"These are elite boars," the mouse replied sedately. "Scouts of the invading horde. They are trained to move silently and without spoor. But if you look, you will find this trace." She plucked from the underside of her gown several thick and dark bristles. "They shed these. If you look for them in the raided field, you will find them."

As wrathful as beavers could be, their character craved justice not vengeance. They dispatched two runners to the ravaged fields to look for boar bristles. While the beavers guarded the captives, shrew and mouse sat silently, backs to the Riprap. They gazed down expectantly at the scurrying beavers on the hills below.

A shrill whistle sounded from below announcing the discovery of boar bristles. The beavers immediately muttered embarrassed apologies to the shrew and mouse, returned Notty's knife without looking him in the eye, and quickly departed.

"Lucky for me ya kept a cool head, mousie." Notty helped the maiden to her feet and cast a nervous glance into the rushing water below. "Maybe now ya can tell me who ya are?"

"I'm Olweena Talkingstone." The mouse took the shrew's paw in her own. "And I'd be grateful if you'd show me the road to Fernholt."

CHAPTER FIFTEEN

An Infamous Criminal

Muspul had marched all the previous day to exit the Mere. By night, he found new strength, summoned from his nocturnal nature as a hedgehog, and he climbed up narrow trails of the mountain that led him into the high meadows of the Rill. All the while, he carried across his hunched shoulders a musket, a gift intended for Thrym.

The hedgehog had traded his tinker's wagon and all its wares for this flared barrel of blue steel. The arms merchant, a one-eyed rat dragging a gnawed tail, had conducted the transaction in the Mere's hinterland, where no creatures resided to question Muspul's lack of a license from the Council of Squires.

The usually circumspect hedgehog had behaved like a rash adolescent. He had spent no time wrangling the price or inspecting the weapon. He was too eager to find and arm Thrym, too overwrought at the thought of losing his best pupil, and too anxious to be rid of his wagon now that invading boars were about to demolish his business and the whole world around it.

A paw shake had sealed the deal. Moments later, the emotional event took its toll on Muspul's old heart. Spasms of pain leaned him heavily against the side of the cart. The rat's one eye avidly watched as the hedgehog groped his pockets before bringing forth a vial of green glass.

"Don't let them crows see ye like this, ye old bristlehide," the rat warned with a sneer. "They will surely take yore eyes."

The blackened cork of the vial came free with a pop, and the stricken hedgehog quickly sipped. As his limbs found new strength, he backed away from the wagon, relieved to catch his breath.

Shaking his head piteously, the one-eyed rat handed over the musket, wrapped in oilcloth, lifted the tines of the wagon, and trundled off as brisk as a thief.

"I traded my livelihood for a single shot!" the hedgehog was still muttering a day later as he labored uphill. "That rat got the better of me, for sure. Unless, of course, this one shot proves better than no shot."

Along the way, he had lost the oilcloth wrap, and he carried the naked weapon with one arm draped over the stock, the other over the barrel. At dawn, he forded a clearwater branch and climbed a nearly perpendicular track toward the northwest sky.

A gruff voice called, "Yaw! Slow down there, Bristle Hog! Where you rushing off to with that gun across your back?"

Muspul looked down and saw nothing but a gully of birch trees stacked with sun shafts.

Peering more closely, the hedgehog noticed that the slants of sunlight amid white trees concealed a large, splotched animal. Tapered orange eyes gazed up at him. Muspul started with fright.

"Don't you go passing out on me now, Hog!" The ferocious beast's thick voice issued from a wide grin of carnivorous teeth. He stood and dead leaves swirled off him. "You got no cause for that green tinge on your snout or them bugging eyes. I might be ugly but ugly never hurt nobody. Besides—I'm no trouble to nobody but myself in this sorry state."

"Sorry state?" Muspul dared to breathe, staring horrified at the gruesome beast. *A polecat!* his startled brain finally registered. *I passed within inches of those deadly jaws and sensed no peril whatsoever! Oh, indeed, I am too old for wilderness treks.* Nervously, he inquired, "What is your state, sir, that is so—so sorry?"

The large polecat rose to full height, tall enough to stare down at the hedgehog perched on the clay stairway. The fleece vest he wore glistened with grime as did his lavender scarf and once-colorful wool boots decked with tassels. "If honey could talk, it would sound like you, Little Hog. What are you, a preacher?"

"A recovering teacher."

"Haw! And a sense of humor like a spit of rain in a dry eye!"

"Yes, well, thank you for the compliment." Muspul nodded courteously and backed up another step. "But I really must be on my way."

"Hold on there, pal. I got me big trouble. I need your help." He raised front paws gloved in black velvet and pointed down at a braided wire looped about his right ankle. The metal cord lashed the beast to two sturdy birch trees. He budged his leg side to side, demonstrating the tautness of the snare. "The trap was baited with the palest blue grosbeak eggs—rigged for a tall fellow the likes of me. It sprung when I stepped in this here noose while reaching for them precious baubles." He shrugged. "Now, you tell me, what evil would think to overwhelm a polecat's confidence by baiting a trap with the most irresistible treats known to all? Addles the brain."

"You're a thief," Muspul surmised. "And a carnivore. What are you doing here on Riversplash Mountain?"

"No competition. That's why I risked breaking my handsome neck in Weasel's Pass to get here." The polecat twisted a corner of his black lips into a sly smile. "Frikee—eggsnatcher, fish poacher, nuts-and-berries pilferer, and all-purpose crook." He extended a black-gloved paw. When he saw that the hedgehog had no intention of shaking paws with an outlaw, he scratched his snout and tugged his back leg hopelessly. "What? You gone tell me you never filched no eggs on your righteous way through this world? Come on, Hog, 'fess up. If you'd seen those cute little blue eggs ogling you from up that tree, you'd be the rascal with your paw in the noose."

"You misjudge me, Mister Frikee." The hedgehog backed up another step so that his spectacles came level with the polecat's eyes. "I am no malefactor."

"You sure you no preacher?" Frikee squinted one wicked eye skeptically. "What genuine teacher don't have no appreciation for the push and pull of good and evil? Hm? We all of us are *malefactors*, Hog. What, you live on air and sunshine like the trees? Them there are the princes of heaven. We just tooth and claw, you and me. Now, show some charity for a fellow beast of prey and untie this skanky snare so's I can avoid concluding my days as a throw rug in some beaver's lodge."

"Beavers are notoriously just, Mister Frikee." Muspul continued his backward climb up the claystone steps. "I'm sure that whatever punishment awaits you in their custody is fitting and proper."

"Yaw, Hog! You are as cold as a vulture's breakfast!" Frikee sat down heavily. "But you're right. Least wise, you would have been right as sunlight before two days *and* nights of me lying here, contemplating my past misdeeds—*malignant* misdeeds—brought a powerful change upon my heart. A hog of the hedge such as yourself, though, probably don't have no truck with changes of heart. That's the stuff of fairy tales, not reason."

"You're mistaken about me again, Mister Frikee. I know that a heart may change when prompted by necessity." Muspul paused. "Perhaps this is not a situation to be decided by reason but trust."

"Hog, your wisdom has outdone itself and found truth!" Frikee waggled the braided wire. "Now, if you got paws nimble as your mind, I'm out of here, tossing good deeds as I go like crumbs to birds . . . "

"Thas a lie, every word!" a shrill voice sounded from the stream. "Frikee Fitch be a varlet and a fugitive hisself."

Hedgehog and polecat looked to where a speckled trout reared his glistening head. "And you are?" Muspul inquired.

"Never you mind 'bout me," the trout spat back bitterly. "Lookee here on the side of this beech an' tell all us what you see."

"Don't pay no heed to that scaly, cold-blooded spawn." Frikee snarled. "He's sore I made a meal of his mama in my vile former days. I tell you true, Hog, I am surely quit of them ways. Berries, nuts, and roots—that there be my fare of choice ever more."

During Frikee's rant, Muspul climbed down to the beech tree indicated by the trout. He found a sun-bleached poster stained by rain.

The stenciled writing read

WANTED

FRIKEE FITCH, POLECAT

FELON AT LARGE:

THIEF—MISCREANT—FOWL MURDERER—BRIGAND—

CRIMINAL DEBAUCHER OF MINK, SKUNK, AND MARTEN—

GOON FOR HIRE—HOODLUM—EGG ROBBER—VANDAL—

ROE SNATCHER—THUG—FISH SLAYER!

THE COUNCIL OF SQUIRES OFFERS THREE PRIME ACRES

OF FERTILE FARMLAND IN THE RILL

FOR THE APPREHENSION—PREFERABLY DEAD—

OF THIS VICIOUS OUTLAW.

BEWARE!

FRIKEE FITCH IS NOTORIOUSLY VIOLENT—

AND A LIAR!

Muspul expelled a soft sigh and wagged his head. "You have a very bad reputation, Mister Fitch."

"Yaw, Hog! I never did deny that," Frikee whined. "I done told you straight up, my past misdeeds was *malignant*. But these two days *and* nights snared up here in this ditch has worked a powerful change for good upon my heart."

"I want to believe you," Muspul allowed. "But this 'wanted' poster speaks grave ill of you. Fowl *murderer*?"

Frikee hung his head shamefully. "I got no defense. All manner of poultry and fowl have been slain with these black-gloved paws and devoured with these jaws. I won't deny I favored a ruthless appetite for cacklers and capon. But I never did kill nothing with fur. Besides, them days are well behind me now."

"You lets him go," the trout piped up, "and he surely will bust you up, old quillback. That hoodlum will leave you bleedin' for the crows to fight over."

"That is a foul lie!" Frikee barked viciously, then softened his tone. "Of course, the carnivore ways of my past would force a small-brained, scaly thing such as yourself to judge me unkindly. Fortunately my fate don't depend none on your slimy judgment. This here thoughtful hedgehog knows I'm worthy of mercy. Ain't that so, Hog?"

Muspul tugged at his whiskers as he ambled to the edge of the gully. "If I release you and you do further harm, Mister Fitch, then I shall be an accessory to those crimes. Such a burden I am unwilling to bear."

"Aw, Hog! Don't be talking like that." Frikee knelt and clasped together his gloved paws. "You know them beavers gone toss me in the Riprap. You walk on by and you kill me sure as them beavers."

Dread at the likelihood of condemning a fellow creature to death troubled Muspul, and he stiffened. Frowning, he staggered toward one of the birch trees that anchored the wire snare. "I've lost enough time dawdling here with you, Mister Fitch. I am on a pressing mission, and I cannot linger further. And as this is a matter of your life or death, my trust in goodness obliges me to believe in your sincerity and release you." He leaned the musket against the birch, knelt, and began untwisting the wire. "I will give you back your life, sir. Please, do not betray my faith in you."

"Hog, you got the undying gratitude of this reformed polecat." Frikee grinned.

"You're a durn fool, hedgehog!" the trout shouted and splashed into deeper water as Muspul began loosening the snare.

Muspul's heart throbbed in his throat as the wire came loose and his belief in this fellow creature faced its test. He watched as Frikee swiftly yanked the wire off his ankle.

Without a moment's hesitation, the polecat bounded to where Muspul stood. "Yaw! Teacher's gone back to school!" Frikee snatched the musket and thwacked it sharply to the side of the hedgehog's skull.

With an anguished groan, Muspul collapsed to the forest floor as Frikee barked with hearty laughter. "Lesson number one, Hog! The heart of the beast don't never change." The polecat dragged the elderly hedgehog to the trees where he had been tied and quickly wrapped the wire around unconscious Muspul's foot.

CHAPTER SIXTEEN

Fortune's Tragedy

Sun cast metallic light upon a bristly fellow, lying among a grove of beech trees. Carried by a chill downdraft, his soft sobs drifted.

"Hullo!" Notty shouted with surprise. He and Olweena had heard the crying from where they hiked alongside the bluff. They hurried, hoping to get a better view of the hillcrest and see who despaired.

"Braid my whiskers! That's dominie!" the shrew said. "That's old Muspul."

"You know that woeful character up there?" Olweena shielded her eyes from the sun with her paw. "He looks injured."

Notty scrambled up the packed clay slope. "Dominie! It's me—Notty! What ya doin' up here?"

Muspul turned a dazed expression upon the intruder.

"Owl spit!" The shrew gasped at the sight of the hedgehog's ensared foot and blood-crusted brow. "Dominie! Ya head's all bust up! And ya tied ta the trees. Wha' happened?"

The hedgehog blinked at the shrew through the cockeyed lenses of his bent spectacles. "Is that you, Notty?"

"Sure 'nough it's me." The shrew removed from his neck a large red bandana and daubed at the gobs of jellied blood on Muspul's forehead. "Ya a lucky quillpouch. It ain't split ta th' skull. Just one big bruise an' a shallow gash not wantin' thread an' needle." Gently, he unwound the wire from the hedgehog's foot.

He tugged free from his belt a wood flagon. Uncorking it released a bleary chemical scent. "Nettle mash," he replied to the hedgehog's groggy frown. "Th' Mere's finest whiskey for all what afflicts ya—inside an' out." He soaked the bandana in the pungent alcohol. "'Fore I apply this binding, ya best take a deep swallow." Not waiting for assent, Notty pressed the flagon to his old teacher's lips and poured a long draft.

Muspul spluttered, gagged, and coughed. "Gah! That is poison!"

"So th' wife an' parson insist. But it awready put th' sparkle back in ya eyes. There's th' snappy dominie I recollect." Notty bound the mash-soaked bandana across Muspul's brow and knotted it behind his head. "That stings a trifle, now don't it?"

Before the hedgehog could answer, Olweena stood beside them, on the bluff clutching her sides and panting.

"Dominie Muspul," Notty introduced, "this here is Olweena Talkingstone, a refugee o' Blossom Vale, fleein' th' boars."

"A lady"—the old hedgehog drew a shaky breath—"of distinguished breeding." He bowed his wounded head and added, "You have suffered—cruelly, I see. Indignities—of flesh and heart— but I think not of spirit."

Olweena's whiskers fanned, impressed by the gentlemanly hedgehog. "You make good use of those spectacles, dominie. But how were you injured?"

Muspul related his encounter with the polecat and humiliating misjudgment of Frikee's character. "Educated hedgehog or not," said he, struggling upright and wobbling on his feet, "I'm quite the fool. Now, I've no musket for my best student. My wagon—and all its goods—bartered for naught." A dizzy spell tightened toward an all-too-familiar pain in his chest. He took out the green glass vial. "But perhaps—perhaps this is for the best." He sipped at the medicine, and the spasm in his heart relaxed. "We shall reason with that foolhardy mouse—when we reach the Holt."

"Not me, dominie." Notty helped Muspul regain his balance. "Thanks ta ya alertin' Unise, my adventurin' goes no further than findin' my runaway son, Wili. He took off ta hunt pig wit' Squire Cheevie. He's out there in th' Rill somewheres."

"Notty, I apologize—for speaking to your wife behind your back." Muspul bowed his head remorsefully. "Now your boy is out there, wandering hill and dale. We shall find him together."

"Oh, no, dominie." Notty guided him along a path that meandered down into a sunlit orchard. "We're gettin' ya some rest at a lodge. There's a proper bandage awaitin' that nick upon ya head."

Muspul stopped and dug in his heels. "Notty, you might as well know the truth. I am dying. There is no point in mending my wound—or resting these brittle bones."

"Dyin'?" Notty's pointy nose bent sideways. "Is this one o' yore intellectual speculations, dominie?"

"The estimable frogs of the Mere's infirmary made the diagnosis. I've a season left me on this mountain—probably less. I'm not wasting a day. Let's go find Wili."

On the orchard path, Muspul attempted to lift the gloom of his announcement by inquiring of Olweena's troubles. The mouse maiden offered curt and evasive replies. Afraid of revealing too much, she deflected the conversation back to him, "I want to hear how a refined hedgehog came to live in the Mere. What could possibly have brought a well-lettered animal to that bog of ignorance and brutality?"

"Fortune's tragedy."

"Now you've positively fascinated me, Dominie Muspul." She regarded him with admiration. "You've suffered so much of late. Can you bear my questions?"

Muspul stiffened, reached into his pocket, and squeezed the medicinal vial for comfort. "My family tale is neither unique— nor enlightening, young maiden. What to say?" He framed this question to himself with a dismal shrug. "Yes, my lineage goes back to Fernholt's founders. 'Twas one of my ancestors invented latex galoshes—when she accidentally stepped into a storm-toppled gum tree. Made a fortune. Huge. One of her great-grandchildren established Fernholt Academy—where I was educated—the last of our line after seven generations to afford such elite grooming. You see, my father was a wastrel. A fanatic of two expensive vices: gaming and drink. Lost everything. And *that* is fortune's tragedy, my dear. Though we were among the most esteemed families, without our fortune we became poor and friendless. And ended up in the Mere. There, my parents died miserably—and I have endured a miserable life."

"I'm sorry to have inquired after such unhappy memories, dominie." Olweena's large ears curled sadly inward. "I understand now why you devoted your life to teaching. Your education—there's the wealth that remains of your noble heritage."

Muspul stopped and gazed kindly upon the dirtied mouse maiden. "Yes. Knowledge is my wealth. And that is why I must find the one student who paid heed to my lessons—for he has inherited all that I have to give."

CHAPTER SEVENTEEN

Castaways

Little birds crossed through the wind before them and fluttered like leaves along the orchard trail. "Ya rest here in th' shade, dominie," Notty suggested. "Olweena's smart company—an' she got a kerchief o' acorn bread an' beetle nougat. I'm goin' ahead an' find th' grove keeper.

"No need to go far, kind shrew." Muspul pointed past the trees to a cart track, where several ram–drawn wagons rattled along. They carried bushels of onions, tubs of dewberries, and crates overflowing with lettuce. "That caravan of produce is most likely bound for the Holt."

"They surely ain't goin' ta th' Mere." Notty ran toward the caravan, waving his green cap in one paw and with the other snatching crickets from under the blossoming trees. "Hullo! Rams!"

The caravan did not stop, yet it rolled so lazily that Notty had no trouble jogging alongside the lead ram. They conversed briefly, and the shrew came charging back, chomping on a cricket. "Them rams awready heard th' boar hordes are comin'—an' they'd be proud ta fetch a mouse maiden refugee ta th' Holt." He skidded to a stop before Muspul and winked at his old teacher. "I told 'em ya was an Academy elder doin' field work in th' Mere an' ya got to get back ta th' Holt for ta serve as military advisor ta th' Squires. Clever brainwork, eh, dominie?"

"Most clever, Notty." Muspul clasped a paw on the proud shrew's shoulder. "But what about Wili? I should help you find him."

"Ya should get ta th' Holt is what ya should do, dominie." Notty looked to the rolling wagons. "They ain't stoppin'. Ya know rams an' their stubborn ways. Don't ya worry none 'bout my Wili. I'll find him sure enough. Now get goin'."

"Thank you, Notty." Muspul shuffled into the grove, then paused to turn and wave. "I shall remember you to Thrym."

"Thrym?" Olweena asked, "Is that the name of Muspul's beloved student? Thrym Seedcorn? A beige mouse with strong arms and eyeglasses?"

"You know Thrym?"

"Met him coming out of the Mere," Olweena replied, backing away toward the caravan. "He's an obstinate mouse."

"Yep—that's Thrym!" Notty fit his green cap back on his head and waved both paws at his departing friends. "Olweena, if'n I hadn't bumped inta ya, I'd have ridden th' Riprap! Ya carry my gratitude where'er ya go."

The mouse maiden ran ahead to the rear wagon. When Muspul hurried close enough, she helped push him into the flatbed, then hopped in beside him. "I met your student Thrym as I was leaving the Mere."

"Did you?" Muspul huffed and reached for the green vial. "I am surprised—" He sucked a long breath of air perfumed with pollen and the crisp scent of the fresh spring harvest. "I am surprised Thrym did not"—he held the uncorked vial to his snout, and the medicinal pungency proved sufficient to ease his heart and allow him to finish his thought—"did not escort you to the Holt. He's a kind young rodent—and you are a beautiful mouse."

"He claimed I was *too* beautiful." Her tail flicked with indignation at the very thought. "And he gave me these pennies."

Muspul's eyebrows bent sadly when he saw the dented coins. "You realize those are all the funds that Thrym possessed. He is very much the kind rodent to have parted with them on behalf of a stranger, albeit a lovely stranger."

"Kind and foolish." Olweena leaned back among the crates and made herself comfortable. "We both realize he is throwing his life away going against the boars. They'll crush him with one trotter."

Muspul winced at the thought. "You've witnessed the wrath of the boars firsthand." His whiskers twitched with worry. "For all my seasons on this mountain, I've never seen a boar. Are they as terrible as the books depict?"

Olweena stared at the hedgehog and could find no words to describe the terror of the boars. The more she tried, the more her fear widened.

"You're trembling." Muspul rapped knuckles against his brow for his idiocy. "You must have experienced unspeakable horrors at Blossom Vale."

"My mother and father . . . " She dared not complete the thought for fear she would blurt out the truth of her spying for Griml.

"You lost your parents to the boars." The hedgehog swung his gaze out over the orchard. "I'm sorry."

They rode in silence. The rhythmic motion of the wagon rocked Olweena to sleep, and she suffered a nightmare of boars clothed in smoke like ghostly beasts. Screeching and howling, the attackers trampled the fallen, swinging ropes of entrails, whole bodies of mice, shrews, and hedgehogs clenched in their jaws. She cried in her sleep, her whiskers quivering in terror.

Muspul moved to wake her, but instead leaned close and

whispered, "Olweena, you are safe on Riversplash Mountain. You are well on your way to a new life in the Holt."

The mouse maiden calmed and settled into placid slumber. He knew that he, too, should sleep, for his aged body craved rest. Even so, he could not forgive himself for allowing Frikee Fitch to dupe him.

The wagon trundled across a narrow stone bridge, and the Riprap swept into view. Staring into that brutal roar of white water, Muspul gradually felt less stupid for the beating he had taken from the predator. He had spared the polecat, a fellow creature, from certain doom.

Yes, he had broken a serious rule of law, but the price for civilization, for its civility and order, Muspul had learned keenly from his father's failure.

" 'Those who do not comply are made to cry,' " the hedgehog muttered, recalling that saying from his privileged childhood.

"The predators have their own law, not sanctioned by any society or judge but by life itself. What we may call good and right and lawful is a fabrication, made up and foolish. And like any fabrication may collapse and be lost. But the predator's freedom is the might of life!"

Muspul drew a large, satisfied breath. "Let the boars come. Let civilization and all its strict rules slide down the mountain into the Mere, where the freedom of the predator shall have its way with us all."

"Is that what you truly believe, dominie?" Olweena mumbled groggily. "That is a hardhearted judgment."

"I didn't realize I had thought aloud." He tucked his chin to his chest sheepishly. "There was a hint of dubiety in my tone perhaps?"

"Dubiety?" Olweena pushed herself upright with her elbows. "What does that mean?"

"Uncertainty."

"No." She rubbed her sleepy eyes with her wrists. "You sounded quite certain. You want revenge on the Holt for exiling you and your family."

Muspul gazed down his snout at her. "Yes, I suppose I do. I see now that it is my lifelong conviction."

"That is an ugly conviction, dominie." Her stare sharpened. "You don't know what you're talking about."

"I'm talking about the inevitable, my dear." The paws in his lap flexed helplessly. "Noble cultures grow old eventually and slide down into chaos—as did yours in Blossom Vale—as will the Holt. The authentic world is wild and unbroken. There is nothing noble about it."

Olweena's fur rose along the scruff of her neck. "*We* are what is noble in the pitiless world. Civilization is nature's flower and fruit."

"And what becomes of fruit, Olweena?"

Olweena crossed her arms. "There are no large predators on Riversplash Mountain. Notty tells me that all the sizable maulers were driven off by your legendary heroes, the Brave Tails. Since then, the remoteness of your mountain has kept you safe. Where I come from, life is very different." She closed her eyes. "*Was* very different."

When she looked at him again, her face had tightened, strict with memory. "We lived in walled compounds. There were no open paddies and fields as you have here. Wherever we traveled, we moved in convoys armed with muskets to fend off lynx and weasels. If dog packs or wolves attacked, we had no choice but to flee and hide. What you have here is good. You should not wish ill of it."

"I do not." Muspul sniffed. "What I express is but a law of nature. All fruit falls and rots. So will the Holt—and all its fine estates."

"You *are* an bitter bug eater, aren't you?"

"We are castaways, Olweena." The hedgehog settled back comfortably and closed his eyes, pleased with this revelation about himself and his heart's despair. "The world's castaways."

CHAPTER EIGHTEEN

The Sea Is a Book Whose Pages the Moon Turns

Thrym retrieved the sack of his possessions hung from the willow beside the canal where he and Wili first met. But the wind had tossed into the mud his floppy hat, and the straw had gotten soaked and come apart. "That hat fit well," Thrym complained in an annoyed whisper and stalked back to where Wili waited.

Together, young shrew and bareheaded mouse stood atop the dike and gazed downhill toward the distant Mere. "I ain't a-goin' back thar," Wili declared firmly. "I'd as soon git et by a snake than go back to that stinkin' swamp."

Thrym slung the clattering sack over his shoulder. "You mean that?"

"Is the rain wet?"

"You do realize if anything bad happens to you, I'm the one who will have to answer to your ma and pa?"

"Then jest fergit we e'er met," Wili replied, unruffled. "I'm so dink, ye kin fergit me jest by blinkin' hard."

"Don't be silly." Thrym nailed Wili in place with a stare. "Your pa and I are old friends. I'm not going to forget I saw his son out here on his own."

"I should ne'er follered ye." Wili jerked a glance along the canal in the direction he intended to flee. "I'd done better on my own."

"You got that right." Thrym's tail twitched angrily. "Now, we're going home. And don't give me any back talk."

"I'm done talkin'." Wili stepped to the edge and bent his knees to jump. "I runned away from you before, an' I'll bolt agin. You'll ne'er see a whisker o' me no more."

"Whoa!" Thrym seized the shrew by the frayed collar of his shirt. "Hold on, little furball. I'm done chasing you hither and yon." The worn fabric of that sorry shirt ripped, and the mouse swiftly shifted his grip to the boy's scruffy neck. "Get your scrawny hide back here."

"Eee-ow!" Wili squealed and squirmed, held fast in the mouse's secure grip. "I ain't a-goin' back to the Mere. No way 'cept in a blue jay."

"You're big enough now to stop worrying about jays." Thrym fixed a stare on the wee shrew. "But you best keep an eye out for owls, hawks, and snakes, or there's going to be scat somewhere with your bones in it." That frightful thought only made the shrew squirm more. "Stop that and listen to me. Look, you stop wriggling, and I'll make you a deal."

Wili hung limp from Thrym's brawny arm and glared grumpily. "What deal?"

"You a shrew good for his word?"

"Is fire hot?"

"All right, then." Thrym released Wili and backed away. "You promise you'll never again run away from me and we'll go on together to the Holt."

"You funnin' me?"

"No, I'm not funning you." Thrym backed off another pace, demonstrating his sincerity by granting the boy plenty of room to escape. "We made an important discovery together. You realize that we are the only two creatures in all of Riversplash Mountain that know where the Dead Riders are entombed." He paused, letting that thought sink in. "It's only right we should share the credit. So, what do you say we both make the trek to the Holt and report to the Squires what we've found down there in that grotto?"

"You doan' reckon thar be a ree-ward fer sech a rare an' mighty find?"

"This is a big discovery." Thrym turned his back on Wili and proceeded across the dike, the boy in tow. "Bigger than big. I guarantee, you'll be a celebrity in the Holt once news of this gets around. But the deal is, you come with me without any tomfoolery." He cast a stern look over his shoulder at the wonder-struck shrew. "No running off on your own. No ignoring my orders. You stay close to me and do what I say."

"An' we a-goin' to the Holt?"

"That's right." Thrym jumped down from the dike and quartered across a clover field. "My sister, Magdi, lives at Bracken Knoll with her husband, Squire Cheevie. We'll report to them. I'm sure there's a place on their estate for an enterprising shrew—especially one of the co-discoverers of the Dead Riders' crypt. Work hard, and soon enough you'll be sending money back to your folks in the Mere." He paused long enough for Wili to come alongside. "You can work?"

"I kin work fast as a bee spits honey!"

"Bees don't spit hon . . . "

Wili danced ahead of the mouse and grinned proudly. "You really reckon your sis gone make a place fer me in Bracken Knoll?"

"I reckon she will."

"Then let's git!"

"Hold up, pal." Thrym scanned the sky with his far-seeing eyes.

"We're not going anywhere until we get a message to your pa and let him know you're safe and with me."

The mouse whistled, and a moment later, a chickadee alighted on a willow branch. Thrym briefly negotiated with the winged courier before it shot away. "Well, that went nowhere. The Avian Guild won't convey messages without payment upfront. We're just going to have to try to meet up with your pa along the way to Bracken Knoll."

"I ain't tore up about it." Wili strode on ahead. "No matter we done made a discovery bigger than big, Pa gone holler at me, and I ain't in no hurry fer that."

The hikers departed the fields by crossing a rapid stream where a drifted tree acted as a bridge. Climbing across acres of barley and strawberries, the shrew foraged a meal. Soon they found themselves ascending a valley ridge too steep for farming.

Thrym surveyed the trail ahead. Beyond a grove of crooked oaks was an expansive clearing. There, several rotund cedars gathered and a chipmunk scrounged among fallen needles. That slick mat of layered needles would make the ascent slippery, and the mouse clipped his pince-nez to his snout the better to read such loose terrain. Trudging slowly, they entered the clearing.

A shrill whistle split the air, and Thrym spun about, grabbed Wili by the shoulders, and pulled him to the ground. Together they slid under the cover of the scrub oaks.

Talons splayed, a kestrel swooped upslope, over the exact spot where they had stood.

The chipmunk under the cedar spun to flee, but claws struck her from behind. Up into the sky the kestrel wheeled, hoisting the limp chipmunk, who gazed downward sadly, bidding farewell to her scampering life.

"Tails 'n whiskers!" Wili stared dismayed at the disappearing raptor and chipmunk. "That prit near was us!"

Thrym swiped the lenses from his face and scanned the skies. "I don't see any other hunters on high."

"You ain't never seen that one!"

"I'm sorry. I'd forgotten how dangerous these foothills are. That won't happen again." The mouse led the shrew out into the clearing, head craning to search the heights. "Come on. We're better off not stopping in the open."

The slippery climb through the long clearing proved tiring for the young shrew. When they finally arrived at the spruce trees cresting the ridge, his heart heaved under his rib cage.

"We'll spend the night in this grove," Thrym decided. "I know it's a bother sleeping by night like we were mongooses or rabbits, but with the boars on the way we have to adapt. So, why don't we rest here and eat? I spy a bee tree in the woods yonder, and after I get a fire going I'll smoke it and gather some honey combs."

"I'm takin' a thirst," Wili announced after he caught his breath. "Why doan' I scout us'n a crik?"

"See those big ferns the other side of the bee tree?" Thrym pointed past the spruce trees. "There'll be a spring back there for sure."

"I doan' see no bee tree, much less them ferns."

"Just stroll in the direction I'm pointing." The mouse began gathering kindling for the fire. "There are still a couple hours of light, plenty of time to forage some early berries and mushrooms. Wild yams thrive in these conifer groves, too. So, we'll have a satisfying meal tonight."

"I got to learn me how you find vittles where I doan' see nothin' but sprucy trees an' rocks."

They ate at twilight. From their high westward view, cloudbanks floated like mountains adrift above the slanted territory of the Rill. Afterward, mouse and shrew slept inside the root cove of a large spruce.

The old moon rose on the far side of midnight. His cool voice called down from star-flung reaches, "Hello there, friend Thrym. Are you awake or all done in?"

The mouse sat up in the dark and sniffed the air. A wind had risen and deposited scents of pine sap and river rock from higher up the mountain. He turned about and squinted into the eastern sky, where the curved moon drooped. "Why'd you wake me?"

"I had to wait past midnight to hear you say I was right."

" *'Before this morning is fully done, an adventure for you will have begun.'* You did say that." He rubbed his eyes and flicked his whiskers, assuring himself the moon's company was not some fleeting dream. "You could have been more specific. You know, something like, *'Once into a hole in the Rill he has slipped—there brave Thrym will find the Dead Riders' crypt.'* "

"Who all ye talkin' to?" Wili mumbled.

"Just the old moon."

"Long as he doan' talk back."

"He's the one woke me with his chatter."

Wili opened one eye. "Git some sleep."

"I'd like nothing better." The mouse got up and sauntered to a downwind spruce to discharge his bladder. "Just let me see what he wants."

"That thar's the moon." Wili rolled over and curled tighter into his sleep position. "He doan' want fer nothin'."

"Don't you believe it." While he relieved himself, Thrym inspected the starry firmament for owl shadows. "The new moon has the sun for company, but the old moon is the loneliest thing I ever met. When he's full, the moon is rising as the sun sets, and he gets a little crazy with the whole night before him, all to himself. That's famous—the crazy full moon. Well, the old moon, all shriveled and tired, is on his way back to his companion, the sun. But that old boy, the moon, is still too far away and too weary. So, you see, he's lonely. And if you pay him some heed, he'll share his secrets with you."

From the edge of sleep, the shrew muttered, "What all secrets?"

"The moon's been around almost from day one." Thrym tightened the drawstrings of his tunic. "He's seen everything."

"It cain't see fer tryin' where them squids an' starfish warsh their draws at the bottom o' the sea."

Thrym chuckled. "You ever seen the sea?"

" 'Course not," the lad answered drowsily. "I ain't no idjit thinks a pond's the sea. But I heard tell 'bout it from them gulls an' plovers visitin' the Mere. The sea's wide 'nough to swaller Riverplash Mountain an' all these here mountains entire an' not even burp."

"It's that big, all right." Thrym climbed into the spruce above Wili and straddled the lowest bough. "The moon pulls the tides in and out and watches the sea's waves, reading them like pages in a book. In fact, the sea is a book whose pages the moon turns, Wili. It reads everything in those riffling pages."

A soft snore sounded from the shrew.

"I don't think he believes me," Thrym confided to the moon. "I hope you're not annoyed."

"The disbelief of a boy is not enough to annoy."

"So, what have you got to say for yourself?" Thrym watched blurs of bats whirring against wild vapors of stars. "Another prophecy I won't understand?"

"No more foretelling, just some advice—for my favorite seer among the mice."

"Well, you better make it clear," the mouse insisted. "I'm sleepy and in no mood for riddles."

"Keep your discovery secret—or it will become regret."

"Hey, that's asking a lot." Thrym squinted at the chipped bone of the moon. "This is the biggest archeological find of modern times."

"If you spread it, you'll dread it."

"What am I supposed to do?" Thrym stood up on the bough, filled with confusion. "Forget I found the burial place of the greatest heroes in history?"

The moon repeated, "If you spread it, you'll dread it," then whispered cool and silver across the night sky, "When mouse shares with his *friends* what he knows—they reclaim the masks and become heroes."

The Holt

Cloudbursts erupt all summer long. Their torrents spill out of the mountain's crater in great mantles of white water that plunge over cliff faces as booming waterfalls. Farther down the mountain, drifts of rainbow spray ascend. Dense vapors gather on upland slopes, sustaining lush, wet jungles and transforming that elevation to a country of fog, a giant's realm of immense trees: the Holt of the Cloud Forest.

—*Geophysical Notes*

This is the high country, doorstep of rain,
Cliff-face kissed first and last by the sun,
Riverbed of clouds, evergreen's domain,
Jade windowsill of earth's horizon.
from "Riversplash Song: Lay of the Land"

—Ki-o-Ki

CHAPTER NINETEEN

Bracken Knoll

Thrym and Wili reached the pike road early, under a gray sky of light rain. Almost immediately, they got a lift from a donkey express transporting mail across the Holt. Riding in the wicker saddle basket among parcels and letters, mouse and shrew watched the dripping trees of the Holt jog by.

The donkey's halter bells lulled Thrym to sleep, and he woke hours later to find the sky clear and Wili hooting at the many wayfarers alongside the road. Stout water rats, a mole in bamboo armor, chipmunks, and toads stood aside—all pilgrims bound for Bracken Knoll. Wili waved to one and all, shouting, "Hey-dee, thar! We a-goin' pig huntin'!"

Around a treacherous, curve of gnarled pines, Bracken Knoll appeared. The estate filled an entire upper valley, backed by peaks hidden in mist. Ghostly waterfalls dropped out of mountain clouds, and their streams poured downhill to power-churning wheels of three large mills. Abundant orchards, nut groves, and apiaries enclosed a baronial manor on a hill.

"Dang!" Wili nearly popped out of the wicker basket with excitement. "I ne'er seen the like!"

Through towering stands of bamboo and whopping ferns, Wili glimpsed greenhouses, nurseries, and gardens. Armed gatekeepers motioned them onto a slate drive and through a stone gateway crested by a wrought-iron sign: WRIGHT COURT.

They rolled past cottages and bungalows with terra cotta roofs and chimney pots. Trade signs carved to the likeness of loaves, a boot, horseshoes identified a prospering community of artisans: baker, cobbler, smithy, wheelwright, tailor, potter, confectioner, plumber, cheese maker, mason, carpenter, weaver, and glass blower.

Wili sucked an awed breath through his teeth. "This here squire got him a whole village!"

"Gardeners and field workers bunk in barrack housing out of sight at the back of the vale . . . " Thrym's voice trailed off at the sight of makeshift bamboo hovels set up behind the gate's long brownstone wall. The volunteers who had come to Bracken Knoll to fight the invading boars thronged there. Some brandished swords, hatchets, and lances and hacked away at straw caricatures of boars. Many others shouldered hoes and scythes and clambered in and out of muddy field wagons. "That's just like Cheevie. He's using the volunteers for farm labor!"

"The squire jest gettin' 'em in shape fer war," Wili speculated.

"Cheevie's going to admire you, boy."

The donkey express ascended a poplar-lined avenue. Among the trees, urns spilled blooming clematis. Topiary of fabulous beasts—micefish and snakemice—graced the rolling lawn, and the hill displayed random statuary of naked, winged mouselings, carved in pink marble.

On the manor's broad steps under fluted pillars awaited a tall, silver-furred hamster, wearing a plum velvet singlet, gray pinstripe trousers and spats. When the donkey express clopped into the roof-covered driveway and the servant spied Thrym and

Wili in the saddle baskets, the monocle dropped from his startled face.

"How you been, Chisulo?" Thrym swung out of the basket to the ground.

"Mister Seedcorn!" Chisulo quickly regained his composure. "What a surprise to see you returned to Bracken Knoll, sir."

"Come on, Chisulo." The mouse removed from the basket his tied-off blanket of possessions. "Lay off the *mister*. It's me—Thrym."

"Very good, Thrym sir." Chisulo motioned with his gloved paw for the donkey to move on. "To the servant's portal with you as usual, my good courier."

"Hey-dee!" Wili hopped out of the basket as the donkey walked on. "I ain't no packet needs haulin' off."

Chisulo peered down dubiously at the scruffy shrew, who dashed among the plunking hooves of the donkey. "And what name shall we call this junior member of the Mere, Thrym sir?"

"This is my traveling companion, Wili Burrtail." Thrym draped an arm over the boy's shoulder and escorted him up the wide stairs. "Wili, meet Chisulo. He runs the manor, calm as a beehiver and twice as busy."

"You a squire?" Wili asked in awe.

Chisulo turned on his heel. "I shall inform the squire of your arrival."

Thrym and Wili sat on the broad steps and viewed the busy estate. Workers tiny with distance tilled greening tracts, pruned grapevines and fruit trees and swung sickles in grain fields. "They all workin' fer one mouse?" Wili marveled.

"He's a demanding mouse," Thrym confirmed. "And I'd like you to do me a favor when we meet him."

"I ain't disrespectin' him none."

"I know that. But I would like you not to tell him about the crypt we found in the grotto by the Riprap. The Dead Riders' sepulcher."

"Why ever? Ain't he gonna be more than a li'l amazed?"

"He'll be plenty amazed. But I'm asking you to keep this important discovery a secret for now."

The boy's tiny eyes narrowed shrewdly. "You'd be proud to tell him yerself, I guess."

"No, I'm not going to tell him or anybody. Not for now." Thrym looked squarely at the young shrew. "Will you do me this favor, Wili?"

"Jest tell me why ever."

"Because I'm asking you." Thrym held the boy's questioning gaze with a wide-eyed look. "Will you do me this favor?"

"I ort to, I 'spect." The shrew's tail flicked indecisively. "You done saved my whiskers from that murdersome bird."

"I did do that."

"But why we keepin' this secret?" Wili squirmed. "What about our ree-ward?"

"Brother Thrym!" Through the crimson doors that fronted the mansion, a portly gray mouse strode onto the portico. He wore jodhpur breeches, black catskin boots with catfur trim, a scarlet vest over a frilly silk shirt, and a blue cravat. His large, jowly face radiated complacence and authority.

Wili jumped up. He stood open-mouthed, transfixed by the squire's poise and penetrating gaze. For the first time in his young life, he realized all that was coarse, uncouth, and vulgar in himself. He shut his mouth and mumbled, "Howdee."

Squire Cheevie transferred his formidable attention to his brother-in-law. "My, my! Huffy Thrym! Look at you, blurry eyed, destitute, and filthy as ever. I actually believed you when you swore you'd never muddy your paws in my fields again. You showed us quite a stiff tail stalking out of here. Yet, here we are again! Ha! I cannot conceive what gall has delivered you once more to my steps."

"Looking at your fat face and hearing your loud pomposity again, Cheevie, I have to agree with you." Thrym cocked his head in disbelief. "What *am* I doing here?"

"You're leaving!" The squire spoke through gnashed teeth. "And you're taking that scruffy clot of shrew fur with you. Or by the whiskers of the Dancing Drunk Red Rodent, I will wring your—"

"Slim, trim Thrym! My own heart's whim!" A corpulent mouse swathed in yellow taffeta and satin ruffles pranced across the portico on apricot silk slippers. "Oh, beloved brother, you've returned to the bosom of your family!"

Wili staggered back before the oncoming barge of shimmering fabric and would have tumbled down the stairs had not Thrym's swift paw caught him by the shoulder. The mouse held the boy dangling while the large woman engulfed her brother in a smothering embrace.

"I knew you would come back to us!" the obese matron squealed. "I assured the squire, my vim Thrym knows his home is here with us. Did I not, plumpkin?"

"Oh yes, dearest," Cheevie replied through a radiant grin, his whole demeanor illuminated by the sudden presence of his wife. "Most every day."

Renowned throughout the Holt for his doting love of his wife, Squire Cheevie delighted in worshipping her. She exhibited everything he desired in a mate: canny yet dignified, imperiously proud of her humble origins, and a robust match for his own large appetites. The fact that she administered devastating tongue-lashings to anyone who crossed her, including the squire, only endeared her even more to her adoring husband, who cherished a partner worthy of fear.

"Hey-dee!" Wili's muffled voice called from under a cascade of marigold cloth where he was confronted with a bouffant set of citron bloomers. "Git me out!"

"*Eek!*" The large woman backed away, chittering with embarrassment. "Plumpkin! A peeper under my skirts!"

"No, no, dearest." The squire moved to her side protectively. "This is the shrew lad Chisulo announced. Our brother's traveling companion. Wally Tailburr."

"Wili Burrtail," the shrew corrected meekly, regaining his footing on the steps and attempting a formal bow. "Kindly pleased fer to meet ye, yer squire lady's ship."

With lacy handkerchief pressed to her nostrils, she nodded queasily and backed off another pace.

"This is Magdi," Thrym introduced. "The sister of mine I was telling you about."

Wili nodded vigorously. "Last o' yer kin."

"Nonsense—oh, you grim Thrym!" The obese mouse swung an arm around her husband and nearly hoisted the large mouse off his feet. "The squire loves you as much as I. He's your brother-in-love!"

"So true, dearest." He kissed her cheek tenderly and released himself from her hefty grip. "Our Thrym is as a brother to me" —he directed a tight, menacing stare at Thrym—"albeit a *prodigal* brother."

"Ah, but his wandering days are done," Magdi proclaimed. "At last, he has come home to stay."

"Actually, Magdi, I've come to join the squire's volunteers." Thrym motioned downhill to the work gangs that had completed their strenuous tenure in Cheevie's fields and had congregated to receive swords, lances, backpacks, hiking boots, and walking staves.

"This is the *third* expeditionary force I've outfitted to cast about the Tarn," the squire proudly said. "We must find those white squirrels who built the rock weirs, if they are not extinct. Who else might know how to awaken the entranced squirrel princess Hati? She's the only one old enough to remember—"

"Yes, yes, the combination to the weirs that will release the boulders to block Weasel's Pass," Magdi rattled off in a bored tone. "That's all I hear about at our teas and brunches. No one wants to discuss culture anymore—the opera, the theater. Weirs and white squirrels and invading boars. I say put this threat out of mind. Those bulky swine will never negotiate Weasel's Pass anyway. The few that get through, we'll dispatch with our musket regulars. Ah, but no! The squire and his cronies won't listen to patience. They're all for action."

"Now, dearest, you know procrastination only plays to our enemy's advantage," the squire gently exhorted. "We've little to lose by—"

"By employing riffraff," she cut him off. "Yes, yes. Send the rabble into the Cloud Forest and up to the Tarn to track down these albino squirrel fellows. But not our own baby brother! The thought's abhorrent!"

"So true, dearest. Our kin belong right here on the estate." Squire Cheevie's already tight stare tightened. "I'm sure vim Thrym, slim trim Thrym, darling heart-brim Thrym will simply be delighted to help us manage all the new workers passing through our fields during these turbulent days."

"Forget it." Thrym turned his back and proceeded down the steps. "Come on, Wili. It was a mistake to come here. Let's grab some food and stuffs from the kitchen and we'll be on our way."

"Fare thee!" Wili lifted one paw in parting to the sizeable couple and bounded after Thrym. Behind, he heard first the snicker of Squire Cheevie followed hard upon by Magdi's shrill complaining:

"Thrym! Where do you think you're going? You've only just arrived! Come back here. Don't you dare ignore me, you little ingrate. You drag your scaly tail back here this instant! I didn't save your life in the Mere for you to throw it away among snakes and owls in the Cloud Forest. Do you hear me? You rat-faced, gerbil-shanked turd gnawer? Do you *hear* me?"

CHAPTER TWENTY

One Deadly Blunder

Notty tramped along the pike road a long time in the drizzle, hoping a vehicle would come by and pick him up. He would have preferred a ewe-train delivering dry goods to Fernholt. He had a knack for the small talk ewes love and was sure he could hitch a ride. But he would gladly have withdrawn the coin pouch tucked inside his pantaloons to buy fare on a pony coach—if one happened to pass.

During the many business travels with his pushcart, he had never ventured very high up the mountain. The larger farms on the Rill's upper slopes remained unvisited by him, because they would never have bothered to barter for the crude goods he found in the Mere. Situated among impressive cliffs and waterfalls above the Rill, the Holt existed for him, and for most inhabitants of the Mere, as a realm remote, unattainable, and fabulous.

The scenery looked strange. He felt uneasy in the light rain spitting down from the Cloud Forest. Cliffs rose ominously overhead. Wild orchids and antler moss sprouted from crevices, exotic flora he'd never before beheld. Only the twitter of green finches consoled him, and he continued on his way humming softly to himself.

Fear that Wili lay dead in a ditch somewhere on the mountainside had seized him from the moment Unise reported their son had run off. He knew well the perils of the road and his fear for the boy grew by the hour.

By midmorning, the light, steady rain ended, and pilgrims who had sought sanctuary in the forest returned again to the pike road. This motley gang of animals paraded along the pike intent on taking up arms in Squire Cheevie's battalion. Several groundhogs loudly shared their opinions on the most deadly martial techniques for slaying hogs.

A rat and a chipmunk hiking in the opposite direction erupted into argument when they learned that Bracken Knoll lay behind them. Soon thereafter, a skulking hare joined the company. Reading the cut of his crew neck and black denims, Notty understood this was an animal looking for trouble.

He realized then that they were all looking for trouble, eager to escape their wretched lives on the lower slopes and kill creatures they'd never laid eyes on. Until Wili had run away, he himself had shared the same ambition as these bloodthirsty nomads, and now that memory stabbed his heart with sadness.

Notty inched away and quit the pike road on the first trail that climbed into the ferny woods. He intended to follow the road from a higher altitude and perhaps even locate a short cut to Bracken Knoll.

Compared to the swamps of the Mere, the green ferns and conifers struck the shrew as a fairy-tale landscape. So wonder struck was he that he anticipated no threat until his sight touched a grubby pair of wool boots decked with tassels.

"Yaw, Rat!"

Notty's gaze lifted to take in a powerfully large and surly polecat wearing a grimy fleece vest and lavender scarf. On his shoulder, he propped an antique muzzle-loading gun. "Hey! Ya th' goon what robbed dominie! That mus' be his musket."

"You know that chump hedgehog? This surely is one neighborly mountain." The polecat's grin shot straight back along his black jaw, exposing many sharp teeth. "Okay, li'l neighbor, take out that plump coin pouch you got tucked into the waistband of them spiffy trousers."

Notty raised the hackles of fur behind his neck, stood his tail straight up, laid ears flat back, and showed tiny but sharp teeth. Though fear urged him to run, anger at the bully who had pummeled his aged teacher fixed him in place. "Ya ain't takin' what's mine wit'out a fight, ya ugly mountain o' fur!"

Though the polecat's wide and cocky grin remained locked, his black lips curled higher, exposing the impressive length of his fangs. "I never did kill nothing with fur, but for you, Li'l Rat, I gone break new ground." Wrinkled muzzle and bared fangs lunged forward with deadly intent.

Notty didn't budge. The draw from inside his vest unfolded with such blurred speed and practiced grace that the blue-steel blade seemed to appear out of nowhere. The slashing, outward motion of the knife carved the air within an inch of the polecat's snout.

"Yaw, Rat!" The aggressor pulled back so abruptly he nearly lost his footing. "That is a pretty move!"

"Pretty *scary*, ain't it?" Notty passed the blade from paw to paw with fluid ease.

Frikee aimed the musket at the shrew and pulled back the hammer. "I'll take that coin pouch now, Li'l R., or I bid you a crispy fare thee."

"Ya best be a crackerjack shot," Notty warned gruffly, ignoring the pounding thunder of his terrified heart. "Ya got one slug, skunk. Ya miss an' I'll carve ya inta a totem pole."

"I ain't gonna miss this close, Li'l Rat." But before he killed the little knife fighter, Frikee wanted to see fright in those tiny eyes. "Toss the coins."

Instead, the shrew tossed the knife. The blade streaked like a prong of blue lightning and struck the polecat in his chest, left of center, at the bull's-eye of his heart.

Frikee looked down astonished to find the wood hilt of the knife sticking out of his torso. Its blinding speed had deprived him of any chance to squeeze the trigger or expel even a gasp of horror.

A cold smile displaced his anguished scowl, and with a gloved paw, he pried the knife free of the fleece vest and tossed it aside disdainfully.

Frikee removed from inside his vest a thick sheaf of pink pages tied off with purple twine, now severed by the impact of the knife. "Mammy's letters."

He briefly regarded the gaping hole in the bundle of his mother's correspondence, and the cold smile fell from his black snout. "When you see her in the next world, you apologize, Li'l Rat."

"Yah!" Notty held up both paws as if they could deflect a burning musket ball and hid his face. "Take them darn coins!"

"Oh, I will, Rat—from your blasted body." With a grimace of intent, Frikee pulled the trigger. The hammer-flint smacked the steel pan containing the gunpowder, and the resulting flash ignited an explosive charge in the barrel that inexpert paws had packed too tightly. With a tremendous blast and a burst of flames, the musket exploded. The force kicked Frikee off his feet and propelled him backward under a hail of sparks.

Notty, eyes closed tight, awaited the fatal impact. After a moment, he figured the ball had missed, and he peeked through the slit of one eye. Black vapors drooped over the spot where the polecat had stood.

Swiftly he retrieved his knife and strode through the gunsmoke.

Frikee lay on his back in a gully, fleece vest blown to lint, his mother's letters confetti, and his chest smoldering. The polecat peered up at the shrew through a blear of pain.

Notty doffed his cap. "Say hi ta ya ma, for me." He sneered and walked away, thinking of the justice of this cruel creature's final reckoning.

Frikee cried for help even though he knew perfectly well that the shrew was more likely to finish him with his knife. Eyes squeezed tight, he felt his lifeblood seeping away.

This realization inspired a terrible fright, and his lids snapped open. He saw then on a nearby branch three crows, beaked heads hanging low, watching him with patience and an appetite.

CHAPTER TWENTY-ONE

The Darling Spy

As Thrym and Wili left Bracken Knoll, they stood aside to let pass ram-drawn wagons bearing produce from the Rill. Thrym felt like shouting to the rams that they were helping feed Squire Cheevie's slave workers.

If he had spoken, perhaps his angry voice might have woken Muspul and Olweena, snoozing out of sight in the last wagon. But he held his tongue. He didn't want to waste another breath contending with his brother-in-law. While Cheevie lived a life of greed and self-importance, Thrym and Wili would take the news of their astonishing discovery directly to Fernholt, the capital.

Three paces onto a narrow trail thick with the scent of juniper Thrym stopped cold. "Mud and garlic!" He turned around. "We've got to go back. I left in such a huff, I didn't think to ask Magdi for the money to send an avian courier to your parents. They need to know you're all right."

"I'll wait on ye here." Wili edged away. "Your sis gives me the witherins."

"I know what you mean," Thrym grunted. "But if we go back, she won't hand over the money unless we agree to stay. And we can't leave your parents not knowing you're alive. Come on. We'll face Magdi together."

Wili strode defiantly up the trail. "I'll wait up yander fer ye."

"Oh no, you don't!" Thrym hurried after Wili, and consequently he never saw the hedgehog or the beautiful mouse maiden rising from their rest in the rams' last wagon.

"Here so soon?" Muspul blinked away fatigue and gingerly touched the blood-stiff bandana wrapped about his head. His paw fell back to his lap as he gazed upon the Holt again for the first time since childhood. In his memory, the journey as a boy had been much longer to these bluffs and their giant trees. "My, my—the scent of the air—that perfume of pine and mountain mist! My youth is restored!"

"What's your business, bristleback?" A gatekeeper intruded on Muspul's memories. "You're too old for the squire's battalion."

"Oh my, yes." Muspul pushed his bent spectacles higher up his snout, better to regard the hare in the brown jumpsuit with epaulets. "This maiden and I are here on business concerning Mister Seedcorn, a prominent member of the squire's family. Summon us a coach, will you? That hill to the house looks daunting."

Chisulo met the doe-harnessed buggy when it pulled up to the mansion. "The gatekeeper informs that you are affiliates of Mister Seedcorn," said the silver-furred hamster. He held open the side panel as Muspul and Olweena stepped out. "He has just now departed the estate from out the kitchen gate. If you hasten, you may yet engage him not far along, for he has a shrew tyke in tow, a Master Burrtail."

"Notty's son!" Muspul spun, squinting downhill, searching among the animals at the main gate to Bracken Knoll. "I shall depart at once." He returned his attention to the hamster. "I assume Thrym sped off subsequent to an emotional tilt with the squire."

"Just so, sir."

Muspul nodded knowingly and expelled a lungful of air. *What did that stubborn mouse expect from Cheevie? Unfurled banners and trumpet fanfare?* "I must find Thrym. But before I go, I should like to see this young refugee provided sanctuary in the squire's household."

"Dominie, you must stay and rest." Olweena clutched the hedgehog's arm. "You're injured."

"Not seriously." He gently patted the bandana across his brow. "A minor scalp wound. The brisk air up here has rejuvenated me. After years of dragging my wagon through the murky heat of the Mere, strolling the Holt will be a delight. But first, we must get you sanctuary."

"I'm afraid that's not possible, sir." Chisulo tapped his monocle impatiently against the back of his white-gloved paw. "The squire requires all refugees to offer service during their stay at Bracken Knoll. This is not a charitable institution but a working estate."

"I'm willing to work." The mouse maiden curtsied. "I am Olweena Talkingstone of Blossom Vale. My expertise is econometrics— statistical analysis of financial data. I served as chief fiscal officer for Blossom Vale."

Chisulo peered down his blunt snout. "The squire manages the estate's finances himself."

"Perhaps then I can undertake domestic chores," Olweena offered brightly. "I have some experience with embroidery, the culinary arts, and childcare."

"The household's domestic staff is replete, Miss Talkingstone."

"We always need more hands in the vineyards, young woman." Squire Cheevie, stoutly straining the ivory buttons on his jacket, stood at the top of the broad stairs under an archway of purple clematis. "You're of a size ideal for pruning undergrowth without damaging the vines. Off with you now. Put in a half day's work, you'll receive a full meal and lodging."

"Squire Cheevie!" Muspul ascended two steps and bowed. "A genuine honor, sir, to meet a mouse of your far-flung renown here on your own most excellent estate."

"And you are?"

"I am your brother-in-law Thrym Seedcorn's professor." The hedgehog bowed again. "Muspul Woo-Havoc."

"Woo-Havoc?" Cheevie stared down at Chisulo with an expression tinged with surprise. "Of *the* Woo-Havocs?"

"A Fernholt founder-family," Chisulo acknowledged with a sudden air of deference. "Muspul Woo-Havoc—last heir of the noble house of Woo-Havoc. First in his class at Fernholt Academy. I believe you served as captain of the fencing team. A perfect record under your hand, if I recall correctly, sir."

"Kind of you to remember." Muspul lowered his bandaged head to hide a small, sad, and demure smile. "That was so very long ago."

Chisulo's eyes shone with admiration. "The record has not been broken since, sir."

"Thank you. I had no idea." Muspul looked up to address the squire. "Since the tragic decline of my family, I have resided in the Mere, where news of the Holt remains scarce."

"My good fellow, you've endured hard times. Come. Freshen up." Squire Cheevie, unwilling to touch the tattered and soiled hedgehog, gestured up the stairs.

"Yoo-hoo!" Magdi drifted onto the portico in her billowy skirt and gauzy yellow ruffles. "What is this about the Woo-Havocs?"

"Dearest!" Cheevie motioned at the old hedgehog in his muddy, torn mantle. "Let me astonish you with the presence on our doorstep of Muspul Woo-Havoc."

Magdi retracted her pudgy chin in disbelief. "Of *the*—"

"Yes, yes. It's the poor fellow himself." Cheevie beckoned Muspul upward one slow step at a time. "Have a bath drawn at once. And prepare a small lunch on the patio—"

"No, no." Muspul stopped his ascent. "Very kind of you. But I cannot linger. I have only returned to the Holt to locate my prize pupil, your brother, Thrym, Lady Bracken."

"*You* tutored my brother? He never—"

"Oh, he wouldn't have." Muspul dismissed the thought with a terse shake of his head. "He is quite the retiring mouse. But I must hurry to find him, for I am determined to dissuade him from participating in the impending fight against the boars."

Magdi heartily nodded. "Yes, you must find him at once, Sir Muspul."

"Simply Muspul, Lady Bracken." He shrugged his silver eyebrows. "My father forsook our family title at our exile."

"I shall have a carriage readied at once, Muspul." Cheevie motioned to Chisulo.

"That won't be necessary." Muspul caught Chisulo's eye and canceled the order. "Thrym most likely has departed the main byways. I know his mind fairly well and stand the best chance of finding him on my own. However, I should be glad for some provisions, perhaps a pair of walking shoes if you can spare them— and, also, refuge for my friend here, Olweena Talkingstone, a noble maiden of Blossom Vale in flight from the boars."

"*Noble?*" Magdi swept down the stairs to the mouse maiden's side and looked closely at the pathetic remnants of Olweena's once elegant garments. "I do need someone of culture and refinement on my personal staff. Come, darling mouse, we shall refresh you. I must hear all about Blossom Vale and your terrible journey here."

In passing, the mouse maiden nodded with gratitude to the helpful hedgehog. "Thank you, *Sir* Muspul."

Before Muspul could reply, Magdi ushered her newfound assistant into the mansion. As they walked, Lady Bracken sustained a constant patter: first pointing out the architectural fine-points of the manse ("That ovolo molding was turned from a single trunk of exotic rosewood. Have you ever seen anything as exquisite, dearie?"); then defining the mouse maiden's duties ("For years I've longed for someone of culture to read aloud classical poetry as I bathe. You shan't mind indulging that whim for me, would you, darling Olweena?"); and not in the least decrying the imminent boar invasion ("Those pigs shall learn quickly and ruefully that Riversplash is not so vulnerable as your unfortunate Blossom Vale. We have our own unique way of protecting ourselves, you know. Have you heard yet of our rock weirs?").

CHAPTER TWENTY-TWO

Treachery

Late that night, high above Bracken Knoll, Olweena huddled at the base of a pine, hiding from the wind. Her paws smoothed the silk fabric of the fine teal gown she had found laid out for her after a bath of perfumed suds. What the mouse maiden intended to do mixed poorly with the kindness of Lady Bracken.

The old moon rose into the sky the third hour after midnight, and Olweena employed its moonbeams and her mirror to transmit a signal of three short flashes and one long. Then, she hugged herself and held dear the thought of embracing her parents again, even as she contemplated what she had called forth upon this mountain, its gentle animals—and her own soul.

She was still brooding upon her treachery when she looked over her shoulder and confronted, not a whisker's length away, the massive, tusked face of Kungu.

A burst of fright started a scream that never sounded, because Kungu pressed a trotter to her lips.

"Hush!" the scout hissed. "In these woods, there be forage hikers—berry pickers, truffle diggers and such—cozy asleep. Speak soft like."

"Kungu!" she gasped. "You frightened me."

"I be good at that." The boar drifted past her and through the evergreen grove, his reed sandals seeming to glide upon the pine needles. He sniffed the air, and his pointy ears swiveled, sampling sounds. He returned to the mouse maiden's side and withdrew from under his cloak a small pair of bamboo slivers. Rubbing them together, he generated cricket-like chirps, which the wind accepted as genuine.

A moment later, the forest floor rasped and crackled, and a dozen boars emerged from the dense undergrowth. Griml swaggered directly to the mouse maiden and, with delicate precision, placed the jagged edge of his broken tusk under her jaw.

"Thee done well by us, Olweena girl?" His kinked and swishing tail signaled his squad to draw lots for who would bite off her head and make a meal of her.

"I have the information you want." She peered anxiously at the boars, their small eyes glowing as white as pearls with reflected moonlight. "When I tell you, you will reunite me with my parents?"

A loud munching noise commenced from deeper in the grove. Griml swung his head around with a growl. "Ull, ye greedy oaf! Get thy hide out here now or I be guttin' thy belly wit' me own tusk."

The munching ceased and the massive hulk of Ull lumbered through the pines. Dripping blossoms hung from the goliath's mouth. "Them tender roots be good. This be our reward, yus?"

"Use thy boar cunning, Ull!" Griml snorted with disgust. "The horde be on the March. Our lads an' sows ain't safe till we knowed wut defense be set against us'n."

"Boilin' tar pots?" Ull rumbled with fear.

"Mayhap, ye lummox! Mayhap indeed." Griml returned his attention to his spy. "Olweena girl be tellin' now wut's set against us an' wut ain't. Well, mousie, be there boilin' tar an' catapults o' fiery pitch awaitin'?"

"I want to see my parents first."

"That ain't near likely, Olweena, as thy beloved ma an' da be held fast amongst the legions awaitin' thy happy return."

"Happy as flowers urgin' up from down under!" Ull gloated.

Olweena's eyes flared with alarm and horror. "What is he saying?"

"Ull!" Griml hurled at the colossal boar a wrathful stare. "Shut thy yap!" The boar lord faced the mouse with a cockeyed smile. "Ull be daft. He knowed better, thy kindly ma an' gentle da be proper captives. Ull ain't right 'tween the ears."

"Me ears be right!" Ull grumbled.

"My parents are dead." Olweena shoved to her feet and peered with cold challenge into Griml's mean eyes. "They've been dead all along, haven't they?"

"Thy ma an' da ain't killt—not yet, nay!" Griml signed with his tail for the squad to remove Ull. As one, the boars converged on their large comrade and budged him out of the grove. "Ull be daft. That be the mortal truth."

"No." Olweena shook her head firmly and backed off, wanting to place the tree between her and those tusks. "You've killed my parents already—and you'll slay me once you get what you want."

"Olweena girl," Griml said throatily, "such suspicions be unworthy of thee. Now, I thank thee for sendin' thy signal so prompt like. Reveal to us'n wut thee knowed, an' Kungu here be escortin' thee to thy beloved ma an' da."

"I was wrong to trust you—that's what I know," the mouse declared sharply. "I should have let you kill me on Blossom Vale. You tricked me with my heart!" She ducked behind the pine. "I'm through with you!"

"Olweena!" Griml snapped and signed with his tail for Kungu to fetch the mouse. "By the Sacred Sow's Swollen Teats, thy folks be fine. Get thee back here!"

Lies! Olweena wailed to herself and crashed through dense undergrowth that wrapped around her. Ensnarled, the mouse maiden collapsed on the forest floor, and the more she struggled the tighter the creepers snared her.

Kungu burst out of a wall of pea vines. hooves churning clots of mulch. Huffing fiercely, he loomed over the mouse. With one swipe of his tusks, he sliced off her tail and sent it wriggling into the air.

Olweena screeched! The hurt that blazed through her wrenched her upright, and she tore free the noose of binding weeds. She skittered under shrubs and over a fallen tree, impelled by shock and pain.

Kungu's tusks gouged the earth where Olweena had lain, but the lively mouse had already disappeared into the forest night.

The scout paused. He knew the boar lord wanted this one captured alive, and that was why Kungu had been careful to sever her tail and not her spine. He burrowed his straw-wrapped head into the underbrush, sniffing among fungus for his quarry's fading scent.

CHAPTER TWENTY-THREE

A Diplomatical Boar

Vidar closely examined a mineral pool of the Tarn. Its trance depths revealed Griml and his boar warriors, watching the sun rise through redwoods in the Holt.

Telepathically, the viper experienced the awe filling the boars' stupefied hearts. Even the dull-witted Ull felt overwhelmed—frightened and elated—at such radiant beauty, and he intoned aloud his comrades' common sentiment: "Life be but a dream."

"Yes, yes, you swine, cherish that thought." Vidar bobbed his faceted head eagerly above the frozen pool. "Your life *is* but a dream—my dream." He took advantage of their pangs of wonder to insert his thinking into their minds: "Go at once to the great estate below the cliffs. Go to the squire there and deliver to him the terror of the boars."

"We be goin' to wut estate we finds below," Griml announced to his squad, believing this was his own inspiration. "It were time we brung unto the squires o' this land the boar horde's right awful terror."

"Unto squires?" Ull spoke dully, still entranced by dawn's splendor.

The rest of the squad murmured uneasily, and one among them dared voice, "Be that wise, m'lord?"

"Wisdom itself!" the snake transmitted. "The mouse maiden is fled! If she escapes and reports your invasion, you will be hunted down and roasted on skewers with apples in your yaps."

"This be wisdom itself!" the boar lord echoed the serpent. "Mousie be escaped. If'n we be found out and stalked by sodbusters, fine roasters we'll make."

"Roasters?" Ull snapped alert. "We ain't roasters!"

"Nay, lad." Griml faced the hot stare in the giant's eyes. "We be elite warriors o' the March."

"We be skewered we showed ourselves!" Ull backed away. "We hide."

"Go forth, you porkers!" Vidar shouted, circling his vision of the boars from every side of his magic mirror. "Go forth under protection of the white flag—to *negotiate*! Go forth into the thick of your enemy, expose their weaknesses for yourselves, you oafs!" The serpent spat impatiently. "If you piggies weren't so cautious, your legions could attack at once! There are *no* defenses on Riversplash Mountain! None! These farmers are stupid with peace and complacency!"

"We ain't hidin'," Griml declared. "We be boars an' we be relyin' on our cunning. Unfurl a white flag . . . "

"We ain't got no white flag!" Ull groused as loud as booming cannon. "The March don't never surrender!"

"Unfurl bandage gauze and tourniquet wrapping then!" Griml touched each boar with his commanding stare. "We ain't surrenderin'. We be *negotiatin'*!"

"Wut?" Perplexed, Ull blinked his wee eyes. "Talk terms? Wut talk?"

"We be *pretendin'* we talk terms, great Ull. That be gainin' us'n time. Time for us'n to be learned in the defenses o' this root wall."

"Aye"—Ull's tiny eyes widened as comprehension penetrated his brain—"time wut for lies and clever spying!"

Griml showed thick teeth in a knavish smile. Still, in spite of his confidence, a vague sense of peril troubled him. Perhaps Olweena's escape had shaken him. Perhaps he should have ordered Kungu to kill her.

"Here be the white flag wut thee ordered, m'lord." A warrior unrolled a banner knotted together from several lengths of gauze.

"Ull! Thee be flag bearer. Them sodbusters see thee comin', they be takin' right proper notice. Smartly now!"

Swinging the gauze flag over his massive, helmeted head, Ull strode out onto the shrubby hill. Griml followed and the other boars in file behind. Soon, they came forth upon the heath above the estate's parkland.

Field workers in the upper pastures spotted the armored beasts, and they hastened away in fright. When the boars paraded onto the deer park above the mills, a small army of Squire Cheevie's battalion arrayed to meet them.

Ull's hulk swayed to a full stop, and he whisked the white flag before the ranks of chipmunks, marmots, rats, and beavers, armed with lances and drawn bows. "Seed thee this white flag, ye stinkin' mud sloggers, ye mush-mouthed fruit pickers, and ye doltish root diggers? Stand off!"

"At ease, mighty Ull," the boar lord whispered as he came alongside the giant. "Let us'n not frenzy the wee critters." Griml upheld his front trotters and advanced slowly toward the skittish soldiers. With well-acted civility, he bowed. "Proud warriors of Riversplash Mountain, greetins from us far travelers an' new-arrived visitors to yore fair dominion."

A brassy fanfare of hunting horns announced the arrival of a battle wagon. Pulled by an antelope, the wagon carried armadillo archers and pink-eyed rabbit musketeers. Squire Cheevie, sporting a shiny brass helmet with a green plume and wearing body armor, stood in their midst, an ungainly flare-barreled blunderbuss cradled in his arms.

"What ho!" the squire shouted as the battle wagon pulled up to the boars. "I am Squire Cheevie, gallant of Bracken Knoll, this estate upon which you have intruded. State your intentions!"

Griml's tail jiggled a gesture of revulsion to his squad even as he lowered his tusks with servility to the ground. "Squire Cheevie, it is! We thort as much when we seed the grandness of this here estate. Thy name be broadcast upon thy neighbor mountains."

"Neighboring mountains to which you gluttonous boars have laid waste!" Squire Cheevie glared with indignation. "We've heard of your ruinous campaigns abroad from woeful refugees—and there'll be none of that pillaging and despoiling here, I swear by the Maker of Beasts!"

"Ah, the Maker o' Beasts wut made boars as well as ye puny critters, aye?" Griml slowly lifted his snout and surveyed the armed creatures before him. "Muskets, lances, and bows ain't worthy defense against the Boar March. Surely, this ye knowed. Aye?"

Squire Cheevie stiffened with the impact of this threat. "Riversplash Mountain is defended well enough, you grunters!"

The boars as one reached for their cudgels and aimed their lances. With a flick of his tail, Griml stayed them. "Grunters, eh?" The boar lord advanced by slow, measured paces toward the battle wagon. "Griml be me name—boar lord o' the March. Me legions sacked twelve mountains, each bigger than this'n, each defended by brave little critters fightin' wit' all wut strength they got. And here

I be—Griml, boar lord o' the March—facing thee, Squire Cheevie, brave mousie wit' yore brave little troopers."

Cheevie leveled the blunderbuss at the advancing boar lord. "Another step, Griml, and I'll blast you to pork hash."

"Will thee now?" Griml's eyes contracted, his tail alerting the boars to ready themselves for hostility, and his fight-trained brain playing out all the many permutations of destruction that would follow his spooking the antelope, jarring the battle wagon, and spoiling the squire's one shot. But before he could implement his violent ploy, he drew a long, slow breath. He and his scouts had not belly-crawled through Weasel's Pass, avoided alligators in the Mere, and escaped detection by the mountain's denizens just to battle farmers.

"Stay thy threats!" the boar lord growled. His tail canceled his combat command, and his warty, whiskered face changed itself to a mask of smiling benevolence. "I be a diplomatical boar—and thy *guest*, squire. Aye, we be that—thy guest—not invaders to be wagin' war. Nay. We knowed from afar that Riversplash be proud unlike any other mountain we seed before. We ain't come to ravage thy proud land. We come wut for to talk terms o' peaceful settlement twixt thee an' the might o' the boars."

Ull shared a look of disbelief with the other boars at their commander's tolerance for insult.

"Terms?" Squire Cheevie closed one eye and sighted down the length of his barrel. "There'll be no terms with you pigheaded vandals!"

"*Pig*headed? *Pig!*" Griml gnashed his molars and snorted rage. "Why, thee stinkin' excuse for a . . . " The boar lord squeezed tight his tiny eyes and sucked a sharp breath through his teeth, reminding himself of his allegiance to the Great Sow and her legions, who awaited news of this mountain's war machines.

The boar's scowl relaxed, replaced by a kindly smile. "Thee stinkin' excuse for a host!" Griml sat back on his rump. "Ain't hospitality a tradition wut thee knowed here on Riversplash?"

"Hospitality for *invaders*?" Squire Cheevie snickered. "We've no tradition of inviting murderers into our homes."

"*Murderers*?" Griml thrust forward and slashed his tusks in disagreement. "We be warriors! We ain't killt none that ain't raised no arms to fight us'n! And thee, puny beasties—" He jabbed a sharp trotter at the fidgety soldiers arranged before him in their makeshift armor. But before he could complete his angry thought, his deadlier intention asserted itself once again and quieted him. *Thrash these weensy blokes wit' words!*

"Turn aside thy arms an' we be talkin' terms an' not spillin' blood. How many here wants to be killt outright instead o' hearin' wut reason we brung—under a white flag? Did we sneaked up on thee? Nay! Did we killt any o' thy kin? Not yet we ain't. Behind us'n there be more than a *towsand* boars readyin' to squeeze themselves through this mountain's narrow pass, an' they ain't carryin' no white flag." He strode directly up to the squire's blunderbuss. "So, wut say thee, squire? We be talkin'—or we be killin'?"

Squire Cheevie glanced at his skittish soldiers, all of whom were staring at him expectantly. No one wanted to die this fine morning. And time—to figure out how to work the rock weirs and close Weasel's Pass—time was far better bought with words than blood. He lifted the blunderbuss to his shoulder. "We will talk."

CHAPTER TWENTY-FOUR

White Squirrel Princess

Olweena hurried as noiselessly as she could through thickets of wild fig and flowering creepers. The pain from her severed tail burned white hot. If she allowed, that agony would knock her unconscious. But then, she knew, Kungu would seize her.

The certainty that the boars had indeed slain her parents cut her more keenly than her amputated tail. She gagged on a sob to keep from making a sound. The restraint she needed to stay quiet shriveled her heart to a lump of intense cold.

Jaw locked with determination, eyes squinted against lashings of fronds and branches, she squeezed herself into the darkest, tightest recesses of the forest. She listened for Kungu.

She peeked through the dense mesh of vines and branches. She would not hear Kungu until he pounced upon her, and that terrifying truth drove her deeper into the brushwood.

Blood continued to spill from her tail wound. She tore a strip of silk from her gown and, gnashing her teeth against the pain, secured a tourniquet about her bleeding stump.

Her pain and the possibility of impending death required her full presence of mind. She realized then that all her training as a cultivated mouse had come to this: to carry her own mind and soul through tremendous amounts of suffering—and not stop. If she stopped, Kungu would torture from her the defenses of Riversplash Mountain. The only way to fight the boars and honor her parents was to keep going until she died.

Crawling and wriggling, she carried herself farther from sunlight. She crept into cramped, somber tunnels, like a cave explorer, her lifeblood oozing out behind her despite the tourniquet.

As if in a trance state, she proceeded a long time, ignoring the savage cries of birds: "Turn back! Sharp pain! Stabbing hurt! Watch out!"

When relentless pain and blood loss had used up all her strength, she collapsed. Through half-lidded eyes, she peered into a web of black bramble, and she thought she saw in there a snowball. The oddity of finding snow confused her bleary eyes.

Sharpening her gaze, she saw then no snowball but fur as white and pristine as snow. She then noticed the contours of a curled-up animal.

Olweena remembered the age-old tale of Hati, a famed squirrel princess in her cage of thorns: Hati's subjects had built the colossal barriers holding back the rock slides that could block Weasel's Pass forever. A vindictive magician among the exiled carnivores had spellbound Hati for aiding the Brave Tails. Bereft of their leader, her tribe of white squirrels had wandered into the Tarn and supposedly dwindled away. Now, none but the bewitched princess knew the secret of opening the rock weirs.

The sight of the legendary white squirrel pushed Olweena to her feet. She wobbled and sank again to the ground.

Before she could find the strength to roll her head around and examine the thorny coop, she startled at the sound of scampering paws. Again she staggered upright and again collapsed. This time, through the slits of her heavy lids, she confronted numerous eyes with voices.

"Look, look! She bleeds!"

"And no warning heeds!"

"Did she not hear the birds?"

"Or not understand their words?"

"Her spilt blood attracts carnivores!"

"Maybe even those invading boars!"

"She puts Hati in danger!"

"We must kill this stranger!"

"No! No! That spills more blood!"

"Then, let us bury her in the mud."

"The boars will certainly root her out."

"We must take her where we have no doubt."

"We will carry her where she can do us no harm."

"We will feed her to the adders in the Tarn!"

Olweena raised her head to address the hidden animals deciding her fate but had no strength to speak.

From out of their hiding places, small figures of sleek black fur materialized. She recognized the plump, short-tailed bodies without ears as voles. They quickly surrounded her—two to either side, one at her head and one at her bleeding tail—and lifted her off the ground.

She groaned from pain and her urgency to communicate, but the voles ignored her. They carried her past the furry white ball of hibernating squirrel and into a warren of spiny passageways. The voles' paws grabbed the thorns with expert ease and moved gracefully through the prickly corridors.

They passed colorful husks of butterflies and pale moths impaled upon thorns, but they bore Olweena without a single scratch. Gradually the gloom dispersed, and sunlight flickered through dense hedges.

In a glaring rush of brightness, they came out from the thorn forest onto an expanse of pines. The voles hurried with her, darting under dwarf spruce and evergreen shrubs. Beyond silent pines, the Cloud Forest rose, shrouded in white.

The sun dimmed then vanished entirely as they hurried headlong into that blinding fog. How the voles could see where they were going, let alone bear up under her weight, she could not guess.

Ghost shadows of trees clipped past, and the crash of waterfalls shivered the air.

Rocked by this jostling ride in such gauzy light, Olweena nearly slipped unconscious. Then, daylight blared over her again, and she squinted into a golden landscape of boulders, bushes of barberry, and carpets of taiga moss.

Above, she beheld the walls of the crater bowl.

On a brittle shelf of the caldera's rim, the voles paused in their speedy transit to study the blue sky for wings of eagles. The old moon hung frozen far in the west above remote valleys.

Surveying sheets of slate and desert rocks within the sprawling interior of the caldera, the little mammals searched for serpents. Satisfied that, for the moment, they were safe, they rushed down between boulders, bearing their limp burden.

"We are here!" one vole whispered crisply and another softly replied, "Snakes are near!"

"Leave her on the ground."

"Leave without a sound."

And they did.

After lowering Olweena onto the rock bed, the voles vanished amid the crater's stony debris.

CHAPTER TWENTY-FIVE

Riddle of the Final Fact

Blue-black flies crawled upon Frikee's inert body. Others swarmed around his skull. His long torment here on his back in a ditch had gone on *too* long. Sprawled under a frenzy of flies, rotting slowly, he felt bereaved.

This is all? Over so soon. And this is all there is?

Mammy! The polecat smiled inwardly. Maybe he would meet his mother in the afterworld. Of course, then, he would have to apologize for having ignored her book-learned wisdom and gotten himself killed on this mountain—renowned as a criminal.

"Harkee, fellers! He's a-goin'! Let's git his eyes afore they gets all gummed up with flies!"

A large, glossy crow alighted on his boot toe and cocked a black eye at the bloodied polecat. "Y'all done in, ain't ye, mister?"

Frikee peeked out narrow slits of swollen eyelids. Fright pumped through him at the sight of that spiteful bird. He groaned.

"What's that thar ye sayin'?" The crow twisted his head as if trying to hear. "Fellers! This here polecat got some testifyin' he's fixin' to broadcast afore we set our beaks to his eyes."

Loud squawking descended from the trees. "Git his eyes!"

"Hush up, boys! I cain't nary hear a word."

Frikee summoned all his strength to gasp, "Beat—it."

"*Eat* it?" The crow hopped from Frikee's boot to his knee. "This sure be one obligin' scratch-cat. Come on, boys! It's surely feedin' time!"

"Nyah-wah-yahhh!" Frikee cried with horror as a dozen big, loud crows danced around him, laughing. "Nyah! Nyah!"

"Shoo!" A small, elderly hedgehog in brown wool jerkin barreled into the clearing. "Show some respect for the dying, you gluttonous scavengers!" He slid down on the pitched bank of the ditch, swinging a makeshift walking stick. "Be gone, greedy birds! Fill your filthy craws with the fetid flesh of some beast already expired! Be gone, I say!"

With shrieks and thrashing wings, the gang of crows quit the trembling polecat. "Yee! He be aimin' to brain us! Watch that thar stick! Watch it!"

The hedgehog flipped his walking stick into the air with intimidating precision and force, driving the black birds high into the forest. He caught the branch as it fell—and dropped it with amazement as he bent forward, eyes widening, on the quivering polecat sprawled in the weeds.

"Oh, my!" The aged hedgehog spotted the shattered musket with its barrel split like a peeled banana. "My, my!"

Frikee stared aghast at the hedgehog. "You!"

"Yes, 'tis I—fool hedgehog of yesterday." Muspul knelt at the polecat's side. "Mister Fitch, I assure you I had no notion that musket was defective." He sat back. "Had you not taken it—it would have killed Thrym." He blinked. "*I* would have killed him."

"Kill—*me* . . . " Frikee whispered through gritted teeth.

Muspul delicately parted Frikee's shredded fleece vest and appraised the polecat's wounds. "You seem to have accomplished that for yourself. I can only grimly surmise what unfortunate victim you intended to dispatch with that musket shot. More capon, was it?"

Frikee writhed, eyes shrill. "*Kill . . .* "

"Hush with that nonsense. I'm not a murderer. I don't take lives. I empower lives. I'm a teacher." Muspul quickly completed his examination of the wounded animal. From the satchel of provisions given him by the cook at Bracken Knoll, he withdrew a canteen of spring water and held it to the wounded animal's snout.

"Slowly. Drink slowly, Mister Fitch." Muspul removed the canteen from the polecat's straining mouth. "Do you know what that means—to empower a life? Ah! Pardon me. I forget whom I address—the notorious fowl murderer, fish slayer, and assailant of elderly hedgehogs. You don't empower lives—you overpower them."

"Just—*kill*—me."

"You may yet get your wish." Muspul shook his head once. "Your sputum is clear, ribs intact, and you are breathing freely. But your pulse is bounding, and your gums are pale." He removed from his mantle's pocket the green vial of elixir and regarded it. "Without surcease of your pain, I am convinced that the intense suffering you've endured will soon render you unconscious and, shortly thereafter, your fatigued and overworked heart will fail. It is, after all, simply a muscle. A heart needs rest."

The polecat stared back at him, dazed. "What?"

"Though your vest protected you from serious injury, your heart has endured a frightful amount of pain, and it is exhausted to the point of collapse." Muspul opened the stopper and smelled the chill, familiar ethers. "You are dying, Mister Fitch—of shock."

Those words inflicted upon the polecat more agitation. "Just—kill me—*please!*"

"Perhaps that is what justice decrees." Muspul frowned at the open vial in his paw—his only anchor to life. He thought of the explosive musket and the death he would have delivered to Thrym had not Frikee interceded. And he decided. "I've always been more partial to mercy. You see, Mister Fitch, my family has tasted the fruit of justice—and it is exceedingly bitter. Here." With one paw, he eased open and steadied the polecat's jaw, then carefully dripped the amber liquid into Frikee's mouth.

The frosty energy of the drug coursed through Frikee, instantly numbing the stabbing hurt. "Oh!" Frikee sat up and blinked with surprise. "Oh! You done delivered me from the pit!"

"Calm yourself, Mister Fitch." Muspul gently urged the polecat to lie back. "Rest. Let the full effect of the medicine unfold." A smile lifted the hedgehog's whiskers. "Your vigorous response implies you have not suffered very much loss of blood. The prognosis is good, Mister Fitch. Very good indeed." He reseated the stopper but did not pocket the vial, knowing that what remained would be required before very long.

From within his straw satchel, he revealed parcels wrapped in parchment paper. "Dishes prepared by a master chef. Now you must recover your strength. While the elixir allays the pain, you shall eat. I have here beetle broth from the kitchens of Bracken Knoll. And a loaf of black and red ant bread. Mmmmm, yum! I regret the squire does not share your appetite for flesh and blood."

With serene exhaustion, Frikee inquired, "Why are you helping me?"

"Would you rather I left you to die in misery?"

"I robbed and beat you and left you to die."

"Hmm, yes." Muspul fingered the lump on his brow. "I sport an achy memento of our initial encounter. And though my night's rest in the bracing air of the Holt has restored my health, I will admit, you caused me genuine anguish."

"So, why?" With a dark and questioning look, the polecat confronted the old hedgehog. "Why didn't you gloat while them crows stabbed my eyes?"

"That degree of cruelty, Mister Fitch, is strange to my nature."

"I don't got no grasp on your nature, Mister—" Frikee squinted. "What might your name be again, Hog?"

"Muspul Woo-Havoc." Muspul broke off a knob of ant bread, tore it to crumbs, and dampened it with beetle broth. "But just 'Muspul' to you."

The felon accepted the soggy bread with trembling paws. "Muspul, what is this nature of yours?"

"An uncommon love for the common creature, Mister Fitch— and the wisdom to accept that before death we are all equals."

"Before death . . . " Frikee devoured the sop and received more in his unsteady paws. "Lying here, I got me fixated on that very thought. But it proved too big for my narrow head. Perhaps you know what I can't figure. Is this all there is, Muspul?"

"Ah, Mister Fitch." Muspul partook of a twist of bread and, while he chewed, placed the flask of beetle broth to the polecat's mouth. "Am I to understand that you are inquiring if our individual lives have purpose beyond our appetites and instincts?"

Frikee gulped the broth and nodded.

"On one level, life is utterly meaningless." The hedgehog soaked more bread. "Each of us singular and alone must seek our own destiny. None may choose the circumstances. Yet we may live a life of joy by largeness of heart and good will."

Frikee swallowed hard and winced as the medicine began to fade.

Muspul trickled more of the amber painkiller into Frikee's mouth. "You are a predator, Mister Fitch. You have been true to your nature. That must have been fulfilling. And yet, here in this ditch, you have encountered the despair and loneliness that every thinking creature confronts. That can either make you or break you."

"Break me?" He huffed a sigh of comfort as the harsh pain again diminished.

"We are broken off from what we know when we die. We are alone. We will die alone. In our journey from birth to death why should we not live just for ourselves?

Frikee propped himself up on his elbows, and said, "We done come to the same idea then, Hog."

"Have we, Mister Fitch?" Muspul leaned his head back and peered down through his spectacles. "I propose that life without meaning or point can break us or perhaps make us whole."

Frikee pressed a paw to his brow. "Why you hurtin' my head, Hog?"

"You're right. Apologies." Muspul bunched together leaves for a pillow and motioned for the polecat to recline. "You should rest."

"Hold up there, wise guy." The polecat's eyes narrowed. "You tell me how the pointlessness of our being here can make us whole."

"We are equals before death, Mister Fitch." Muspul softly pressed him to the ground and whispered soothing queries, "Why not express this equality with our lives as well as our deaths? Why not *share* the pointlessness? Why not care as much for all others who suffer this fate as we care for ourselves? Why ever not?"

"I don't know," Frikee breathed drowsily and closed his eyes. "You tell me."

Muspul smiled and laid a paw on the sleeping polecat's heart. "By my life, Mister Fitch, I believe I have."

CHAPTER TWENTY-SIX

Heart of the Beast

Wili hightailed it through tunnels of pine and across a log bridge spanning a green gulch. In the hazy cold above droning waterfalls, Thrym eventually caught up with the winded shrew. The two glared at each other, bent over and huffing, too spent to speak.

Staring down from this high country onto plummeting streams and wild mists blowing through dark spruce canyons, they found nothing familiar. And when they peered upward, the Cloud Forest hung white, dressed as a ghost.

The rest of that day, they wandered trying to retrace their steps. They passed stairway streams and walnut groves and limestone walls—and they lost their way worse. At one point, they popped out from a fir forest of mist and stared across a measureless spread of glaciers.

"There's Notty!" Thrym's voice soared out into the silence. "I see your pa down there. He looks as lost as we are."

Hard as Wili labored to see, he saw only the sprawling mountainside. He could barely make out the aqua Riprap as it hurtled through rock gorges in the Rill. "That's so fer it'd pop a hawk's eye."

"Trust me. He's down there looking for you, terrified you're going to turn up dead in the underbrush."

Wili leveled an accusing look at the mouse. "I reckon I jest might if'n we keeps to ramblin' these heights."

That night, they hunkered together grouchily under granite ledges as rain sputtered in the pines. The next morning, when Thrym awoke to Muspul's familiar abrasive laughter in the forest deep, he almost cheered with relief.

Mouse and shrew clambered down rock shelves into a grove padded with green moss. On an old rotted log, Muspul, wearing a natty jerkin and cork-soled walking shoes, sat sharing termite biscuits and black honey with a large, dangerous-looking polecat.

Before the hedgehog noticed their approach, the beast watched coolly as they staggered into the grove.

Thrym lowered his sack and quickly slapped on his eyeglasses. "Dominie—"

"Thrym!" Muspul stood, his elderly and spectacled eyes big with surprise. "Frikee, this is the student of mine I've been lauding—the crofter from the Mere. Thrym! Come. Don't be afraid. Frikee is a friend."

Wili poked his wee head out from behind the startled mouse. "That ol' bristleback's a-needin' new goggles. Sure enough that he a killer what'll eat us all three in one chomp!"

"Is that Notty's lad?" Muspul adjusted his crooked spectacles. "No reason to be afraid, boys. Come along and meet my latest stalwart— Frikee Fitch, reformed malefactor and budding philosopher."

The polecat's black mouth leaked a laugh. He rose, towering over the hedgehog, and exposed a chest crisscrossed with bloodied strips torn from Muspul's old green mantle. "Death had his fat chance with me, fellas. Yaw! But this here quill-hog made Death swallow his lunch!"

Thrym edged closer, keeping Wili behind him. "How were you wounded?"

"With a weapon intended for you!" Muspul hacked a hoarse laugh. "Come. Join us, and I will tell you all."

Thrym and Wili reluctantly stepped to the near end of the fallen tree most remote from that brute with the dark smile and orange eyes, and sat. They declined Muspul's termite biscuits and offered from out of Thrym's provisions fried earthworms in sunflower mix, wedges of aged cheddar crusted with cricket legs, crunchy mustard-dipped waterbugs, and a crock of grasshopper and beans.

Frikee helped himself and ate heartily while Muspul relayed what had transpired. When the polecat, talking around a mouthful of food, explained how he wound up nearly dying in a ditch, Wili stood up. "That's my pa you done tried to killt!"

"Your pappy is right handy with a knife, young fella." Frikee swiped another cracker with grasshopper and beans. "And he'd a killt me deader than a curried egg if not for my tender mammy's letters pressed to my heart." He cast a mournful look at the colorful bits of paper strewn across the mossy ground. "She saved my life— and that busted musket whittled it to a more useful shape."

"What all useful shape you talkin' 'bout?" Wili scowled at the evil-eyed polecat. "You look more tore up than useful to me."

Frikee gave Muspul a huge wink and addressed the youth, "Fang and claw was all I ever knew until I grown wise on my own pain. Then, I asked myself, 'Yaw, cat—is that all there is for you? Is that all?' Now, brother Muspul come by earlier this extraordinary morn and has entrusted me with an opportunity to see if there is more. And I aim to learn for myself."

"Learn what all?" Wili squinted. "Learn you all worn out chewin' off chicken haids? That declaration sure got no stayin' power!"

"You think murdering poultry is all there is for a polecat, little mouse?"

"I ain't no little mouse, mister. I'm a shrew. You ort knowed that, seein' as you likely et more than one in yore less kindly days."

"I never did kill nothing with fur." Bland and patient, Frikee held the truculent stare of the little shrew. "And now my homicidal ways are well behind me, son. I'm just a bug chewer and admirer of fruits like you all. And I'm resolute to prove myself useful."

"You reckon you right useful 'nough to carry a mouse an' shrew to Fernholt? We got busyness big time thar, an' I'm plum tuckered."

Thrym shot Wili a quick look of reproval, then gazed up at the polecat's molten eyes. "You have to forgive Wili, Mister Fitch. He's a little grouchy today." Wili opened his mouth to contest this judgment, and Thrym grabbed the shrew with his tail and firmly yanked the youngster behind him. "We didn't get much sleep up there under the Cloud Forest, what with the spitting wind and no real shelter."

Frikee tested his recovered strength by stretching both arms above his head as if to grab one of the wands of sunlight aslant in the morning air. "Brother Muspul and me was just marveling how quick I heal. Fernholt is it? I got to deposit you rovers outside the city gates—there being a warrant outstanding for my arrest and subsequent neck-stretching."

Wili leaped out from behind Thrym. "Fer real? Fernholt aimin' to hang ye?"

"I'm kicking in the wind, boy, they get their paws on me." Frikee set his shoulders proudly. "I'm an *authorized* outlaw. Several hunnert trees across this mountain wear paper attesting to my numerous and sorry misdeeds." He got down on all fours. "Hop on, critters. Let's see how far to Fernholt old Frikee can jaunt before he gives out."

Muspul frowned so hard his rickety spectacles slid down his snout. "Fernholt is a long and arduous climb from here. If you are to test your strength at all, I propose we journey downhill. We must find Notty as quickly as possible. And then I believe a return to the Mere would behoove everyone."

"I ain't a-goin' back thar," Wili whined. "I'd as soon git et by this bust-up polecat than go back to that stinkin' swamp. Besides, we got awful big busyness in Fernholt."

"What business might a tyke shrew got with Fernholt?" Frikee leered with disbelief. "Swamp trash like you got no business with them fat-bellied squires."

"Them squires gone make us swamp trash heroes once they all hear what we fell onto in the Rill."

"Wili—" Thrym put a restraining hand on the boy's head and drew him back by the fur of his scalp. "Let's not rattle on."

"Ow-eee!" Wili glared hotly at Thrym. "I ain't a-goin' back to no Mere. Not e'er! We done fell onto somethin' worth hollerin 'bout, and we gone holler 'bout it in Fernholt to them fattest squires what'll listen."

"Thrym?" Muspul lifted curious eyebrows. "What is the lad carrying on about?"

"It's a secret, dominie." Thrym struck Wili with a stiff look. "We discovered something that will astonish everyone—even the squires."

"Well?" Muspul budged his aged head forward. "What is it?"

Thrym darted a nervous glance at Frikee, and the polecat tilted his eyes upward, aggrieved.

The old hedgehog shuffled closer to Thrym and Wili and passed a tired expression between the two. "Secrets feed on our hearts." Muspul swung his weary stare toward the hunkering polecat and back to the mouse and shrew. "He looks cruel. But fate, through this boy's father, emptied Frikee's heart of that vileness." He nodded knowingly at Wili. "What irony if Notty's own son should employ a secret to gnaw a hole in that polecat's heart and let that cruelty pour back in."

Thrym peered down at the youth, and shrugged his whiskers. "Muspul's right. What we found belongs to everyone on Riversplash Mountain. But you'll always be renowned as the one who found it first."

Tail swishing uncertainly, Wili contemplated this. "You reckon them squires might keer to name it after me?" His small eyes gleamed. "Wili's Holler?"

Frikee's pointy ears perked. "You boys uncover a treasure cave?"

Thrym and Wili shared a knowing glance, and the mouse said, "First, we find Notty. Then, I think it's best you see for yourself."

CHAPTER TWENTY-SEVEN

Brave Tails

Rain sparkling in sunlight accompanied the four animals out of the fern glade. Frikee impressed them all, including himself, with how easily he carried his wee companions on his back.

The animals held on tightly and gazed astonished upon the wilderness. Emerald butterflies rioted across slashes of sunshine between trees. Flocks of rose finches swirled into blue, frozen atmospheres among the snow peaks.

"Hey!" Thrym shouted from behind Wili. "I spy Notty!"

Frikee slowed to a stop on a ridge. "What you looking at, mouse?" The polecat gazed across the pastoral vista. "I don't see that knife-happy shrew nowheres."

Thrym pointed to a shadowed creek so distant that the sunny hillsides there looked like scattered flower petals. "He's on a footpath following that stream west."

"Looks like a pitcher book," Wili declared, admiring the snowcaps above foggy cliffs and rainbows and a mountainside of forests and fields. "But I ain't yet seen my pa."

Muspul tilted the lenses of his spectacles, hoping to telescope a better view. "Let us exchange places, Thrym, and you can guide Frikee."

With Muspul behind Wili and the mouse lying flat atop Frikee's scruff and imparting directions, the polecat swiftly descended. He bounded creeks and fallen trees, gliding through the pollen haze and slant light of the forest. Before long, Notty jogged into sight.

"Thrym? I ain't never!" The shrew removed his green cap and slapped it against his pantaloons. "Wili! Wili! I near died wit' fright lookin' for ya!" The joy on Notty's face slipped away. "Boy, what ya doin' atop that varmit polecat? And dominie!"

"He ain't no varmit, Pa!" Wili rolled off the polecat's back and flung himself at his father. "Frikee be our kindly friend."

"Yore *friend*?" Notty swung his son behind him and stared coldly at the polecat's charred face. "What mischief ya up ta, skunk-cat?"

"Yaw, Li'l Rat—don't get your fur all in a poof." Frikee showed his many sharp teeth in a prodigal grin. "I done killed myself when I tried to extinct you, tough guy. And now I'm new as the morning dew and twice as sweet."

"Ya 'spect me ta believe that stink?" He threw a querying look at his son. "Wili, what this murderin' cat doin' wit' ya?"

"We be adventurin', Pa!" Wili's clogs scuffed the ground excitedly. "Thrym an' me, we done found where at them Brave Tails be a-buried. An' we hied us quick to the squires up thar in the Holt fer to stake our claim. An' as we was a-goin', a goodly sizable talon bird near hook me! But Thrym he throwed me down an' saved my hide. An' we got to the squire by a donkey wagon, pa. An' the fancy-pants squire there toll us git. An' so we hiked ferny woods somewheres I doan' reckon where. An' then we come upon the ol' bristle-back wit' this here kindly polecat. An' Thrym he done seen ye from afar. An' now here we be."

"Ya said *what* 'bout th' Brave Tails?" Notty jammed his fists against his hips. "Ya know I don't respect no lyin'."

"They ain't no help fer it, pa. It were a secret." Wili thrust an arm at the mouse. "But Thrym'll own up it's true."

"The Brave Tails?" Muspul rocked his jaw. "Is that what this mystery of yours is, Squinty?"

"Nothing we say will convince any of you." Thrym motioned for his companions to mount the polecat. "If Frikee's got the strength, we should all go take a look, and you can decide for yourselves."

"Strength?" Frikee smoothed back the fur from his sooty face. "I'm wearing my strength comfortable as silk underpants."

Notty and Wili rode together between Thrym and Muspul, and Frikee sped so quickly through the corridors of trees that none could hold their breath still long enough to speak. With grace and speed, he vaulted thorn hedges and young conifers.

Frikee galloped out of the Holt down hillsides of tall grass. Thrym's far sight selected a sheep-worn trail that led most directly across the Rill, and the polecat charged ahead.

The Riprap's white water rushed alongside, scrolling around rocks far below. By then, Frikee's strength no longer fit his limbs so well. The afternoon sun glared his vision, and his run felt suddenly out of control.

Howls tore loose from the animals on his back as he scrambled along the crumbling stone brink of the Riprap.

"Stop!" Thrym pulled at Frikee's ears, and the polecat braked to the very edge of a rockfall above the roaring waters of the river. The abrupt halt ripped the sack of Thrym's meager possessions from Muspul's grip, and it plummented into the cold blue gulf.

"I am sorry, Squinty." Muspul tilted his lenses and peeked unhappily into the lonely abyss. "I will miss those tasty crackers."

"Sorry you had to lug that, dominie." Thrym forsook his grief for the loss of his one book, *The Chaunt of the Dead Riders*, figuring this was somehow fitting. He searched out a safe path down the canyon wall. "We can walk from here."

Gulping oxygen, leg muscles trembling, Frikee gratefully let the animals dismount.

Thrym led the way down zigzag stone platforms all the way to the gravel banks of the Riprap. Fear grabbed at the hearts of the animals following, because they couldn't see very far along. They held one another's tails and avoided staring down at the exploding current by keeping their attention on the snow crests above.

Frikee teetered at the rear, bewitched by the wry thought that fate had foredoomed him to die in the Riprap despite his change of heart.

With spray driving like rain, the travelers hiked over gravel banks to the cave. A gigantic fanged mouth gaped, framing the shining limestone crypt of the Dead Riders.

Awed silent, Muspul, Notty, and Frikee stared with big eyes at the sepulcher of winged pigs and hognosed snakes. Thrym and Wili left the stunned newcomers behind and scrambled over boulders to enter the burial vault.

"Hey-dee!" The small shrew turned and beckoned his companions onward. "Ye ain't seen nothin'! Them dead critters be in here!"

The astounded creatures staggered into the grotto. Toothy mineral drippings over-arched the burial chamber. From somewhere deep in the cavernous dark, perpetual drops of diluted limestone pinged and gonged.

Frikee stood tall enough to peek into the crypt. "Yaw! These critters been dead so long even worms gone look the other way." He helped Notty and Muspul onto the carven lip of the vault and both stood, gaping at the mummies within. Vacant eye sockets gazed back above caved cheeks and wide, yellow grins.

"Hey-dee!" Wili staggered under the weight of an orange, white-tipped foxtail. "This here the scalped hide of Rumner the Swift!" His cries rebounded in wobbly echoes. "Ye gotta see all the ol' timey swords an' lances a-hid in this here stone box. Some shoulders and arms could shove this open. Come on, Pa!"

Frikee held Rumner's pelt in his gloved hands and dolefully inspected the empty eyeholes and missing snout. "The gloss on this hide glistens like it had wind in its ears yesterday."

Notty strained to shove open the stone bin, and the slate lid yielded with a raucous shriek. While Notty and his son marveled at the timeworn weapons of the mythic Brave Tails and Frikee draped the fox pelt across his shoulders like a cape, Muspul searched the grotto for Thrym.

The mouse had scanned the dim-lit cavern with his far sight and had located an alcove cut neat and flush into a distant wall. He had shinnied over cone-shaped rocks to reach the carved niche. Only his big round ears stood visible above the dribbled boulders. "Dominie!" he called, his voice pounded with echoes. "Notty! You'll want to see this."

Wili led the other animals across the stony enclosure, leaping over fissures and dodging stalagmites.

Muspul followed the others more slowly. He had to be careful not to insult his weak heart, which was tripping madly against his ribs. But when he confronted what Thrym had discovered, his knees buckled, and he sat down heavily on a bench of curving flowstone.

A cleanly cut recess reached three mouse paces into the cave wall. There, illuminated by reflections from the Riprap, a plate of amber glass tall as Frikee gleamed. Beyond its orange transparency, shadow figures stood.

"They shadder bodies in thar, Pa!" Wili shrilled. "Let's git!"

"Hush, Wili." Notty stole into the alcove and pressed a paw

against the amber glass. When he withdrew his touch, a paw print impressed the layer of dust upon that pane. "Ya e'er seen th' like?"

"Naw!" Frikee wrapped the fox pelt tighter about himself. "Ain't nobody intruded here in an uncommon spell."

"What do you make of it, dominie?" Thrym inquired.

Muspul clutched a fist upon his thin chest, and knuckles touched the thump of his heart. "'From out the Mere they came, hard riding loose and quick—'" he quoted from *Chaunt of the Dead Riders*.

Thrym nodded, enchanted. "'They made their fame and shame abiding by black magic—'"

"Yeee, Pa! This be devilment!" Wili tugged at Notty's arm. "Come on away! This place given me the witherins!"

"'They rode a red fox fast, these riders who were dead—'" Muspul droned.

The young shrew could no longer abide shadow beings or the blood-beat drum of the river or the ghostly flickering of sunlight in this subterranean shrine to the dead. He yowled and ran.

Notty snagged him by the shoulder, and Wili spun free and slammed into the stone jamb of the alcove.

With a steamy hiss, the amber plate slid down, vanishing underground. Wili bounced wailing into the air, and his father caught and secured him under his arm. Limbs swimming, the boy struggled to get free until he saw the niche held not ghosts but an enormous elk skull with a scroll shoved through both eye sockets. Its antler rack filled the flinty alcove, and from each of its many horned points dangled a crimson mantle and matte black cowl.

Under this massive skull, upon a round dais, seven gold swords gleamed. The tips of the swords touched so that the mirror-bright blades rayed like spokes and the sturdy hilts evinced a wheel rim.

No one moved.

"Dominie—" Thrym whispered.

Up from a chasm of dreamy disbelief, Muspul rose. He plodded forward stiffly, paw still clutching the fabric over his aching breast, the knot there tighter than ever. But as soon as he entered the chamber, a wondrous tranquility saturated him. The scented air, spiced with remnant incense of some ancient ritual, dilated his sinuses and eased the tightness of his heart.

He bypassed the dais of swords and went directly to the skull of the giant elk. The bony visage reared over him, a weighty, august emblem of death. To either side opened larger chambers, catacombs, wherein lay niches crammed with boots, gloves, sword belts, and sheaths.

Muspul had to stand atop a stray rock on toe tips with arms outstretched to reach the elk skull. From its sockets, he slid forth the large scroll, and it rasped open under his paws like a carpet. He stared a long moment transfixed at the document, bespectacled eyes still and shiny as black agates.

"What all it say?" Wili squirmed to get free, but Notty held him fast. "Ol' Muspul's stricken, paw. We ort fetch him."

The company remained still. A fragrance like summer tedium, like a dazzle of honeysuckle, like a lazy frenzy of butterflies seeped from the alcove. Those soporific fumes calmed all, including Wili.

Charmed witnesses, they stood unmoving as Muspul tottered toward them and pulled the scroll around for all to behold six bold words scripted there in a large and florid hand:

Now you are the Brave Tails.

The Tarn

With winter, Riversplash Mountain's caldera freezes to a giant glacial bowl, full of silver light and clouds of powdered snow. Spring melts the drifts, and the caldera brims at its center with diamond-blue water in a mountain lake called a tarn.

—Notes

You've crossed into the land of the dead.
These rocks are whetstones of heaven
That hone wind and the moon and shed
Sparks of stars as they sharpen
Darkness to a razor edge of dread.

—Ki-o-Ki

from *Crater Canto*

CHAPTER TWENTY-EIGHT

Slitherhole

"Shore we ain't no Brave Tails!" Wili twisted free of his father's hold and dropped to the ground, giggling. "Them shadders scared us all purty bad."

"Speak for your own self, li'l shrew." With both arms, Frikee dramatically spread the fox pelt across his shoulders, extending it like a knight's mantle, and bowed to the scroll under Muspul's paws. "This here polecat ain't slamming no door in the handsome face of adventure and opportunity when destiny comes a-knocking. We are now Brave Tails!"

"What ya yammerin' 'bout, skunk?" Notty entered the alcove and leaned close to the dais, studying the swords for booby traps. "Ya ain't no Brave Tail. Ya just a common criminal."

"To the puny mind of the shrew, the heart of the beast don't never change." Frikee faced the elk skull with an expression almost of rapture. "My joy is I got good deeds in me. And fate knows it, else this ain't never would've happened—not to the woolly likes of me. Here be magic, little critters. Don't none of you doubt about it."

"Ya crazy!" Notty dared pick up one of the swords, and anxiety melted to wonder when nothing dire happened. "The only magic is how rich we'll be once we sell these gold swords ta th' squires."

"Unhand that, Notty!" Muspul's bark made Notty's heart jump. "We are, none of us, looters."

Notty immediately replaced the sword and muttered, "Yeah, well, we ain't none of us Brave Tails neither."

The aged hedgehog conceded this with a curt nod. "Surely not. We are, by fortuitous circumstance, stewards of a tremendous treasure. We shall report our discovery forthwith to the Council of Squires at Fernholt."

"Whoa, Hog!" Frikee jabbed a thick claw at the scroll. "You done read what is writ. We are now the Brave Tails. And we've got adventures and daring deeds to perform. This ain't no accident, fortuitous or otherwise. Look at them capes and hoods, critters! Smell the air! Yaw! This is magic!"

"Place all thoughts of magic firmly out of mind, my dear Frikee," said Muspul as he rolled up the scroll, "and spare yourself heartsick disillusionment."

Notty honked a laugh at Frikee, but Thrym silenced him by placing a gentle paw on his shoulder. "Wait." The mouse stepped into the alcove and gazed at the swords and elk skull. "The old moon told me this would happen." He swung an abashed look among his companions. "He told me I'd have an adventure. Then, dominie and Notty showed up, and I got . . . "

"Ya known this all along an' ya ne'er said nothin'?" Notty looked hurt. "Wished I'd known th' ol' moon had a say. I wouldn't a-feared ta bust our necks on that cliff comin' down here."

"The old moon told me if I spread it, I'd dread it." Thrym then turned slowly about. "He also said in these exact words, '*When mouse shares with his friends what he knows—they reclaim the masks and become heroes.*' He jerked a thumb at the elk skull. "So, I'm sharing."

"I dare say." Muspul's whiskers twitched with emotion, and his tail thumped the ground. "That settles the issue." He slowly spread out the scroll, blinked at it for a breathless moment, and then held up one corner for all to see better the writing. "Now we *are* the Brave Tails."

"What?" Frikee spoke through feathers of laughter. "Magic ain't a right reason for us to be here, but word from the *moon* makes us Brave Tails?"

Wili shared in the polecat's chuckle. "They funnin' us, Frikee."

"Thrym ain't funnin' us," Notty corrected his son. "Ya know that mouse got th' far sight. That's why th' moon talks ta him. That ol' moon been foretellin' true as sunrise wit Thrym since we was shavers—when Squinty un'erstan's him, that is."

Wili absorbed this news, recalling a sleepy memory. "He done toll me he was chattin' wit the ol' moon, but I jest reckoned . . . "

"So that's it? Frikee interrupted. "The *moon* says we got a destiny and so now we are the Brave Tails?"

"You wear that fox pelt well, Frikee." Muspul leveled a weighty stare on the incredulous polecat. "But Rumner the Swift's hide is a heavy coat to bear. Do you believe you're up to it?"

"*Up to it?*" Frikee drew the pelt over his brow. "Frikee Fitch is dead in a ditch. I *need* this moon prophecy to pick me up." He fitted the mask around his muzzle, and his dangerous eyes changed character, to sparks of shrewdness, with little of their original cruelty. "A moon prophecy, a skin flayed from legend, and one of them razor swords—that's plenty enough to endorse me a Brave Tail. I could also stand more of this nook's smell. What is this bouquet, this blossom wind that's looted summer?"

"Ya think it proper I take up a blade now, dominie?" Notty circled the dais, examining the apparently identical gold swords for differences.

"Choose your weapon, Brave Tails." Muspul turned to the elk skull and breathed deeply of the fragrant air. The congestion in his breast had vanished entirely, replaced by a tingling energy. "Frikee is correct. There is indeed magic in this place. And by that magic, we must define the terms of our alliance as Brave Tails. We must do so with sensitive regard to fairness, righteousness, and camaraderie."

"What all he sayin', Pa?" Wili whispered out of the corner of his mouth.

"I 'spect he's wonderin' who oughta lead us Brave Tails." Notty spoke to his mirror likeness in the sword he grasped. "He's rightful curious 'bout our purpose."

"Our purpose remains the same," Thrym said. "We must quest in the Cloud Forest and the Tarn for the last of the white squirrels. How else to discover the combination of gear turnings that will spill the rock slides and close Weasel's Pass?"

"That is quite the drama, mouse." Frikee plucked a sword from the dais—a mere dagger in his large paw—and waved the shining blade overhead. "But why all the bother? Some barrels of gunpowder will blast them rock weirs!"

"Ya e'er seen them dams, skunk?" Notty asked. "Each one of them dams is bigger than Fernholt itself! Ain't 'nough powder in all Riversplash ta dent e'en one."

"Well, then, forget about them rock dams." The fox mask sneered. "There sure to be some surprised swine if the Brave Tails be layin' in lurch atop Weasel's Pass." Frikee crouched as if to pounce. "We'll cut them porkers to sausage as they squeeze through the pass!"

"We gone stick some pig!" Wili squealed like a grunter and reached for a sword.

Notty sprang quickly and grabbed his son's wrist. "Ya ain't no Brave Tail, wee 'un. Ya gettin' back to th' Mere 'fore ya mama come after *my* tail."

"I ain't a-goin' back to Ma." Wili tugged his arm free. "I'm the one found this holler in the first place. Thrym knows it. And sure 'nough I jest now opened this here magic closet."

"So ya think that makes it right for ya ta run 'round wit' a cape an' sword an' get ya own self killt?" Notty met his son's defiant stare with a peevish look. "What am I ta tell ya mama when ya show up dead dressed like some circus caper?"

"Well, Pa, if'n I'm dade, I ain't gonna much care what all you tell Ma." The little shrew snatched a sword from the dais and raised it high. "I be a Brave Tail! Ol' Muspul sez so!"

"Ol' Muspul ain't ya papa." Notty grabbed for the sword in his son's grip, but the boy evaded him, dodging to the other side of the dais. "Dominie! Tell Wili he ain't no Brave Tail."

In the eye blink that Notty turned away from his son, Wili bolted out the alcove, brandishing the gold sword above his head. "Yeee-haw! Ketch this here Brave Tail if ye kin!"

"Boy!" Notty charged after the youngster. "Ya gonna get it now!"

Wili spun about and ran backward along the rock ledge, swiping at shadows and slaying make-believe boars. "Ho, pigs! Ye astin' fer it an' this here blade goin' to . . . Yeeee!" The young shrew dropped out of sight into a slender crevasse. With a dull clack, the gold sword stood blade up in the fractured stone floor, hilt wedged tightly in the crevice.

"Wili!" Notty fell to his knees among melted stumps of rock. His head disappeared in the slender seam through which his son had fallen, but his shoulders would not fit. "Boy!" his muffled voice reverberated. "Wili!"

From very far away, Wili's voice chimed bright and tiny, "Pa! I ain't ne'er seen the like!"

"Ya got ta climb up outta there, Wili!" Notty's shoulders hunched together and still would not fit into the cleft. "I can't get through!"

"Ain't no way up!" Wili's wee voice threaded out of the rock fault. "I done felled nowheres! Ain't nary a tree—ain't nary a blade o' grass! Jest rocks, all red an' yeller."

"Lichens," Muspul muttered, kneeling beside Notty, his whiskers wavering with amazement.

"An' ponds! They be ponds o' water green as trees!"

"The lad's describing the Tarn." Muspul bowed close to the crack and shouted, "Wili! Run and hide! Hurry! Get away from where you fell. Be quick!"

Notty squirmed and wriggled, and his head popped free of the narrow fissure. "What for ya tellin' him that?" The shrew pulled an unhappy face. "We gotta get him outta there!"

Muspul placed a consoling paw upon the shrew's shoulder. "Notty, your boy has fallen into a slitherhole."

"Ya say what?"

"Yaw! I heard tell of them." Frikee hurried to the shrew's side and fit one eye to the crack in the stone floor. "A short tunnel to far off."

"Ya crazy!"

"No, Notty." Muspul said. "A slitherhole crosses dreamspace."

"It's viper magic." Thrym emerged from the alcove. "Remember? All those bugaboo stories about the evil viper spirit, Vidar. This must be one of his slitherholes."

Terrible understanding formed in Notty's eyes. "Wili!" He pressed his mouth to the tight crevice. "Wili! Run an' hide! Ya in a snake den!"

CHAPTER TWENTY-NINE

Dream Den of the Viper

Wili explored the Tarn, keeping to the hidden places—rock crevices and narrow shelves. He slaked his thirst at rock flats of trickling water, then raced for cover under layers of slate. From his coverts, he watched giant red-winged eagles circling over the world—tiny in the sapphire sky above snow ranges.

Fear trilled in him like an electric current. He knew fright could kill a shrew. His parents had taught him to practice courageous thoughts in the face of peril. "I be explorin'!" he told himself. "I done found the grave of them Brave Tails an' now I be studyin' this here grievous land."

He hurried among boulders. Crouching in their shadows, he discovered odd new plants, rubbery blue succulents. They tasted bitter, and he spat them out and rushed off through the crater rubble. In this thin air, he tired easily. By nightfall, all strength exhausted, he crawled into a cranny just big enough to hold him snugly and slept till dawn.

Wili continued his explorations the next day. He was hungry. Shrews had to eat a lot each day to stay alive. But the soil here was poor, and he could pick up no scent of beetles or bugs. He followed a thin rivulet of snowmelt under slabs of granite and through angular crawl spaces underground that he thought might lead to either a trove of water bugs or another slitherhole and escape from the Tarn.

An odd, acrid odor tainted the air. It gradually thickened, and Wili, paw over snout, turned about in the cramped passage to retreat—then paused. A breeze tweaked the small hairs of his ears and tail. He poked his head around the next bend and gaped amazed at a skyline of glaciers and blue heaven.

The shrew advanced into a bright and marvelous chamber. Sunlight poured through a broad opening and illuminated a grotto cluttered with copper cauldrons, painted chests, wood-bound books, polished bronze mirrors, hide drums, and winged serpents of imposing ceramics.

"Well, lookee here!" Wili laughed softly. "Durned if I ain't luckier than a two-tailed lizard!"

The windowsill served as a rough-hewn altar: A long shelf of quartz displayed seashells and bloodstones in ceremonial patterns.

The sharp stink that had nearly turned him away came from brass lamps burning lumps of dung. The lamps spotlit frescoes of hairless, savage apes. Something of the snake in their hairless bodies gripped his attention—but what they held in their furless hands turned him away: a dangling raw heart with severed pipes and the bloody sponge of a lung.

Pins of fright prickled his hide. Alongside the quartz altar, the trickle of water he had followed pooled into an icy mirror. Something stirred under its glossy surface. He leaned over to see his reflection.

Wili's face of streaked fur vanished. Wobbly light firmed to a thick snake, and Wili zipped away. After he peeked out from behind the altar and realized that the serpent itself was not in the pool, only its image, he approached again.

Twin scarlet pinstripes trimmed the length of the black snake from jaw to tail. Around the predator were boulders of the Tarn. And under the viper's chiseled head gleamed an ice green pool. Yellow eyes stared hypnotically at their likeness in the mirror surface.

Wili's heart panted as he understood that he could also see what the transfixed snake watched. A figure moved there. And distantly he heard—music?

No. The young shrew's ears perked. *That thar the wind!*

Peering closer, Wili saw that the serpent gazed upon a reflection of a mouse maiden in a torn and stained gown, just stirring awake.

"Hey-dee!" Wili called and the sleek head of the black snake lifted.

The shrew hid behind one of the ceramic figurines and peeked out at the magic puddle and its vision of the thick black snake. A tongue flick tasted the air. Then, the viper's stare returned to the green waterhole and the drowsy mouse maiden within.

"Ah, Olweena,"—the snake's quiet voice oozed. "You escaped Kungu . . . to find your way to my gullet."

Wili watched the black serpent watching Olweena.

The snake muttered to himself, "Vidar—Vidar—stay alert. Do not let this mouse's drowsiness entice you into dream . . . " His head swayed over the green water as if trying to decide if he also should nap. "Awake!" His sinuous body slapped the surface of the water. "Awake and eat!" Swiftly he flowed away across the stony floor of the Tarn.

Wili crept out from his hiding place and cautiously approached the reflecting water. He stood over it and confronted merely his own reflection. The magic resided with the snake.

"Vidar," he whispered, wanting to hear aloud that despicable name. He had often listened in the Mere to gossip among the traveling peddlers who visited his father's dray shop to barter for goods—and Wili knew the name Vidar. *Sorcery Snake—Magic Viper—Dreamcaster*—a hobgoblin creature that might slide forth from any crevice in the Mere in the night's most dreary hour and swallow whole a water rat, let alone a shrew. "Vidar," Wili repeated.

The sound of the dreamcaster's name blurred across the surface of the pool. The young shrew's reflection wrinkled away, and Wili stared at the jumbled, broken slabs of the Tarn—and Vidar wriggling swiftly among them.

"Olweena," the shrew breathed, repeating the mouse maiden's name that Vidar had spoken so hungrily.

Immediately the vision within the water pulled back to an aerial view. The naked rocks of the Tarn looked like melted ice cream. Vidar appeared as a squiggle of licorice in a landscape banded chocolate, cherry swirl, and butter pecan.

Blocked from Vidar's sight by a rocky hill not far ahead, the mouse maiden sat up and rubbed her eyes sleepily.

"Hey-dee!" Wili hollered into the visionary water. "Olweena! A big ol' snake is a-comin' yore way!"

His warning cries bounded out the cave and thinned away in the mountain air with no effect on the mouse maiden.

"Mousie! Vidar's comin' at ye!" Wili yelled, but Olweena didn't hear. Frustrated and angry, he whirled about and shoved at the earthenware figurine that had hidden him. It spun on its pedestal, then tipped over and shattered with an explosive burst that lifted the shrew out of his clogs.

He tumbled to the pool of ice melt and saw Vidar jolt to a stop.

"That got yore 'tention!" Wili stood on toe tips and swept all the bloodstones and seashells off the altar. Then he dashed to the frescoed wall. With quick paws, he picked up a hot brass lamp and hurled it at the paintings of the hairless apes. A sheet of blue fire rippled up the wall and seared the violent images. Smoke twisted out a small hole in the ceiling.

"Hey-dee, Vidar!" Wili yelped when he noticed that the serpent had curled around. "Yore snake den's gettin' all tore up!"

CHAPTER THIRTY

Magic Restores the True Dead Riders

"We'll never squeeze ourselves through this crevice." Thrym pulled Notty away. "If we're going to save Wili, we've got to go find him in the Tarn."

"Yaw! To the Tarn! As the Brave Tails!" Frikee hooked the white gloves of Rumner the Swift's pelt to his dewclaws.

Notty stood staring at the narrow crevice. "I'll hire th' Avian Guild ta send fliers through th' Tarn. Them birds'll find him, an' we'll know where ta go."

"No, Notty," Thrym said. "The Avian Guild won't go anywhere near the Tarn. The eagles . . . "

"Brave Tails ain't afraid of no eagles." Frikee removed Wili's sword from where it had wedged near the slitherhole and pointed it at the cave's entrance. "To the Tarn!"

"Wait." Muspul motioned the animals back into the alcove. "We are not to depart this place of legend any less than legend ourselves."

"My Wili is in a snake den!" Notty wailed. "I ain't listenin' ta no legends. I'm goin' ta th' Tarn—*now*."

"Notty, hold up." Thrym put an arm around his friend. "Our best

chance of getting Wili back alive is if we go after him together."
Beneath the elk skull Muspul had stationed himself, a gold sword
in his paw.

The scholar-hedgehog pivoted on one heel and the gold blade
flashed among the antlers. Two crimson mantles swirled into the
air, floated across the chamber, and settled upon the shoulders of
Thrym and Notty.

One more flourish of the sword launched two black cowls. They
arced over mouse and shrew and plopped onto their heads.

"Haw, Hog!" Frikee reared back, awestruck. "You some kind of
dueling maestro?"

The hedgehog answered by whisking his sword overhead and
flicking another mantle and cowl from the antler rack. When the
garments fell, the mantle draped Muspul's shoulders and the cowl
hooded his head.

From within his mask, a darker voice resonated, "We shall not
portray the Dead Riders. That would be a pathetic sham—for we are
no Brave Tails, we feeble creatures of the Mere. To be worthy, we
must cease to exist as our former selves. In our place, beneath these
vestures, let magic restore the true Dead Riders."

The cowled hedgehog pointed his sword at Frikee, who was
taking in the ritual scene with a bemused air. "That goes for you,
as well, Frikee Fitch. When you don the fox pelt, you *are* Rumner
the Swift."

The polecat abruptly stood erect. "Yaw!"

"I grant no credence to providence or fate. Yet, here we find
ourselves—root farmer, dray shrew, felonious polecat, and worn-out
hedgehog. Chance or heaven—whatever we call that which gathers
us here—chance or heaven gathers us here and no others. And so, we
have a destiny. We must use these weapons as one under heaven
with no leader save heaven itself. Agreed?"

The other animals offered slow nods.

Notty's voice came forth timidly from under his cowl, "Uh, what 'bout Wili? He a Brave Tail?"

"Wili Burrtail is of our company—a Brave Tail," Muspul declared forcefully. "Did not he discover this grotto as well as the entrance to this chamber?"

Notty's cowl nodded. Then, he added meekly, "Wili ain't so good wit' secrets."

"He must learn. As soon as we find him, he shall partake of our oath." The hedgehog opened his arms. "Now, creatures of the Mere, are we all agreed upon the rightness of heaven's selection? Are we Brave Tails?"

The four animals shouted with raucous resolve.

Catacombs to either side of the elk skull contained the Brave Tails' equipage: wolf-hide boots, scabbards and sword belts crafted from zigzag snakeskin.

Notty stomped out of the chamber in fur-trimmed buskins, cinching his sword belt about his waist. "Now, let's get goin'! Where's dominie?"

"I'm here," the hedgehog called from atop two rocks he had stacked to reach the elk skull. With the edge of his sword, he scraped shavings from its horns into a cork-top vial. "The lovely fragrance we smell—the perfume of summer's twilight—exudes from this mysterious antler velvet. We are stronger for breathing it. I believe it is the source of the chamber's magic."

"Ya got an answer for everythin', don't ya?" Notty chided impatiently. "Well, what's ya answer for my boy, Wili?"

"Magic." Muspul stoppered the vial and climbed down from the stacked rocks. "To the Tarn!" Cape snapping behind, the invigorated hedgehog led the way out of the alcove.

CHAPTER THIRTY-ONE

Threats and Lies

Large folding doors with inscribed panels of sphinx mice and griffin rats slammed open. "Cheevie!" The boar lord barged into Squire Cheevie's book-lined study. "Thee dwells in a ridikilus big maze for a wee mousie. I beed wanderin' lost midst thy clutter o' rooms an' halls a rageful long time!"

Squire Cheevie looked up startled from where he sat behind his desk. "Lord Griml!"

The armor-clad boar strode to the center of the room with mud-caked boots. "Ah, but I ain't finded thee for to bellyache. Nay. Thee beed a right proper host, Cheevie." The boar exhibited sharp teeth in a hairy grin. "Thy victuals be too fancy like, wut for the boar's wild taste, but ample, squire, plenny ample. I an' the lads be thankin' thee for thy grub an' hospitality."

The mouse smiled weakly while grinding his molars. In the doorway, he glimpsed Chisulo grovel apologetically as he closed the folding panels. *Did I not instruct that hamster I was to be forewarned when this brute sought audience with me?*

"Do come in." Unobtrusively as he could, the squire slid beneath his ledger book the cipher parchment he just received by avian courier from the Council of Squires at Fernholt. "We have much to discuss now that you've sated your hunger."

The Council's coded instructions had denied Cheevie's request to destroy these intruders. They wanted to keep alive the possibility of a negotiated settlement in the likely event that efforts to open the rock weirs and block Weasel's Pass failed. The instructions were as clear as they were vexing: Stall for time until the Council could either unlock the rock weirs or agree upon terms for a settlement with the boar legions.

"Before we get down to brass tacks, my lord Griml, perhaps you and your—*lads*—would enjoy a steamy and fragrant bath. Soothe those travel-weary haunches, right? Shall I have Chisulo draw you a hot one? What say you, my good boar?"

Griml said nothing. He stood in the middle of the study, full of disdain for the opulence of the squire's chamber. This was an immense, high-raftered room for one dinky mouse to occupy. Ceiling murals depicted mice gods among rainbows and thunderbolts. Each painted panel was framed by beams of rare and polished woods. Cheevie's broad desk of petrified wood could seat half a dozen squires amply. The inkwell gleamed silver, the quill squibs pure gold, paperweights crystal. The boar lord looked down in disgust and confronted his reflection in the waxed cedar floor.

"How can thee abide this gilded cage, Cheevie?" Griml moseyed to the window bay behind the squire's desk and tapped a trotter upon a sill of coal-black marble. "It were bad to lose thy home in the untamed world an' find thyself here, soft an' fat an' locked up tight in a maze o' vaults an' chambers an' windin' halls."

Squire Cheevie, his pudgy face impassive, looked up from the ledger book he had opened to hide the Council's cipher parchment. "I'm a mouse, Lord Griml. I relish residing indoors surrounded by beauty and finery." He returned his attention to the ledger and added wearily, "My wife lived her childhood in the Mere. She assures me it is a joyless existence."

"Beg pardon, yore squireship, an' no disrespeck meant unto thy formidable missus, but there ain't no finer life than wut be had in the wilds." Griml eased his big rump onto the cool marble sill and raised his eyes to murals inlaid with ivory mouse divinities. "Ah, ain't no ceilin' grander than the stars . . . "

The squire snorted, "Until it rains."

"Aye, squire." The boar nodded dreamily. "That be finer yet. Rain dancin' in the trees be the loveliest music in this lovely world. Aye! An' the sky full of lightnins an' the dark closin' round deep in thunder then lit again an' lit again! Aye, that be the *Life*."

Pretending to blow his nose, Squire Cheevie held a lacy handkerchief to his snout and breathed in its lavender perfume, hoping to cut the musky stink of the boar. "My lord Griml, while I have you in attendance, I must draw to your attention the intrusive misconduct of your squad. They have positioned themselves throughout my estate as *overlords*. Boars have imposed upon my fields and vineyards and presume to supervise my workers! Other of your *lads* interfere in the manor, and with the authority of my butler, who tells me that he and my other servants are subject to random and rather brusque body searches. Also, there is the matter of the refugees who have come to Bracken Knoll for asylum. Your soldiers have seen fit to intimidate these refugees and to mistreat my volunteers. I cannot tolerate such behavior."

"Now, squire, doan' be gettin' thy whiskers in a tangle." Griml leaned forward and made no effort to disguise his scrutiny of the squire's desktop. "We be here negotiatin' 'mongst wee creatures wut as soon stick us in the troat as say g'day. We've to have security for our own selves, aye? So, we needs to search thems wut draws nigh our persons an' handles our victuals. Thee would do same were thee a guest o' the legions."

"I should think not!" Cheevie turned full about in his swivel chair. "Your safety is guaranteed by my honor, sir."

"Nay, squire. Our safety be vouched by our own boar vigilance. Takes this here cipher thee be takin' pains to keep from me eyes." With nimble speed, the boar lord snatched the Council's parchment from where a corner of it peeked out beneath the ledger book. "By the Holy Sow, what have we here? *Code?* Be it orders? Wut be writ here, squire? Tell me that."

Cheevie stiffened. "Sir, that is a private communiqué."

"Thee be negotiatin' wit' the Boar March." Griml turned the parchment upside-down and scowled at the cryptography. "Wut be writ here?"

"That, sir, is a charter from the Council of Squires in Fernholt ratifying my authority to negotiate binding terms with the boar legions, represented by you, lord Griml." The squire casually flicked some nonexistent lint from the silk sleeve of his ruffled blouse and elaborated on his lie, "This document grants me sole discretion in deciding your fate here on Riversplash Mountain. Hence, I urge you to behave yourself."

Griml's warty snout wrinkled in a derisive sneer. "Thee farts with thy mouth, squire."

"I beg your pardon!"

The boar lord slid off the sill, turned, and directed his tusks at the windows. "Cast thy eye upon thy yard, Cheevie!"

The squire viewed the mossy courtyard and hedged gardens below his window. Among fountains and walkways, volunteers with lances and bamboo armor patrolled, coming and going under the fierce gaze of two spike-helmeted boars.

"There'd be no puny soldiers here 'cept thee knowed for some time we boars be marchin' on thy mountain." Griml rapped his tusks hard upon the desk. "Thy lords in Fernholt knowed as well. They ain't trustin' no wee mousie to talk terms with the March. Nay! They be hunkerin' down in them big houses, draftin' war plans whilst wee mousie here sets to distractin' us wit' fancy feasts an' steamy baths. Aye?"

Cheevie felt the blood flare in his jowls, his whiskers tighten against his snout, and his tail stiffen, yet he forced a civil tone, "My lord Griml, I shall ignore your insulting my honesty."

"There be talk from them in this house wut we've leaned heavy on—talk 'bout rock weirs an' blockadin' Weasel's Pass." Griml's tiny eyes screwed tinier. "Wut be the meanin' o' such talk?"

"Poppycock, my lord. The fabled white squirrels of ancient times built massive bulwarks to hold back the mountain's avalanches. That's all. But folklore has amplified history to myth and made those bulwarks into more than they are. Stuff and nonsense." The squire spoke quickly, almost squawking in his eagerness to change the subject, "I, however, am prepared to offer your legions something genuine. In return for the sovereignty of Riversplash Mountain and the Boar March not entering Weasel's Pass, we shall agree to provide biannual tribute of a yet-to-be-brokered quantity of orchid roots, truffles, and earthnuts. I am certain I can carry this resolution by a full majority at the Council of Squires in Fernholt—if you will but agree in writing to these terms."

"Aye—in writin'." Griml flapped the encrypted parchment in the squire's face. "But first, I be findin' out wut be writ on this scrap, eh? Kungu be right smart at crackin' code. And, squire . . . " The boar grimaced threateningly. "If thee lied to me—it be bad for thee an' thine. Un'erstan'?"

Cheevie swallowed hard and replied in a small voice, "Indeed."

CHAPTER THIRTY-TWO

Death Improvises

Wili raged. His fury surprised him. Finding himself in a snake den, even one as marvelous with treasure as this one, should have terrified him. His shrew instincts screamed to get out and hide among the rocks of the Tarn before the serpent returned. But anger overwhelmed his instincts. The moment he realized he had distracted the horrid Vidar from devouring Olweena, he flew into a tantrum of vengeance for all the little creatures that monster had eaten.

Wili smashed figurines and flung open painted chests. Inside, he found masses of molted snakeskin—Vidar's hides, as colorless and light as fluff. Grabbing fistfuls, he whipped those streamers into the air, shredding them to a flurry of floating bits.

Hide drums, he bonged off the altar. Brass lamps, he tossed out the window to get rid of the dung-burning stench. He kicked over copper cauldrons, spilling quivering contents as clear and goopy as jellyfish.

Squealing, he danced away as the gelatinous stuff gummed together into one thick mass. It reached blindly forth with queer, blobby tentacles that slapped the walls and sluggishly pulled itself onto the altar.

The shrew scooped wooden books from their wall niches and heaved them with both paws at the sticky thing. The heavy volumes impacted with a wet, sucking sound, and sank into the giant amoeba—then spewed forth with projectile force.

"Cat's claw!" Wili ducked to avoid a flying book. "You plumb near took off my haid!"

Bending to retrieve the book and rip its pages, he glimpsed the magic pool and saw Vidar's black tail whip out of sight into a rock cleft. The next instant, the viper's head squirmed up in the den from a nearby floor fissure, jaws unhinged, fangs splayed to strike.

"Yeee!" Wili shrieked and seized a bronze mirror almost as big as he, pulling it in front of him as a shield.

The cold grasp of an amoebic tentacle enclosed his tail, and the young shrew leaped away from the shapeless attacker with another shrill cry. Holding tight to his shield, he collided with Vidar's striking jaws.

Vidar clanged loudly off the bronze mirror and reeled away. Pinpricks of hot light twinkled before his crossed eyes.

Wili dropped the large mirror and took hold of the smallest one in the heap of polished bronze, intending to pitch it as hard as he could at Vidar's head. Then he felt again the gruesome touch of the blob slurping toward him, and he recoiled and slammed into the cave wall.

His frantic eyes fixed on a jagged seam in the rock beside him, just large enough to squeeze through. He shoved himself into the fissure with bone-squeezing compression and fell into a void of silvery darkness.

Vidar's fangs sliced the empty space where Wili had stood. The viper's angry gaze fitted itself to the fracture. It was a slitherhole that widened in summer when the ice of the Tarn melted and the rock wall relaxed. But this was too early in the season for the viper to fit. Of course, he had ways of tracking down that violator of his dream den, that insolent shrew vandal, and devour him—one limb at a time.

First, though, he had to assess the damage done to his magic. He swirled through the shambles and came to a sharp halt before the burned frescoes. That heretic shrew had smashed the lamps of perpetual homage!

For the first time in Vidar's adult life, the lamps of sacred dung had ceased to burn. The burning coprolites, fossilized lumps of waste, of the hairless apes of ancient lore no longer filled the den with their power! Such a breach disrupted Vidar's bond with the sorcerous force that fortified him. If he did not act quickly, this rupture would soon strip away all his dreamcasting might and reduce him to a common, belly-crawling viper.

"Gob!" he shouted impatiently. "Retrieve the sacred lamps and clean up this mess! Quickly!"

The colorless slime split with a wet noise like rending flesh, and half slid out the window while the remainder reached with numerous slippery feelers for the scattered books, cauldrons, shards, and power stones.

Vidar writhed among the chaos of his dream den, hissing and spitting. Without his magic, he could not use his ice-melt pools to observe the movements of the destructive shrew. Rage boiled in him and would have flared to a fit of hysteria if he could have seen where the young shrew had fallen.

Far across Riversplash Mountain, Wili sat up in a musty cave. He stared into the baleful gaze of a shaggy brown giant. The beast's mangy hide glittered with rubies of raw red cankers and open sores.

"Yaaa!" The shrew kicked backward till he struck a wall. "Git away from off me, ye ugly ol' bar!"

"Hmmm." The giant gazed down with small moist eyes full of quiet watchfulness. "Yes, little shrew, I am ugly—and old."

That tender, feminine voice made Wili peek between his upraised arms.

"If one lives long enough without succumbing to accidents or predators," the she bear continued gently, "death improvises. She has embroidered me with wounds of great age. Indeed, I am worn by the humiliations of time. But how, may I inquire, does a wee creature as short of days as you know that I am a bear? I am the sole bear on this mountain these many years."

"I know a bar when I seen one." Wili sidled along the wall, making for the distant entry to the cave. "I seen bars in pitcher books."

"Ah-h-h-h . . . " The bear stepped back and sat down heavily, providing ample room for the shrew to scoot out of her cave. "Then you are a learned shrew."

"I know some." Wili got to his feet and cast a look to the exit.

"Good. I don't get many guests, and I am grateful to have visitors drop in who can hold up their end of an intelligent conversation." Tiny chandeliers shone within her kindly eyes. "I am Bestla, and I have come to Riversplash Mountain to spend my final days in sublime meditation." Her warm words melted over the shrew. "And who, may I ask, are you?"

The ragged youngster stood up taller. "I'm Wili Burrtail."

The old eyes softly studied the dirty, shabbily clothed shrew, taking in the proud angle of his tail and confident steadiness of his whiskers. "I can see your parents love you very much. What are you doing so far from home?"

"I reckon I come a fer piece," Wili acknowledged. He took a modest step closer, curious about this benevolent beast. "But what all ye know 'bout my folks an' how kindly they think on me?"

"When a youngster is loved, it shows." Amused by how seriously the young shrew pondered her reply, she exposed mauve gums in a near-toothless smile. Her close-set eyes brightened, as if the scabs and wounds on her torn hide were mere decorations. "So, tell me, young Wili, what occasions this inadvertent visit?"

The shrew glanced anxiously at the cracked cave wall through which he had arrived. "I done come through a hole gittin' away from Vidar."

"Vidar! My!" Bestla rocked back, genuinely surprised. "No little creature has ever escaped his devouring jaws in the time I've known him."

"You knowed that evil monster?" Wili scurried backward three paces toward the cave mouth. "You ain't gonna give me o'er to him?"

Bestla shook her large, scarred head. "No. I don't feed Vidar. He feeds me." She inhaled deeply, filling her lungs for a sigh. "As for Vidar being an evil monster, well . . . " Her sigh sizzled like oats crackling in a fire. "To a shrew, yes, I suppose Vidar must seem evil. But he's not all bad, you know."

"Vidar near et me up!" Wili protested. "Warn't fer a crawlhole to this here cave, right now I'd be gittin' personal familiar wit' that snake's innards."

An orange claw in Bestla's right paw pointed at the little oval of polished bronze the shrew held. "What's that you're holding in your paw, Wili?"

"I 'spect I done stoled this off a Vidar." He regarded the shiny disc with wonder. "I don't know but that it looks much like a lookin' glass. Ain't glass, though."

"No. That's bronze. It's an alloy of copper and tin. Do you know about alloys?"

"Not even nary a little." He made a goofy face at himself in the mirror. "But I got a reasonable suspicion it's some kind a metal."

"An alloy is a mixture of different elements that blend together and make something new." Her words sounded as sweet and soft as carved butter. "Sometimes those elements are metals. Sometimes not."

Wili angled the bronze mirror so that it reflected Bestla. "Looky thar, Bestla! This alloy here can shore make you look pret-near young agin." In the convex surface, the bear appeared swollen to her former fluffy magnificence. "Keer to hold it some?"

"No, thank you, Wili." Bestla slimmed her eyes with exquisite pleasure at the playfulness of the young shrew. "Vidar will be looking for you. I think you should go back home now, as quickly as you can. Show the bronze mirror to your parents. They will tell you more about alloys."

"I ain't a-goin' back to the Mere." Wili widened his stance. "I cain't. I'm a Brave Tail."

"Is that so?" The diminutive lights in Bestla's eyes motioned to a shadowy corner of the cave mouth. "Why don't you take a seat, and tell me about this? You seem a most interesting young shrew, Wili Burrtail. Tell me your story."

"I would proudly if'n Vidar warn't a-huntin' me." Wili strode to the opening and faced a horizon of silver mountains under a deep sky. "I best skedaddle afore he come along."

"Vidar is my friend." Bestla shambled across the cavern floor and sprawled out on a rectangle of sun in the entrance. "I won't let him touch you." She closed her weary eyes. "Tell me your story." In a whisper dangling into silence, she added, "Maybe I can help you."

Wili doubted this decrepit beast could help herself let alone him. But the world beyond loomed vast—full of steep ravines and precipitous bluffs. He felt no urgency to get lost in that enormity. So, he sat in the shade and told the drowsy old bear his story.

When he finished, he leaned over the recumbent bear to see if she was asleep—and she opened one nutshell eyelid. "Wili, I think we better get out of here—right quick."

CHAPTER THIRTY-THREE

The Brave Tails' Perilous Stratagem

Stars twitched in an indigo sky when Frikee and the Brave Tails trotted above Bracken Knoll on their way through to the Tarn. Thrym called a halt, and the polecat wearily sagged into the tall grass atop a bluff.

"Squire Cheevie has guests." Thrym tugged off his cowl and peered down through purple air into the dark fields. Alongside streams gray and wrinkled under evening, a torchlight procession of animals hauled bushels and baskets brimful with spring grain. They trudged toward one of the mills and its faintly clanking paddle wheels. Among the workers marched three large boars in helmets and body armor. They flailed at the laborers with quirts, and their big voices bounded up the bluff with anger.

"Boars!" Notty jumped off Frikee, and his sword hissed from its sheath. "Them swine invaders are upon Riversplash Mountain awready! Let's stick 'em good, fellas!"

"Notty, stop!" Thrym grabbed the shrew by the collar of his windblown mantle. "What about Wili?"

Notty stood rigid, battle fury draining into the earth, displaced by recollection of his son. "What hope for Wili alone in th' Tarn at night?" His raised sword arm wilted. "What hope for any o' us now th' boar hordes come upon us?"

"The Boar March is not upon us. Not yet." Muspul removed his cowl and angled his spectacles to survey more distinctly the acreage around the mills. "If the hordes were present, those fields would be entirely ravaged. The March doesn't oversee field workers but tramples them under hoof. These are advance guards—scouts. Their presence here in Bracken Knoll suggests they have been received by the squire. Why would Cheevie suffer swine—or they him—except to broker a deal?"

"A deal?" Thrym's acute vision reached across the estate to the mansion with its many lanterns. He browsed patios, balconies, and bay windows with chandelier-lit interiors for a glimpse of his sister or brother-in-law. "What kind of deal?"

"Exactly." Muspul's voice dimmed as though speaking to himself. "Boars do not make deals." Then, in a voice of conviction, "These boars are here to test our defenses. There may well be other scouts this very night investigating the squires at Fernholt and Mole Baileys. We must send these swine a message."

"I surely do hope it's a short message." Frikee sighed tiredly from where he lay in the high grass. "I ain't got the strength for no message more bigger than a fare-thee-well."

"This can be a brutally short fare-thee if we have the courage." Thrym pointed to the dam upon the stream above the mill. "That dam's at maximum pool level. Dominie, go there with Notty. Shortly the last of these field workers will cross the stream and mount the higher ground of the mill. When they clear the embankment, you and Notty raise all the sluice gates from the dam's gatehouse. Do this quickly."

"A flood?" Muspul asked with alarm. "Do you understand what you're proposing?"

Thrym surveyed the path the flood would follow across the vinery and then over the bluffs at the edge of the estate. "Grapes are day work. At this hour, no one is in the vineyard. But Frikee and I will see that our piggy visitors are positioned to the tall side of that bank under the mill—where they won't observe the flood until too late."

Notty's hood shook with disapproval. "Tons o' water will explode 'round that bend faster than any polecat can run—let alone wore-out Frikee."

"Haw, there, li'l rat!" Frikee's head bobbed up. "Who you calling wore out?"

"This could work." Muspul rubbed his chin whiskers contemplatively. "But I must go with you, Squinty. You'll need my sword skills."

"We're not going down there to duel." The mouse donned his black cowl. "Frikee and I will be in little danger if you open those gates in a timely fashion. Now, go. Hurry. There's no time to debate this tactic. Speed and surprise are our allies."

With a crisp nod, Muspul and Notty scurried down the bluff, low to the ground, hidden behind grass and weeds. Soon, they reached the stream and the walkway along the dam. Odors of moss mold, algae and river kelp filled the gatehouse, a small shed containing the workings of the sluice gates. Notty took hold of the oaken wheel that dominated the hut.

Muspul laid a paw on the wheel. "Not that. It controls the bypass pipes. They release water into the stilling basin, to quiet the flow before it enters the stream channel. Squinty is expecting something more dramatic." The hedgehog took hold of a pinewood lever taller than he. "I'm going to need your help pulling this jimmy stick. I don't think it's ever been used before."

"How ya know so much 'bout dams?"

"There's a peculiar invention that can teach one just about anything." Muspul flexed his paws to get a better grip. "It's called a book. I cannot commend it highly enough to any who want to understand how this world works."

Notty poked his head out of the hut and peered over the bulwark of the dam into the high, still water that it held back. "That's a rambunctious amount o' water, dominie. Ya sure Squinty knows what all he's doin'?"

"Get over here, Notty." Muspul stripped off his cowl to see better into the night. Torchlights flickered in the distances of the gloaming, and by their quavering glow he observed diminutive shadow figures plodding across the stream's stepping-stones.

"Dominie, spot Squinty an' the polecat?" Notty pushed his face into the window slot, striving to see. "It's dark as a crow's underbelly at midnight."

"I don't see much either. But we've got to do what we're here for. Get a good grip, Notty." Muspul watched the last of the workers tramp onto the far bank. "Heave!"

Hedgehog and shrew, strength amplified by magic antler dust, pulled with all their might, and the lever juddered in their paws and did not budge. Muspul spun around and pushed at the pinewood stick while Notty continued to yank. The hedgehog's face smeared with effort almost to tears before the lever stirred and began to slide.

With a sorrowful bong, the sluice gates jarred loose from their beddings. The sudden force of the escaping water shoved the gates open, and the lever keeled hard over, tossing hedgehog and shrew into the air. They banged into the shed's wall, splintering planks.

"Owl's spit!" Notty's shout disappeared in the bellow of gushing water. He shimmied to his feet, clutching at the shaking walls to steady himself. "Spittin' owls!"

Muspul pulled himself to his knees at the window slot. Spray nearly blinded him, and he peered through fisted paws to watch water slam into the stream banks and kick rocks and gravel to the stars. The flood nearly toppled the stones of the dam, then heaved downstream again in cascading waves, mounting into a massive surge of black water.

Notty hollered as the bucking dam kicked his feet out from under, "Here comes your high water, Squinty!"

That was exactly what Thrym counted on. He had ridden down the bluff on Frikee's back, both animals hooting and shouting at the boars. "Hey, you hairy-butt grunters! Stinking squealers! Your fat Holy Sow got twelve *moldy* teats!"

Thrym had directed Frikee to the far bank of the stream, where the hill's twists blocked the dam from sight. There, they took their stand, hurling more insults at the boars.

One of the boars immediately charged across the stream, shooting spray off the silty, sandy bars. Frikee fled. Thrym waited, heart thrashing against his ribs, wondering frantically what to do. He drew his sword so forcefully that he staggered. His movement flung him to the side of the boar's attack, and his flailing sword slashed the boar's jowl and flank.

Their comrade's wounded cry inflamed two other boars, and they tore across the stream with hideous battle shouts. Not until they reached midstream did they notice the rolling mass of water, as tall as the hills, bearing down on them.

Frikee heard the boar's pained shriek, and he swooped along the bank for Thrym. The polecat rammed into him, and the mouse clutched the fox pelt as the flood wave slung around the stream bend.

As fast as his terrified legs would carry him, the polecat whisked his rider up the embankment. At the crest, they toppled to the ground and lay just above a massive slide of black water pouring across the land.

The torrent pitched all three boars high into its current. The swine warriors tried to race away in the flood, legs churning, helmeted heads straining above the flow. Their cries were lost in the squall of torn earth and trees ripped from their roots.

Briefly they hung stationary in the deluge, eyes beyond hope, mouths open in soundless howls. Then, the might of the swollen river catapulted them through the vineyard. Trellises, clods of earth, twisted trees, and three stiff-legged and screaming boars pitched over the cliffs of the Holt in a long arc of falling water.

Almost at once, the pandemonium hushed to silence. The land lay still and glistening under remote stars.

From beside the mill, awed laborers raised their torches, cheering in spontaneous salute. Their jubilation reached the mill and soon workers emerged, drifting silent, stunned by the brash demise of their masters.

On the hillcrest of the far shore, a caped mouse atop a rearing fox stamped their silhouette upon the sky. Astonished murmurs ran through the crowd, watching fox and rider turn swiftly into darkness.

CHAPTER THIRTY-FOUR

Under the Black Flag

From the rooftop of the manor house, Griml gazed west at a sky banked with orange clouds. He inhaled fragrances of twilight and willow mist, large nostrils quivering.

Kungu stood respectfully in the door of the companionway that led below to the penthouse suites. Still wearing his camouflage mantle of woven vines and headwrap of straw, the scout edged into the open, the better to look around. His heart enlarged when his stare settled on the boars' black flag. It flew from a bamboo staff lashed to roof tiles above the front courtyard.

Griml sighed loudly, and the happiness in his whiskery face hardened. "We be brainless, simple creatures afore the vast fathoms o' the world. Aye. Simple beasts rootin' in illusion, diggin' in stink, searchin' through misery for wut beauty there be—wut scraps we be findin' of infinity."

Kungu agreed with a pensive nod. "Elsewise cannot be. Elsewise could not be. Elsewise never can be."

"Ah, aye, Kungu. Aye." Griml watched the last light on the mountains—dusky red crossing to purple to that moment when heaven reveals its stars and darkness. "Ain't thee mighty amazed with thyself to be walkin' the earth a boar?"

"Mighty amazed, m'lord."

"Where be Olweena?" Griml asked without budging his stare from the luminous west.

"Olweena I could not find." Kungu shuffled uneasily. "In the forest o' clouds, I lost her."

Griml turned slowly, tiny eyes hard. "*Thee*—clever Kungu—*thee* lost a bleedin' mousie?"

"Upon a forest o' clouds, m'lord." Kungu came forward and removed his straw headwrap. "In a vale o' thorns afore a great cedar, her scent vanished." The scout quickly added, "A white squirrel be drowsin' there, m'lord. Myself, I seed her, all caged up in prickers— like unto the fables o' this mountain's wee beasties."

"Hati be real?" For a monent, Griml could not think. "Cheevie sayed not. Cheevie sayed wut them wee beasties be tellin' us o' white squirrel princesses an' rock weirs an' closin' Weasel's Pass be fable." He withdrew the cipher parchment taken from the squire. "Wut be sayed here?"

Kungu inspected the parchment and shook his big head. "Considerable time for unravelin' this code be required. Mayhap, I . . . " Kungu glanced past his lord, and his diminutive eyes bulged. With a startled grunt, he lunged forward and nearly toppled over the parapet of the roof. "By our Holy Sow! M'lord! Look!"

Griml turned and stared upon the night-held estate. At first, he could not be sure what he saw. In the high fields, the dark land itself seemed to unspool. He snatched the spyglass from his utility belt and telescoped it in time to behold a deluge of tree limbs and trellises surging over the cliffs—carrying three boars.

"Me lads!" Griml bawled. He swung the spyglass up the course of the flood to the dam and there observed two black-hooded animals in billowing capes fleeing along the dam. The boar lord's frantic search soon revealed another hooded animal in a fluttering cape, this one astride a fox. "Who be these devils?"

Kungu accepted the spyglass and scrutinized the ominous figures of black cowl and hide boots. Against the night sky charged with mist from the flood, they appeared as ghosts. "Wreckers the like I ain't ne'er seen, m'lord."

"Cheevie!" Griml bellowed. "Bring me the squire!" The boar lord paced a fast, tight circle. "An' his fat wife!"

At that moment, Squire Cheevie and Magdi awaited Griml and his soldiers before a sumptuous banquet table. Bedded on ice shavings, shellfish glistened: whelks, cracked sea urchins, cockles, and oysters among tangles of seagrass. A harp and flute ensemble of woodchucks attired in ruffs and satin festooned the air with tranquil music.

The feast had been set up in the gallery above the lotus ponds, where afterward servants could easily hose away the spillage and disarray left by the uncouth boars. Magdi smoothed a wrinkle from the damask tablecloth of embroidered white birds. For table service, she had chosen plates and dishes of beaten gold (less likely to be broken than her fine painted porcelain) and goblets of silver etched with feathered goats. Albeit a thankless gesture among boars, platinum cutlery fitted with grips of green jasper gleamed beside the plates—and silk napkins folded to resemble swans complemented each setting.

"Welcome, boars!" The squire, appareled in chartreuse breeches and a buff dinner jacket, mistook for guests the two guards sent to fetch him. When one of them seized him by the collar and hoisted him like baggage and the other grabbed Magdi similarly, her copious yellow crinolines crackling, the mice yelled for help.

Ermine lancers rushed into the banquet hall and collided with the exiting boars. The boars, knocking the smaller animals to the floor, trampled them under their boots. Moments later, the squire and his wife stood shuddering with indignation on the rooftop flanked by the two gruff guards.

Torches along the parapets shed light across a triangle of rooftop wherein Griml stood, a riding crop in one trotter, the cipher parchment in the other. Concealed by darkness, Kungu watched from a distance, eyes glinting.

"Griml!" Magdi squeaked angrily. "Griml! Your filthy brutes violated our persons! These mud-clotted, blundering oafs tramped down our guards! You vulgar swine may delight in the chaos of a pigsty, but I assure you, you—you big, stinking . . . "

"Dearest!" Squire Cheevie seized the satin arm of his irate wife. "We are dealing here with a delicate matter of state."

"There is nothing delicate about these churls!" Veins bulged against the jonquil ruff at her throat. "These are not guests or diplomats. They're vile bullies, foul scoundrels, nasty . . . "

In three quick strides, the boar lord closed on the mice. He roughly inserted the handle of his crop through the back of Magdi's bodice, lifted her off her feet, and carried her to the edge of the roof. "Cheevie, I took oath none o' mine be killt on this mountain. But now I seed three o' me lads swept to oblivion on thy land by masked devils! *Three* good boars killt! Diplomacy be done! Now thee be tellin' me wut treachery thee plots!"

"Treachery?" Cheevie stared stupid with dismay at his imperiled wife. "Griml, I've plotted no treachery. Masked devils? I have no idea what you're accusing me of plotting—but you are mistaken! Please! Return Magdi to me! Now!"

"Wut be writ on this here paper! Wut wickedness be the vermin o' Riversplash plannin' against the March?"

Magdi peered down at the garden far below and spluttered, "Squire! Oh, my! Plumpkins! This brigand—this gruesome—"

The squire rushed forward and stopped immediately when the boar lord swung Magdi farther out. "Give her back to me, Griml. I'll tell you all."

"Aye. 'Tis a turrible long way down." The boar dangled Magdi briskly over the drop, eliciting her sharp and despairing shrieks. "Wut be writ here, squire? Wut be the defenses o' this mountain?"

"Tell the swine nothing!" Magdi kicked and squirmed defiantly. "I love you, plumpkins!" she shouted passionately and flung herself into the night.

Griml gawked, amazed. "Crazy gnawer!"

"Magdi!" Cheevie spun about and plunged down the companionway, wailing in despair.

Before she impacted, Magdi moaned the first syllable of a prayer. Then, she smacked backward onto the flowery surface of a lotus pool. Dense vegetation and her copious skirts broke the fall, and she shot up out of the water and stood tangled in lily stems, gaping like a stunned frog.

Cheevie found her in the mud, shivering with shock. He dropped to his knees and pressed her tightly to him. "Thank the Dancing Drunk Red Rodent, you're alive!" He pulled away from her at once, his face awry with worry. "Are you hurt?"

Magdi blinked and her drooping whiskers suddenly perked, flicking droplets from a snarling mouth. "Those fat-rumped, turd-gnawing, hairy hides of bacon! Squire"—she gazed up wrathfully at the rooftop where the menacing silhouettes of boars leaned—"I just got me a strong hankerin' for sausage."

CHAPTER THIRTY-FIVE

A Baleful Prophecy

Dawn streaked the sky; the old moon hung there, slender as a fang. So close to his companion, the sun, he had nothing to say to Thrym. The mouse sat, unmasked, on a rock where his pal Notty had fallen fast asleep. Muspul lay below, snoring against the shoulder of slumbering Frikee. Though nocturnal animals, they had spent all their strength fleeing Bracken Knoll after their successful raid, and they had decided to rest at night in the deep woods above the Holt before continuing at dawn through the Cloud Forest up to the Tarn.

"Hey, you old bone," the mouse whispered to the moon above ragged pines. "I found the hidden masks, just as you prophesied. I'm a Brave Tail now."

After a lengthy pause, a small voice spoke out of the cold sky, "What you are is what you do. And what you do defines you."

"Wise as ever." Thrym gave a dour laugh. "The boar hordes are marching on Riversplash Mountain. How about a prophecy? Will we stop the March?"

"Chew your knuckles while the viper chuckles." The moon sounded remote, distracted by the rising sun. A prolonged silence ensued as morning inched down the mountains. Then, the moon's voice returned, choked with distance, "I see the frightened Brave Tails blunder—and the mighty boars march like thunder. If you are unmasked in the suspense, then all of your lives become past tense."

"Hold on there!" Thrym stood up. "Give us some hope!"

The emaciated moon melted into the sun's glare. "If you insist on possessing hope, you put your neck in the hanging rope."

"Listen, you pocked and gnawed old bone," Thrym whispered through gnashed teeth. "We're the *Brave* Tails! Not the Frightened Tails! We're not going to blunder in fear of . . . "

"What ya yammerin' 'bout?" Notty sat up groggily. "Oh! 'Tis morn!" The shrew sprang upright. "Dominie! Skunk! Get yaselves up. Wili's awaitin' on us in th' Tarn."

Neither hedgehog nor polecat complained as he struggled awake, and Thrym said nothing about the moon's disturbing prophecy. Whatever doom awaited them lurked in the future, while Wili's peril worsened with each hour. The mouse donned his cowl, less to hide his identity than to draw strength from the fabric's gingery scent of sun and shadows.

Silently Frikee carried his companions among misty conifers creaking in the wind. In that chill, damp, and bone-colored light, the Brave Tails were glad for their garments, and they proceeded swiftly up the foggy mountainside.

Far above that dismal weather, another mouse stared into the heavens, not for the old moon but for the eagles that ascended with the rising sun. Olweena had survived one harrowing day in the badlands of the Tarn by paying close attention to the sky.

Shielded by a ledge of shale, the mouse maiden had curled up during the night while hailstones as big as marbles bombarded the stony terrain. The ice melted at dawn, and Olweena drank greedily. Cold air and blood loss from her severed tail had dehydrated her.

Yesterday the bleeding had stopped. She had staunched the wound with mats of moss found flourishing in the shadow of a boulder.

At this altitude the sky appeared violet, the sun as white as a star. Much reduced by her injury and hunger, she just wanted to lie down and stare up at that purple heaven until her life evaporated. She had woken up dying, abandoned in this wasteland where the voles had deposited her. She would gladly have left her bones right there except for what the boars had done to Blossom Vale. The child weeping within for her slain parents offered no peace.

Attentive to eagles and ignoring the pain of her stump, she had staggered among a maze of trenches carved out by rivulets draining the crater lake. For food, she smashed scorpions with a stone and sucked their salty juices. Prickly pears grew along the dunes, and she gnawed them while listening to the moaning wind and whistling eagles.

Several times, she caught the scent of snake and dragged her hurt body up onto stone shelves and rusty slabs, avoiding belly crawlers but exposing herself to raptors and the smiting sun. Asps skimmed over the Tarn floor and swayed upright when they saw her, triangular heads bobbing, frustrated that she had eluded them. "We cook your death in our glands," they each had sung. "One kiss locks you in a diamond of emptiness forever."

Late that first day, she had crossed a dry lake littered with corpses of rats, marmots, chipmunks, gerbils, beavers, and hares, some of whom wore the uniform of Squire Cheevie's battalion. Dry winds had exposed the skulls and clawing ribs.

Wedged in the cranny of a rock wall, she had studied that terrible scene—and she had spied what the dead had not: asps lurking in the sand drifts. "Look upon the dead!" they sang when they tasted her scent on the wind with their flitting tongues. "Behold the many we have slain! More than we can eat! Look at them with their empty eyes and empty skulls no better than the rocks. They are you."

She had crept off at sundown and had located shelter under a shale ledge. Next morning, when the mist peeled away, she observed with numb surprise that she had found her way to the edge of the Tarn. Sand and sharp rocks led down toward a forest of fog-shrouded black yews.

Out of that murk appeared a sight that tested her eyes' credulity: three black-hooded and crimson-caped animals straddling a fox. She blinked and rubbed her sockets and blinked again. The fabulous menagerie proceeded uphill directly toward the sandy banks where the merciless asps waited in ambush.

Olweena stumbled out of her hideaway, and the strength in her legs drained before she reeled three paces. She questioned if she was still asleep until she thwacked her head on the ground. She crawled to a blurry boulder and pulled herself upright. Her exhaustion sat her down again, and immediately the pain that shot from her lopped tail shoved her back to her feet.

Small, stiff steps brought her near the fox and his riders at the very edge of the sand hills. "Stop—" she panted. "Asps—hiding—"

Lurching from around a tall rock, the broken mouse, tailless and anonymous with pale dust, appeared a deathly specter in rags, and the fox reared back from her. "Yaw!"

Olweena squinted at the three hooded animals, fitting together puzzle pieces of a hedgehog's silvered fur, a shrew's twitchy tail, and a mouse's stout forearms. "Muspul?" she croaked. "And Notty?" She tilted forward, certain now she was dreaming. "Thrym? Squinty Thrym? Why—why are you masked?"

Behind the mouse maiden, an asp swirled upright from out a

sandy rift. The fox's eyes flared with fear, and Olweena glimpsed death across her shoulder—needle-thin fangs and bronze eyes of vertical slits.

A flash of golden light swiped past her face and carried away the gaping jaws of the asp. Its supple body lashed headless for an instant, squirting scarlet threads, before collapsing to writhe frantically in the dirt.

Olweena stared at the thrown sword embedded in the ground. Sunlight flared off the twanging blade. Those sharp rays seemed to slash the last, frayed cords holding her up, and she toppled like a string doll.

CHAPTER THIRTY-SIX

Charity of Dreams

"Give her room to breathe." Thrym poured a capful from a flask of beetle broth and waggled his tail at the other animals crouching over Olweena, signaling them to step back. "She's fainted."

"Ya think so, Doc Thrym?" Notty whisked off his hood and used it to fan the unconscious mouse. "She ain't got no tail! It's cut clean off! I think she's bleeded out."

"She saved our heroic hindquarters." Frikee stood lookout atop a tablestone. "There got to be a score of Cheevie's voluntaries yonder. And all got wind whistling a jaunty tune through their ribs."

"That was a deft toss of the sword, Notty." Muspul retrieved the blade and kicked away the amputated head of the asp. "Half inch off, Olweena would be missing a nose as well as a tail."

"Nose ain't no use ta a corpse." Notty braced Olweena's head while Thrym wet her lips with broth. "I owed her a life th' Rill beavers near took off me. Now, I'm paid up. If'n she lives, that is."

Thrym wiped sand grains from her fluttering lids. "She's coming around."

"Put your cowl back on, Notty." Muspul ordered, handing the shrew his sword. "We're Brave Tails."

Notty sheathed his weapon and looked up at the masked hedgehog with an expression of disbelief. "Olweena knowed us on sight, cowls or no."

"Notty's right." Thrym removed his hood and looked around at the desolate land. "There's no one else up here to recognize us."

"We wouldn't even recognize ourselves about now if that tailless mousie hadn't stopped us tramping through them snake hills." Frikee's black lips grinned at the hedgehog. "Give up the masquerade, Hog."

"Ah well." Muspul sighed. "Seeing as she saved our meager lives . . . " He tugged off his cowl. "May this garment's charm help her as it has me." He crouched beside the frail mouse maiden and pressed the black fabric to her nostrils.

Whatever mightiness the perfume of that garb contained, it gently roused Olweena. "I'm not dreaming?" She sat up. Around her, Notty, Muspul and Thrym watched expectantly. A large, predatory creature in a fox pelt towered behind them, surly smile pressed into his sooty snout. "You're not a fox."

Frikee's grin widened. "Hail that fact to the heavens, mousie. I'm sure my mammy's listening."

"We best get ya inta some shade." Notty fit his paw under her arm. "Can ya stand?"

Olweena held Muspul's cowl to her face and strenuously inhaled its fragrance of summer haze from a long twilight. "Dominie, what is this magic?" She floated upright unaided. "What is it doing to me? And who are you dressed as?"

"We are the Brave Tails." Muspul took her arm and guided her away from the gaze of the eagles. They sat in the blue shade of the caldera's wall, and the other Brave Tails joined as the hedgehog told their history. While he spoke, he applied to her torn flesh pinches of antler velvet. Notty fed her fried earthworms and crumbled termite biscuits. And Thrym plied her with beetle broth.

Frikee meanwhile climbed the ridge of the crater and surveyed the interior. Since arriving at Riversplash Mountain, he had oft heard tales of the Tarn but had never before seen it. A thousand acres of rubble and folded rock made a labyrinth of gullies, luminous pools and dwarf forests. Far back against the rim wall, the crater lake gleamed.

A creature of the forests, the polecat shivered in the icy, thin atmosphere. Overtaken by a faint despair, he eagerly scampered back to his companions and found them listening to Olweena's confession of spying for the boars. In the midst of recounting how she had fled Kungu and found a white squirrel slumbering among thorns, Muspul moaned softly and keeled over.

The chill altitude had convinced his body that the cold season persisted, and the hedgehog slid back into hibernation. The other animals—none of whom ever experienced winter dormancy—panicked.

"His heart!" Thrym cried and knelt beside Muspul, rhythmically pressing clasped paws against the hedgehog's chest. "Get the antler dust!"

Notty found the vial packed with aromatic shavings in a pouch of Muspul's cape and wafted it under his teacher's nostrils. The scent of sunlight arrived with the force of a dream—a premonition of warmer days to come—and wrapped the hedgehog even more tightly in his seasonal repose.

Notty pressed his paw against Muspul's neck. "I ain't feelin' no pulse!"

Frikee lay on his belly staring at the hedgehog's nostrils. "Hog ain't breathing either!" He tugged hard at Muspul's whiskers, and the elderly animal continued to lay inert. "Old Muspul—he gone."

"No!" Thrym pried open Muspul's jaws and huffed several strong breaths into the hedgehog's lungs before Olweena took him by the shoulders and pulled him back.

"Let him go, Thrym." She inserted her bedraggled body between the mouse and Muspul and gave Thrym a weighty look. "He was dying. He told us so. Now his suffering is ended. Let him go."

Thrym budged Olweena aside and cradled his dominie's head with great gentleness. Shock gave way to bereavement, and his vision of Muspul's face smeared to a blurriness no lens could focus.

Notty and Thrym removed the Brave Tails' gear from the hedgehog—his cape, scabbard, and sword—but left him in his knee-high boots of cougar skin. They laid him to rest upon a basin of sand situated under the rim wall. Then, they covered him with ferrous red rocks stacked as a cairn. While they worked, each took turns sharing a memory of the beloved animal.

Muspul listened from his bed of sand. He couldn't understand their words, but he recognized the grief in their voices.

Dreaminess soaked his brain, and he did not at all mind finding himself cozy in a rock lair hidden from the wind. Nor did he despair that the others thought him dead. Hibernation left him free of exasperation. His body hummed softly, drowsily. No need for food or water troubled him. He levitated into a restful trance with eternity near.

The others left. They had to find Notty's boy, Wili. That was the right thing for them to do. The compact energy that was Muspul's body hummed agreeably. When summer climbed Riversplash Mountain and finally reached the Tarn, he would sit up from this sand basin, shove aside the cairn rocks, and rejoin his friends. Perhaps with the aid of the antler velvet and some luck, he would live long enough to see the weir gates opened and Weasel's Pass closed against the boar legions.

Muspul's quiet body lay hidden in a chartless fault of the crater wall, but his consciousness—strong and tranquil—pulsed like a magnetic beacon. Vidar sensed him.

Among the shambles of his dream den, the serpent assessed the damage that Wili had inflicted. Gob, the protoplasmic menial, had cleared away toppled books and fragments of shattered statuary. But the sacred frescoes of the hairless and ferocious apes remained marred. Their pitiless faces veiled in lampblack no longer recognized Vidar.

To test his dreamcasting powers now that the magic images were scorched, the viper stared into a puddle of ice melt and detected a hedgehog resting in the rim rock. Many animals roamed the Tarn but no mammal so large lay still in the broad plain, and so the viper noticed him at once.

"Who are you?" Vidar asked.

A hedgehog.

"I can see that from here, fool." Vidar's tongue-flick touched the dream image in the puddle and tasted the creature envisioned there. Usually that was sufficient to know the deepest thoughts of the animal he beheld, but now he tasted only acrid water. "Who are you, hedgehog?"

I? I am like you, a living thing—and, like every living thing, a secret hidden from myself.

"Bah! Don't you dare riddle *me*!" Vidar slithered around the ice melt. "Why are you in the Tarn? What do you want, hedgehog?"

The charity of dreams.

"Enough!" The serpent lashed across the puddle, spitting rage that his dreamcasting powers had been so diminished a hedgehog could baffle him. "Gob! Work harder! Faster! I want my magic back!"

Vidar slid out onto the bright sill that opened upon frost

mountains and high cirrus clouds. "I must go down the mountain," he said to himself firmly. "My magic has become too small to direct those oafish boars from here. I *must* go down now and bring cold vengeance upon my family's murderers. The swine legions will march! And I will taste the blood of my enemies."

The Brave Tails in Death's Doorway

Risen from their graves by a wizard owl,
They lived again with sorcery—
And through that magic mystery,
They made what killed them their might:
Silence of tiger, dread of wolf's howl,
Swiftness of lynx, and the viper's bite.

—Chaunt of the Dead Riders: Book the First

CHAPTER THIRTY-SEVEN

Serpent's Wings

Night enclosed Bracken Knoll. From a slitherhole behind one of the estate's waterfalls, Vidar rushed forth. His sinuous black length wriggled swiftly under blaring water and across flat rocks.

Observing Vidar sliding through the heather, a brown rat on patrol raised his lance and chittered harshly, "*Tsk-tsk-rrrr-tsk!* Viper on the prowl! *Tsk-tsk . . .* eek!"

Vidar knifed forward, jaws agape, and swallowed the rat whole before he could launch his weapon. For several long minutes, the serpent lay still working his squirming prey down his gullet. He scanned for other witnesses and saw none. In the dark, he could hear the slap and splash of the three mills. The clanking waterwheels and their paddles swung darkly across the sky.

His meal snug inside him, Vidar proceeded down the parkland, scattering before him a small circus of crickets. Though Wili had broken the viper's power to dreamcast from afar, Vidar could yet cast his spell upon those in reach of his velvet voice. "Sing to the night's stairways of stars, you tiny fiddlers and forget me . . . Forget me, fiddlers."

Likewise, the serpent spake to the toads policing the fields and orchards. Soon, he crossed lantern-hung gardens where boar sentinels patrolled. The first boar that slouched past on the white gravel path met the viper's yellow stare.

"Stay." Vidar's command stood the boar motionless on the path. The bloated snake skirled up the sentinel's brawny, mud-clotted body and, once upon the spiked shoulderplates, whispered in his hairy ear, "Take me to Griml."

On the rooftop of the manor, the boar lord and his aide Kungu sat before a tilted drafting table whereon cipher parchments overlapped. Two more ciphers had arrived that day by avian courier from Fernholt, implying some urgency, but the boars had been unable to break the code. If Cheevie's armed militia had not outnumbered them, the boars would have wrung the code out of the squire by now. Griml gnashed his teeth wondering if an elite regiment of musketries marched on Bracken Knoll this moment.

Most of the boars on the rooftop, including the giant Ull, seemed unconcerned by this. They gorged themselves at a trestle table laded with eels and crawfish and bushels of truffle biscuits.

At the sight of the zombie sentinel wearing a black snake swollen with the shape of a swallowed rat, the feasting pigs froze. Kungu reeled from behind the drafting table, a hooked dagger carving a bold attack.

"Stop, Kungu." The viper spoke in a voice soft and remote. "Stop and study those names writ in cold light upon the black doors. Study them."

Kungu halted in mid-stride and raised his gruesome face to the stars.

Ull roared with indignation and fear at this display of deviltry. Food bits and spit flying like gunshot, he toppled the trestle table and rose up, enormous head thrown back, bellowing throat braided with veins.

"Ah, Ull," Vidar addressed the massive boar intimately. "Death is a garden in the eyes of flies. Sit, great Ull, and think on this."

Ull sat. His small eyes lidded heavily, and his broad, warty brow beneath his war helmet creased with the effort of thought.

Griml reached for the musket under his body armor, then stayed himself. The absurd sight of Kungu intent on celestial observation and Ull pondering big thoughts forced the boar lord to regard this black viper more closely. "Wut art thou, snake?" Darkly Griml's eyes met the serpent's stare, and something unspeakable entered him. "I likes not thy look."

Vidar unwound from the sentinel. He flowed across the rooftop and swirled up the legs of the drafting table and onto the slant desktop livid and black.

"I have feathers." The silk of the snake's voice clung to silence, just perceptible. "You cannot see them. My wings are dreams. With these wings, we rise above all the desires and longings running away from us. Want is a long road, Griml, ambition a journey of many paths. But with these wings, we have already arrived!"

"Wut's thee sayin'?" Griml wanted to back away from this stark apparition but could not. "My ambition be wut it ever were. To live fearless an' be tastin' o' life's honeyed secret ere we be ripped to pieces in the Holy Sow's hungry jaws. Aye. All wut lives, She devours."

"Yes, yes, lord Griml, life is but a dream." The viper gave a laugh like a sigh, weightless and unhappy. "You are old, the veteran of many campaigns. Soon, your dream will end."

Griml lifted his tusks defiantly, hackles prickling. "Art thou Death come for me?"

Vidar grinned delightedly. "No. I am the wings of the dream. I am *life*, lord Griml. And I am come that you and your legions may feast upon this mountain's bounty."

"Why? Wut devil wizard sent thee here 'mongst us boars?"

Vidar required complicity from the boars greater than he could now command, so he explained in his soft, intense voice, "The denizens of Riversplash Mountain murdered my clan. I alone am survived, and I will have my vengeance when the boar legions march through Weasel's Pass and devastate this land."

Griml nodded gravely. Blood lust he understood, and he leered with one side of his mouth. "If wut thee sayed be true, then thee be a mighty ally for the boars. Aye?" He brought his scarred face closer, bracketing the viper in his tusks, and asked, "Wut be thy name?"

"You will call me Master."

Griml's face pulled sharply away. "Nay! I be warlord o' the March! No snake masters me."

"Lord Griml—*please*—" Vidar hissed. "Regard your minions, clever Kungu and mighty Ull. With a single word each, I proved their master. Do you doubt I could command you likewise? Why have I not?" The viper's glossy head veered closer, flitter tongue tasting the boar's fear. "You *are* the boar lord, and I would not usurp your authority. I have no desire to command legions of boars. I desire to command you alone. And only until your horde arrives. Then, my revenge is complete, and you will never again see me. You and your multitudes shall feast upon snow orchids and truffles. And that triumph before all your kind shall belong solely to you—*Lord* Griml—because when I depart I will expunge from the minds of your comrades every memory of me. You alone shall retain the dignity of remaining wholly untouched by my magic."

Vidar hovered before Griml's stare for an extended moment of silence before inquiring, "Are we agreed?"

CHAPTER THIRTY-EIGHT

The Truth in Beauty

Thrym led Frikee, Notty, and Olweena up the stony lip of the crater wall, avoiding the sand hills of asps. From on high, the mouse would search the Tarn, hoping to spot Wili. But for now, as he trod along the steep and narrow ledge, he grieved for Muspul.

He remembered learning his ciphers among a twig fire's ashes in the twilight, peeking up at Muspul's grizzled face watching him study. What might have happened if he had listened to the old hedgehog and had stayed on his croft? *Would Muspul still be alive?*

"Yaw, Squinty, mind your step!" Frikee caught Thrym by his cape and kept him from stepping off the rim into empty air. Dislodged pebbles bounced and pitched into the abyss. "This ain't no holiday jaunt."

"Thanks," he muttered and avoided facing the polecat's sneer by casting a glance upward, searching for eagles.

Death above and below. The shaken mouse upbraided himself for daydreaming about the dead. He strode more swiftly along the crest. The sooner he found Wili, the sooner they all could quit this bleak and frozen terrain.

The mouse glanced back frequently to make certain Olweena

was all right. The antler velvet powered her with an agile grace that defied the loss of her tail and so much blood. He worried she might collapse again at any moment.

She returned his looks with a brisk, comradely smile. To keep warm at that frosty altitude, she wore Muspul's cowl secured at her throat and the oversize cape folded snugly around her. At one point, she sashayed close to him on the windy brink and whispered, "Courage."

Do I look scared? Or is she consoling me for dominie? Or maybe she's just telling me not to worry about her.

He was still pondering what she had meant when he spotted Wili. Far across the mountain, the little shrew appeared, astraddle a haggard bear.

"A *bear*?" Notty squawked. "There ain't no bear on Riversplash Mountain."

"Well, I've never seen a bear either, so maybe I'm mistaken." Thrym stared harder at the bruin and its rider, questioning his own eyes. "But whatever it is, it's big. And it's old."

"I thought you said that young Wili fell through a slitherhole into the Tarn." Olweena squinted where Thrym indicated and saw no creatures in that soaring landscape. "Are you sure that's him down there?"

"That's your boy, Notty." The mouse nodded. "His little face is no mystery to me. Maybe he crawled through another slitherhole out of the Tarn."

"Ya tellin' me we gotta go back down there?" Notty griped when Thrym tried to point out Wili among the evergreens and mists from the Cloud Forest. "That's near a whole day back th' way we come!"

Frikee swished his foxtail. "Don't li'l shrew know better than to consort with predators?"

"His name is Wili." Notty descended the ridge, his heels

crunching gravel in furious stride. "And he's o'erdue for a serious tongue-lashin'."

Thrym edged alongside Olweena. "Are you strong enough? We can stop and rest here awhile. The view is stunning."

The view is stunning? Thrym flinched. *Why don't I just ask her to dance? Maybe a jig will help her forget that the boars ripped away her tail, her family, her whole world?*

"The view *is* lovely," Olweena agreed.

On the tundra plain below, thaw runoff spread highland flowers in a golden haze of gorse, groundsel, and zinnia. Olweena took his paw in hers. "I feared you were going to hate me, because I spied for the boars."

"Ya told 'em nothin' an' lost ya tail for it," Notty shot back before Thrym could reply.

"Gullibility—that there's your problem," Frikee added. "Desperate hopes funded my felonious life, so I know well how you got gulled."

They came down the crater wall opposite where they had interred Muspul. From there, Frikee carried them across the flowery fields.

Far off, on the far side of a forest of stunted pines, Wili and Bestla ambled. The she bear carried the young shrew on her back, between her large scissoring shoulder blades.

As they shuffled along, they stripped shrubs of new-grown leaves and tender shoots. But that sustenance wasn't ample enough for the bear. When they came to a stream, she lay down so the shrew could dismount.

"Wait for me under that juniper tree," Bestla requested in her buttery voice. "We are going to find the white squirrels and do what we can to thwart the boar hordes, as I promised. But to climb to the Tarn, I need strength. And for that, I must eat."

"What you fixin' to eat?" Wili asked, surveying the quick-running stream with its turtles sunning and air hazy with pollen and spinning gnats. Then, he noticed salmon quivering together under the water. "Oh."

"There's no reason you should watch this." She turned her shaggy back on him and leaned over the murmuring water. "Life devours life. That's the grave truth."

"Ain't no need to get all in a fix 'bout eatin' 'round me." Wili moseyed up the riverbank to a juniper, sat, and observed with rigid fascination as the bear swatted the water and came up with a writhing salmon impaled on her claws. "I reckon you must be somethin' of a large eatin' gal."

The salmon warbled a piteous fragment of a prayer, "River spirit, water of light, take me whole unto . . . ."

Bestla bit off the salmon's head. "I swore I would not hunt when I came to this mountain. I came to die," she spoke with her mouth full. "But your story dissolved my vow, Wili. Now, I see my coming here has a greater purpose. A destiny. Before my time ends, I will do some good for the denizens of this mountain. That is my new vow. A vow that will last me a lifetime."

Wili watched with an air of wonder as the bear waded into the stream, batted the water, and again extracted a thrashing salmon. "We're doin' a right important thang, huntin' them white pouch-cheeks in yander Tarn." He looked away as Bestla continued to feed and preoccupied himself with the bronze mirror. Sunlight through the conifers played across the shiny disk. "If'n Pa an' them other Brave Tails knowed what we was about, they'd be ample proud."

Sun rays flaring off the metal disk guided Thrym and Frikee through the torturous territory. Dusk had buried the sun among clouds when the polecat finally came in sight of the aged bear and her wee companion.

"Pa!" Wili kicked his heels against the hide of the bear, urging her forward. But, at the sight of the polecat and his caped riders coming through the leathery light of nightfall, she sat. "Hey-dee, Pa! Lookit me a-ridin' this here bar!"

Frikee came to a weary halt and goggled. "Curl me up like a rabbit and I'll lay an egg! That *is* a bear!"

Notty hopped down and charged toward his son. "Wili! Boy! Ya get down off that beast."

"Don't be afeared, Pa!" Wili slid to the ground and dashed to his father. "This is Bestla. She's sweet as butter. And ain't they nothin' she don't know!"

Notty clasped Wili so tightly the dray shrew collapsed backward and sat rocking his son in his arms. "I thought I lost ya," he murmured into the fur atop the boy's head. "For sure, I thought I lost ya, my Wili, my little Wili."

"So, when's the tongue-lashing to commence?" Frikee said with a grin and approached the docile bear. "Frikee Fitch, reformed desperado. Bestla, is it?"

The bear nodded softly. As the others drew close, she told her story. Wili interrupted often with his observations about slitherholes, Vidar, and his trek with Bestla through the uplands. The little shrew squinched his eyes in the dusk. "Ol' Muspul ort to hear 'bout all this adventurin'. He could study some from what I seen. Where he gone?"

"Where rain rises, youngster, and the hawk don't hunt," Frikee volunteered.

"Ol' Muspul dade?" Wili slumped and his father leaned close to whisper consolation.

The scent lifting off the Brave Tails' garments filled the silence with the perfume of a summer's eve. Bestla stirred and reaffirmed her mission, "I came to Riversplash Mountain with no burden in my heart, prepared to die. But I have witnessed the boars' plundering on other mountains, and those ghastly memories weigh heavily now that I have found peace here. We must locate the white squirrels and recruit their help."

"Days now, we been scurrying like cockroaches up and down this dirt pile," Frikee complained. "We ain't got either the vittles or the lack of sense to make a spectacle of ourselves in the Tarn. We just come from burying the best of our own up there. And besides"—the polecat gestured grandiloquently to Olweena, who sat in Thrym's arms against a crooked pine—"this here maiden is direly wounded and needs doctoring."

"Ya should go ta Fernholt." Notty rose up in the dark, full of resolve in the presence of his son and the soft-spoken bear. "Olweena, get th' care ya need. And rile th' Council ta arms!"

Olweena sat up. "You're not coming with us?"

Notty nodded to the old bear. "Bestla, ya strong 'nough ta trek th' Tarn?"

"Strong or not, I am going. We must waken the sleeping princess, Hati."

"You're going with her?" Thrym asked Notty. "What about provisions?"

"Forage as we go." The shrew met his friend's concerned stare proudly. "Ain't we survived th' Mere?"

Wili tugged urgently at his father's cape. "Me too, Pa?"

"Ya a Brave Tail, ain't ya?" From beneath his cloak, Notty produced the cowl and mantle Muspul had selected for the young shrew. "I just hope th' scent o' magic on these don't get ya any more rambunctious than ya already are."

Wili threw the crimson mantle over his shoulders and stuck his head in the cowl. The garment's incense of summer twilight filled the child's heart with a loneliness thicker than he had ever felt. His body shivered like wind in ditch grass.

He tugged off the black hood—"Dang!"—and sniffed the cowl again, inhaling honeysuckle banks, pokeweeds, and black sumac all dusted with sunfall. The fragrance was so beautiful that his heart hurt, and he knew then for sure, for the first time ever, that someday he would die.

CHAPTER THIRTY-NINE

Despair of Mice

Squire Cheevie had not visited Wright Court since his mouseling days. The hamlet of artisans at the base of Bracken Knoll bustled with activities that had fascinated him throughout his childhood. Carpenters hammered, smiths clanged, masons tapped rhythmically and continuously as wagons and carts trafficked the cobbled lanes. He had loved roaming cinderpaths behind the bakehouse and cheese works, peeking in through knotholes at workers muscling dough and sieving curds.

"Plumpkins, your eyes look like glazed fruits!" Magdi approached her husband where he stood in the chandler's shop gazing absently out a round window. "Snap out of it!" She shook him by his shoulders till his large ears wagged. "Your militia awaits your decision."

"Yes, dearest," he replied but did not turn from the window. Through hanging racks of wax tapers, he peered out at the chimneys atop Wright Court and, rising above them, masses of thunderhead clouds. When the spring rains had arrived during his childhood, he had loved to visit the weed lots behind the brick kilns and dye hutch. There, he had sated himself on droves of millipedes hiding from the downpour. How his mother had railed at him for returning to the manor house soaked and muddy!

"'Yes, dearest'—'yes, dearest'—do you hear yourself?" Magdi turned him brusquely about so he could feel her hot words on his face. "Will you give the order to slay those swine who have invaded our home or not?"

"I suppose I must." Cheevie brushed wrinkles from his waisted frock coat and smoothed his whiskers. "They are belligerent."

"They are *evil*, squire." Indignation agitated her, and the frills and flounces of her orange gown flapped as in a sudden wind. "Evil!"

"Yes, yes!" Anger stiffened his arms and fists at his sides. "Griml nearly killed you, my beloved! For that alone, I am willing to cut him to pork rinds!"

"*But*?" She drew her head back so that her ample, rampant bosom shoved him against the windowsill. "*But*?"

"Many of our fellow creatures will die in the conflict, dearest. Many more will be bloodied." He looked away from her searing stare. The chandler's workshop seemed suddenly a pathetic place to draft battle plans. A disarrayed worktable occupied most of the front room. Tacked to the wall above the table, crewelwork in a frame of acorn shells declared: *Patience has the sun for a candle.*

"Perhaps negotiations are still possible. We are civilized animals."

"Squire, those hogs have forced us out of our home and into hiding *here*—among our servants! What's next?" Her look changed from infuriated to vulnerable. "Are we going to skulk through the fields to escape Griml and—and then crawl into some mudhole under a log in the Mere?"

"We shall never abandon Bracken Knoll to these swine!" He embraced her shivering, wimpering girth and cringed with anguish that their romance had come to this deplorable test of his virility against brutes bent on destroying everything that had made him important in her eyes.

Steady yourself, Cheevie. Think strategically. After all, you are a mouse not a cockroach.

"Dearest, we are safer here in Wright Court. Let the grunters have the manor house whilst we ponder peaceful means to preserve Riversplash Mountain from the boar horde. We are secure here surrounded by our stalwart guards." Paws firmly gripping his wife's shoulders, the squire stepped back, chin high, rousing himself to defiance. "Those pigs will never touch you again."

An urgent rap on the door turned their heads. Chisulo entered, his hamster face long with worry, white-gloved hands wringing. "Sir, forgive my intrusion—but lord Griml requests an audience" —his whiskers vibrated with fear—"*immediately.*"

"Chisulo!" the squire growled. "Go at once and tell that bullyragging, pompous Lord Pork Butt that—"

"Sir!" Chisulo motioned nervously with his eyes. "Lord Griml is—"

The door whanged open. A trotter hooked Chisulo's collar and hauled him up and out of sight.

Griml filled the doorway. "Thee be a rare one, squire."

The boar lord shoved into the cottage, his tusks knocking aside a workbench and drying racks to make room for his armored bulk. "Most wee critters knowed the savvy mind o' the boar ain't suitable for triflin'. Wut possessed thee to think thee might bamboozle me— Lord *Pork Butt*?"

Cheevie staggered backward, eyes bugging, whiskers twanging. "Holes of cheese! Griml!" The squire backed into Magdi and would have drooped to his knees if she had not grabbed him under his arms and bolstered him. "My guards . . . ," he spluttered.

"Aye—where beed thy guards?" Griml swiveled his whiskery ears left and right with feigned curiosity. Then, he swung about, clearing the entry, and crashed into the worktable so forcefully it exploded to splinters.

The clangor of shrieking wood and banging trays struck the mice as harshly as a blow. They rushed to the doorway, shouting "Guards!"—and laid eyes on armored gerbils, moles, and chipmunks sprawled in the street, eyes blank as hardboiled eggs. Boars plucked muskets, lances, bows, and quivers from the entranced animals.

Shocked speechless, Cheevie and Magdi careened into the yard with expressions at once amazed and enraged.

"Wicked bad luck it be, squire, losin' thy weapons to Lord Pork Butt, aye?" Griml's heart pounded with delight. "Nout thee can do but trust in boar mercy now. Aye!"

The boar lord glimpsed a black lash of serpent's tail whip out of sight. He felt elf-knots of anxiety loosen in his chest. Vidar frightened him, and he was glad to see the viper, exhausted from casting Cheevie's guard into dreams, hurrying away to recuperate in some obscure crawl hole.

Yut, that snake be right cunning—and knowed how to defang these chesty mousies smartly!

"How dare you assault our militia by such—such—by however such!" Magdi reeled, heart dizzy in her chest.

"I knowed what be hid in these ciphers." The boar lord extracted the parchments that Vidar had decoded. "These sayed thy Council o' Squires be needin' time to open the weir gates an' bury Weasel's Pass forever. Thee ain't negotiatin' wit' the boars. Thee deceivin' us!"

"Dee-dee-deceiving?" Cheevie squeaked.

Magdi hefted him to one side and strode contemptuously close to the boar lord. "You flung me off a rooftop, you brute! Do you actually think we are so stupid as to believe you swine intend to negotiate?"

"Dearest!" Squire Cheevie seized the satin arm of his overwrought wife. "We are dealing here with a delicate matter of state."

"There is nothing delicate about these brutes!" Magdi spoke through gnashed teeth. "How did you overwhelm our militia?" She narrowed her eyes. "And why?" *Why are we not dead?* she wondered. *This porker needs us for something.* She glared at her husband. "Ask him why we are disarmed. Does he intend to kill us?"

"Hush, dearest. This is a political concern."

"Aye, squire. We be talkin' politikul like." The boar lord inserted his broken tusk between the mice and swept Cheevie out into the lane. The sight of twenty groggy troopers weaponless brought a despairing sigh from the mouse—and solicited a broad grin from Griml. "Ne'er thee mind wut measures we be takin' for defendin' our own. They be effektual, aye?"

Cheevie made no reply. He craned a desolate look over his shoulder at Magdi.

"Thy missus got unkindly notions." Griml frowned with mock concern. "I were trubbled grievous when me lads got worshed off thy cliffs. An' thus, I dangled thy wife to affright thee. No harm were to come of it. An' I were most painful distressed when she shoved herself to a mighty fall. Bless the Holy Sow, thy Magdi took some few bruises an' no more."

"My guard"—the squire motioned feebly at his dazed soldiers—"you must return their weapons."

"Aye, squire. But not till we be away."

Cheevie's limp ears perked. "You're leaving?"

"O' course, squire," the boar lord said, almost absently. "I be conveyin' to our Great Sow, who be commandin' the mighty legions, thy generous terms for peaceful settlement."

"Verily?" Cheevie stopped in his tracks. "The boars will accept terms?"

"Just soon as thee secures safe passage." Griml pointed his long, blunt snout at finches and larks blowing in flurries across the mountain sky. "Thy Avian Guild be right watchful. I knowed they be tellin' all wut asks where us boars beed on thy mountain. Wut wit' them masked bandits, wut thee be callin' Brave Tails, layin' in wait to inflict more injury an' death 'pon me lads, I be needin' assurances from thy Council o' Squires."

"Letters of transit," Cheevie acknowledged with an energetic nod, waddling his jowls. "Of course. The elders are sure to agree. In fact, I shall recommend an armed escort led by myself, to see you safely back through Weasel's Pass."

"I thank thee, squire." He bowed cordially. "An' now, we be draftin' a cipher requestin' letters o' transit. After wut, for to demonstrate thy sincerity, thee an' thy missus be returnin' to thy manor house. There thee be servin' thy boar guests as gracious hosts till thy Council makes reply. Aye?"

Cheevie's eyes met the boar lord's, and to the mouse's shame he discovered in them what he feared—mockery.

"Aye, squire." Griml barely stifled a gloating smile. "Now thee be takin' full measure o' mercy from Lord Pork Butt. Aye, indeed!"

CHAPTER FORTY

Thrym in Love

Bestla, carrying Wili in cape and cowl across her nape, was eager to depart, to cross as much of the taiga as she could before sunrise.

"Let's git, Pa!" Wili squirmed and flapped the folds of his mantle like wings. "We cain't be jawin' all night. Them nastiest pigs ain't waitin' on us. Best we find them bushytails in the Tarn right quick."

Notty waved his son to silence. Bareheaded, he stood on a root shelf in the woods concluding a transaction with a night heron. Frikee leaned over them, arms crossed, watching warily from behind his fox mask. A heron might just as soon gobble up a shrew as conduct business. The Avian Guild strongly discouraged members from eating clientele, but small mammals knew better than to approach Guild couriers without witnesses.

"Ya just make sure my wife, Unise, un'erstan's Wili an' Notty got pressed inta heroic service by th' squires for ta save Riversplash Mountain from th' boar horde." Notty clinked his coins from paw to paw under the heron's greedy gaze. "Ya tell her we're right together. But don't ya chirp no word 'bout us wearin' capes an' swords an' such, ya hear? Otherwise, ya Guild gonna get a sore earful from me."

"Pay yer coin, shrew, an' I doan' keer what all ye tell yer wifey." With his beak, the black-capped heron opened the feather-pouch cinched about his waist. "Come sunup, I'll jest shout down her chimney so as not to provoke no suspicion I come to get aholt o' her an' yer young 'un, 'Hi-dee thar, Unise Burrtail! Avian Guild got ye a message from Notty Burrtail. He done found Wili safe an' of a piece, an' the squires got 'em drafted, Notty an' Wili both, for to serve the defense o' Riversplash Mountain agin them boar hordes threatenin' to ravage our land. Notty an' Wili be goodly an' together, an' so don't ye fret none 'bout 'em. They sendin' ye love an' hearts full up wit' kindly thoughts fer ye an' the infint.'" The heron showed its sharp profile and sealed their agreement with a wink at the caped shrew in boots and sword belt. "Yer dress-up folly ain't nothin' to me. Our secret. So, pay yer coin an' I'm away to Burrtail Dray Stall in the Mere."

Satisfied, Notty plunked his coins into the bird's pouch.

Sadness leaked through Frikee's mask as he watched the heron glide away. "Wish my pappy had diverted himself from the world's sorrows long enough to post me and mammy so gentle a fare-thee-well."

"You sure it's a good idea to take Wili into the Tarn?" Thrym approached from behind a broad oak, where he and Olweena had watched, well away from the heron. Notty had feared that the scent of blood from the mouse maiden's wound might frenzy the omnivorous bird. "That tyke's talking about the Brave Tails as an *alloy*—a term he learned from Bestla. He says that mice, shrews, a polecat, and a bear make a strong alloy. He's an intelligent little fellow. Don't you think he'll be safer with us in Fernholt?"

"Ya ask Olweena if any place on this here mountain stay safe wit' them boars comin'." Notty spoke with uncharacteristic gloom. "I wanna be wit' my son. Ya un'erstan', Squinty."

The mouse fit his nose-clip lenses in place.

"Ol' Muspul wanted Wili ta take our secret oath," Notty recalled with a soft snicker. "But I figure, that youngster ain't no good for secrets. An' besides, where we're goin' ain't no one ta know anyway. Right, Squinty?"

"We'll do the oath at the Dead Riders' crypt when you and Wili get back," the mouse said with conviction.

They embraced, and Thrym held on to Notty. The warmth of his friend mingled with the Brave Tails' fragrance of summer's crushed grass at the brim of night—and he didn't want to let the shrew go. The mouse reluctantly stepped away. "You better get going. Stay ahead of the rain."

Frikee's own heart enlarged watching the two friends part. As distance widened between mouse and shrew, the polecat felt certain some invisible and pure emotion shimmered in that prospering space.

Then, his wondering eyes touched on Olweena. She had hooked her soul, her purpose, in the Tarn, on some mythic squirrels who might thwart the savage boars. She moved to follow Notty.

"Olweena—" The polecat rose up before her. "Makes my scalp freeze to think what them squires of Fernholt gone make of me if you ain't there. A doormat, I 'spect. A toothy thing to intimidate riffraff. But with your testimony of the true intentions of them boars at Bracken Knoll, those squires will be too shook up to notice this polecat skulking in the corner."

"We must go with Notty." Olweena shouldered past Frikee. "The Brave Tails must stay together."

"Frikee's right." Thrym took hold of Olweena's shoulders. "The white squirrels are a possibility at best—and perhaps only a fiction. But what you know is fact. We've got to report at once to Fernholt."

She shrugged off his paws. "Send a bird."

"No." Thrym shifted to block her. "They have to hear from you. You can convince them."

Notty climbed on Bestla, and as the she bear marched down a dark tunnel of trees toward the starry sky, Wili shouted, "See yins later!"

Too tired to pursue the ambling bear, Olweena accepted with wistful helplessness her place atop Frikee. Within minutes, the polecat's rolling gait gentled her to sleep.

When she woke, she lay in the grass looking up at the moving branches of pines. Frikee snored nearby, where exhaustion had dropped him. Thrym stirred beside her. "Go back to sleep," he mumbled drowsily. "We've a long trek to Fernholt ahead."

She sat up and laid her paw on his, her eyes hollow with fear. "Will they find a way to open the weirs?"

He pushed himself to one elbow and clipped his lenses on his nose. "They stand a much better chance now that you've warned them about the asps." He wanted to say something comforting. *What can I say? Nothing is certain.* "Get some rest. You'll need your strength when we meet with the Council."

She nodded tiredly, grateful that he had not tried to mollify her with false hope. "Here." From a pocket in her torn gown, she produced three pennies. "You should have these back."

He regarded the bent coins with surprise. "I want you to keep them." He searched her face and saw fear was gone. Her whiskers fanned, and her eyes shone. He knew if he told her the truth then— that he had felt stupid with love for her the day he'd given her these pennies—that his love for her was a mansion in his chest where he wanted to live with her forever—she would receive him. But he stopped himself.

Her grief, her pain, was deeper than he could imagine. How could he toss his love for her into such a chasm and genuinely expect to reach her? Loss of blood, lack of sleep, and the Brave Tails' scent of summer had robbed her sobriety. More than his love, she needed honor, justice—vengeance. "Keep them, for luck."

She clasped the coins to her heart. "My luck has changed for the better since you gave these to me. It's this mountain that needs luck now." She met his soft, deep stare with a smile. "Let's plant them here."

She inserted the pennies edgewise into the loamy ground. "Let their luck belong to Riversplash Mountain." She lay down, curled up atop the coins. "All right?"

He turned playfully to the sheltering trees for agreement, and when he looked to her again, she was fast asleep.

CHAPTER FORTY-ONE

A Deeper Darkness

Kungu moved swiftly through the Holt in dry sunshine—yet none saw him. He kept clear of cultivated orchards and fields and avoided the stepping stones set into steep hills to assist wayfarers.

Instead, he traveled along small creeks where tall ferns and weeds received his camouflage in near anonymity. Lichens and moss muffled his grass-wrapped hooves. Red finches bounding among the pines never spied him.

Atop a high ridge, he gazed down at the Rill, where a party of beaver women caught rockfish and prawns with wicker nets. He gloated that they labored in ignorance, with no notion that these chores marked their final days, their last meals.

The boar lord had sent him forth on this treacherous journey, and Kungu had been glad to go. In spite of the danger posed by climbing a mountainside of fierce little animals eager to skewer him over hot embers, he felt relieved to get away from that sorcerous snake, Vidar.

Kungu's bristles stiffened at the mere thought of the dreamcaster. *Wut allies the March finds, we takes*, he consoled himself and shivered in the heat of day.

The boar horde would swarm across these slopes as out of a fevered dream. Muscular desire beat in his heart as he envisioned the fearsome boar legions charging up fields and terraces, the cries of their puny enemies trampled by thunder.

Let Griml distract the Council of Squires with bogus pleas for safe escort. Let those frantic squires debate the merits of holding the boars at Bracken Knoll. Before this mountain's soil turners and manure carriers could waken Hati, the white squirrel princess, Kungu would slip through Weasel's Pass. The Great Sow herself would appoint him to lead the March—and with his return to Riversplash Mountain, the slaughter would begin.

As a shadow, he passed among crooked oaks and hardwoods. The Cloud Forest drifted above him, its fog woven amidst bleak trees and dizzy cliffs. No threat could descend on him off those ghostly heights. Eagles alone might perceive him from above, but the raptors kept to themselves and, having no affiliation with the Avian Guild, fostered no interest in boars. That was why he had chosen to traverse the Holt despite its many landed estates. He was invisible from on high—or so he thought.

Sitting on a bluff far above the Cloud Forest, Thrym peered at the wide expanse of mountains and gorges beneath him.

Upon the Holt, well below the fog of the Cloud Forest, a ghost trespassed. Thrym blinked hard and squinted. Something moved across a slope of tangled weeds. The grass swished, parted, and folded again, disturbed by some invisible specter. *A trick of light and sleepy eyes*, the mouse figured and tilted his head for a second look.

"What are you doing up?" Olweena sat down beside him on her hip, protecting her wound, and glanced back at Frikee, butterflies bounding over him like fugitive dreams. "Did his snoring wake you, too?"

"Dreams of dominie." To steady his voice, he slapped his lenses onto his snout and analyzed the rock under him. His paws touched lichens and spirals, of fossilized mollusks from an ancient sea. "Old Muspul didn't want to climb up here."

"He wanted to find you. Instead, he found the Brave Tails. Destiny is like that."

"Like what?" His grief for Muspul made him speak without thinking. "Surprisingly cruel and arbitrary?"

"Sometimes."

The sadness in her eyes froze his heart. "I'm sorry. That was insensitive. Dominie was old. At least destiny gave him a glimpse of something noble. But your parents—your whole world . . . " Words felt mealy in his mouth. "I'm truly sorry. We'll get you to Fernholt soon as Frikee's rested. What you have to tell the squires—"

"Will make no difference," she said, pulling Muspul's crimson mantle tighter about herself. "Surely they've heard from many other refugees by now. And the Avian Guild must have delivered graphic reports of what the Boar March has done to Blossom Vale and how many other mountains?" She faced him, all sorrow lifted, displaced by austere clarity. "No. All our hope travels with Notty, Wili, and Bestla. We should have gone into the Tarn with them."

"Your wound—"

"The bleeding has stopped," she spoke stiffly. "The antler dust dulls the pain. I will survive. But will Riversplash Mountain?"

"This is the best decision." He skimmed a look at the sleeping polecat in his wolf-skin boots and fox pelt. "Frikee is tired. And we don't even know what we're looking for in the Tarn."

"I understand." The mouse maiden squeezed his paw for comfort. "Perhaps I only dreamed of the snow white Hati. Maybe there are no white squirrels. And if there are, maybe they know nothing of the rock weirs. I should be dead from misery. Yet, I'm alive." A distracted look crossed the mouse maiden's face, a shadow of insight, and her white fur fluffed.

"I don't want to go to Fernholt," she decided. "Why tell them what they already know?" She stood, and her red mantle snapped smartly in the mountain wind. "We must return to Bracken Knoll and kill Griml and the other boars."

"Whoa!"

"The boar legions will not invade until they know your defenses." She grabbed his arm. "If we prevent Griml from reporting to the March, we will buy time—perhaps enough time to open the rock weirs!"

Thrym could see she had already committed herself to this unthinkable mission, and his tired expression mustered all his skepticism. "How are two mice and a polecat going to kill a squad of elite boar warriors?"

"We're Brave Tails."

"We'll be *Dead* Tails."

"You're afraid." Her grip on his arm tightened. "Of course. There's no other way to be brave unless you're afraid."

A breeze delivered news of approaching spring rains, and Thrym inhaled deeply to calm himself. " *'I see the frightened Brave Tails blunder—and the mighty boars march like thunder. If you are unmasked in the suspense, then all of your lives become past tense.'* " He compressed his whiskers against his snout. "That's what the old moon told me. He hasn't been wrong yet."

Her ears flicked, interested. "The moon?"

From the corner of his eye, Thrym caught again a strange movement in the distance below. He tore the lenses from his nose and peered past the woods of the Cloud Forest to the groves of the Holt.

A movement in the windless grass fixed his attention. Like an optical illusion, the weeds gave way all at once to a garish figure clad in ivy and plaited straw. The round-shouldered beast ran low to the ground, glancing sideways. Tusks brushed the earth and a large, slouched body followed.

"What is it?" Olweena knelt forward and reached with her eyes beyond the Cloud Forest, below to the meadows and plowed fields of the Holt. "What do you see?"

Needles of fright pricked Thrym's heart. "I think it's a boar."

"You *think*?"

"He's big, all right—and he's got tusks." In the clarity of his far sight, the black beast in his straw and vines stirred feelings of disaster.

"Yes. He's a boar." He gnashed molars to keep his voice from cracking. "But he's not wearing armor. He's cloaked in some kind of rig of ivy and stalks."

"Kungu!" Olweena heaved herself upright. Her brazen fury perched her at the very edge of the bluff. "Thrym—wake Frikee."

CHAPTER FORTY-TWO

The Mapless Country

Frikee sprinted through the Cloud Forest with Olweena and Thrym astride. He felt stronger for the pelt's scent of a summer day.

Paws drumming mossy ground, he loped easily. Was he roving the dreamworld? This descent felt effortless—a twisting jump into space.

Was that Muspul beckoning from a leafy tunnel? *No, no—a stump bristled with ferns merely looks like a hedgehog!*

The reckless wonder of the polecat's charge across the Cloud Forest vanished the instant he burst into sunlight. At the edge of a drop-off, he skidded to a sharp stop; his frightened howl yodeled across horizons.

"There's the boar!" Thrym stood on Frikee's shoulders, his excited voice muted by his cowl. "On that knoll of gravestones, he's moving quickly through the spear grass."

"Gravestones?" Frikee panted. "That ain't no happy omen."

"Not for Kungu," Olweena stated. She, too, wore a black cowl, her mouse body almost entirely hidden in Muspul's oversize cloak. The costume's odor of twilight quieted her blood just enough for her to think strategically. "I don't see the knoll or the graveyard down there, let alone the boar. Is he near enough for us to catch up with him?"

Frikee stared across the Holt and made out only cedar groves and bamboo brakes interspersed with orderly parks and manses. "Do tell me we got some kind of plan for when we meet up with the big fella."

"Yes." Olweena patted the polecat's flank. "We're going to kill him."

Frikee edged away from the cliff. "Them boar boys I saw at Bracken Knoll looked a whole lot more familiar with killing than getting killed."

"He's taking the high course through the Holt to Weasel's Pass." Thrym read the staggering landscape of cascades and chasms. "If our Rumner's got the strength to scoot along the margin of the Cloud Forest, we can get ahead of him. Kungu has to go through the boulders above the rock weirs to reach the pass. We'll ambush him among those rocks. The trails there are narrow for a boar. He won't be able to outmaneuver or trample us."

"Shovel that antler fur up my nozzle, Squinty." Frikee wearily faced the earthen wall of buttress roots and great trees. "And I'll run down the moon."

Like a chill, telepathic breeze, the murderous intent of the Brave Tails raised the stiff hairs on Kungu's neck, and he paused in his flight. For a moment, dread filled his heart. Somewhere ahead, his death awaited him.

Forsooth, but a dream be our lives. But a dream. And life but an emanation of death.

All boars had to declare that truth in the presence of the Great Sow before she permitted them to join the March. Kungu moved on through the rough grass repeating this truth until his foretaste of doom thinned away.

He hastened past waterfalls and their foaming pools. Streams of fog flowed down from the Cloud Forest and crept after him like ghostly refugees.

Briefly, upon a granite peak, he peered above the cloud world and glimpsed Fernholt.

Imperial columns upheld pink imperial domes, arches and marble vaults. He squinted against flashes of sunlight reflected from glass rooftops and bay windows. Smashing this metropolis of outlandish stone would prove a festive event for the boars, who held in contempt every road, fence, building—everything that scorned life's brevity with pretense of permanence.

Kungu turned away in disgust. Soon afterward, he came in sight of the rock weirs. Four titanic bulwarks, each larger than the city he had glimpsed through the clouds, spanned the mountainside above Weasel's Pass. Built across whole valleys, the weirs shaped the very landscape, holding back miles-long drifts of boulders and rocks. Yet from below, the ancient rockslide barriers appeared as innocent as scenic bluffs.

Dazed, Kungu nibbled on tender black branches from the underbrush while contemplating these earthen contraptions. Where the weirs met the gorund, wood cogs and sprockets constructed from sequoias as reared as tall as cathedrals. Bindweeds and briars flourished between the gear teeth, ivy hung off the high span of wheels, and flocks of birds came and went from within the dark keeps of the mechanism.

More dimwitted than we thought, these wee critters wut thinks ancient gimmicks be savin' them from the March.

Kungu gave a bemused snort and came out beside the rock weirs. Among boulders piled tall, the boar seemed tiny even to himself.

His blood humming in his ears, he scampered downhill, negotiating as quickly as possible the narrow passages between the mammoth stones. When he smelled his adversary, he was not surprised.

He side-slipped to a halt, inhaling a scent incongruous to this cramped, stone corridor: a lordly loneliness of blossoms shaken by a summer wind. From a crevice, a grungy mouse in an outsize crimson cape and black hood strode into his path. "Die, Kungu!" shouted the puny assailant, pointing a small gold sword at him.

"Olweena?" The boar's long face bobbed with tragicomic wonderment. "'Neath that mask, that be thee, mousie?"

"You destroyed my home." Olweena yanked off the cowl and transfixed him with her blood-burned eyes. "Now, I'm going to destroy you."

"You looks a fool 'neath that big mantle, mousie." Kungu took out a hooked knife, casual as a bored hiker resigned to whittle. "You be fitted out as wut?"

Olweena paced to her right, away from the curved blade. "A Brave Tail ends your life, Kungu."

"A Brave *Tail* be you?" A cruel laugh seeped from him. "Brave Tail without yore tail!" Kungu slinked forward. "And now—without yore head!"

Hurling a cry, Thrym bolted from between two rocks, sword raised high. As he pulled up short before the lethal slash of the boar's blade and tusks, his cape and cowl filled with air and bowled him over. Under his hood, his spectacles popped off, and he gawped blurrily at the giant descending on him.

"Thrym!" Olweena dashed toward her fallen companion and, propelled by the force of her tackle, the two mice landed within a shallow crevice.

Kungu shouted, "Mouse turds!" and angled a tusk to spear them out of their hiding place.

Distracted by the trembling mice, the boar did not sense Frikee emerging from a niche downwind. Eyes set on the mice, Kungu braced his hind legs for a skewering thrust as the polecat rushed up behind and drove his tiny sword into the boar's flank.

The boar reeled about, a howl pounding echoes from the gigantic rocks. Frikee staggered back and tripped over his fox tail.

"Yaaaah!" He flailed the minuscule bloody sword at the distorted face glaring over him.

A ferocious tusk knocked the sword from his grip. Kungu's knife was poised for the polecat's masked eyes.

The blade slipped past Frikee's popping stare, and another brute cry ripped from the boar. The wounded beast sprang away from the polecat as Olweena fled, leaving her sword plunged in the boar's rump.

Thrym whipped the cowl from his head and slammed his lenses onto his face in time to behold Kungu descend upon Olweena. There was no evading that rabid predator now that his blood had spilled. Bunched shoulder muscles unknotted and slid fluidly into a sweeping attack.

Thrym's heart splashed in his chest, dousing him in a blaze of raw heat. He knew then he had found his death. In one instant, all the insights and fears of his life resolved to this—he could never live as witness to Olweena's doom.

"Ya-a-ah!" Thrym charged out of the rock crevice in a crazy-legged stagger. He took the mouse maiden's cape in both paws, and flung her away from the rush of the boar.

Through his spectacles, he watched the great hulk of the beast crash toward him, too close to dodge.

Kungu, powered by wounded ferocity, piled toward the bespectacled mouse, tusk aimed to split ribs and toss the broken body over the fallen maiden, smashing her and her companion to gory bone meal under his pounding hooves.

Then, loneliness entered his body.

Again, he recognized the misplaced scent of a lordly loneliness of blossoms fluttering to the ground at a summer day's end.

That thought brought him to the earth's surprising weariness, wrenching his knees out from under. Majestic shoulders sagged, and down he went, kneecaps pounding the ground. His deep-hulled chest followed.

Whiskers twitching, ears laid flat, Thrym stood rigid, electrified by a sharpened tusk two narrow inches from his heart. The mouse watched malice go out of Kungu's eyes. His pupils widening to admit death's darkness, Kungu gazed right through Thrym into the mapless country beyond.

As if from underwater, Thrym listened to Frikee's hurrahs and Olweena's angry sobs. He was puzzled. *How did our small woundings, not really more than scratches, bring down this full-grown boar?*

With cold astonishment, Thrym realized, *The swords are poisoned!*

He understood then how those small creatures had prevailed. Not with bravery or noble cunning . . .

Thrym was still standing paralyzed when Olweena crossed to the fallen boar. Chuffing angrily, she sawed at Kungu's backside and hewed free his skinny, tasseled tail. In a dazzle of blood, she swung her dark trophy overhead and shouted with triumph to the rocks and shadows and the boar's fleeing spirit.

CHAPTER FORTY-THREE

Secret Corridors

Vidar abruptly lifted his sleepy head and peered into the dusty light of the manor house attic. *Kungu is killed.*

Behind lidless, glazed eyes, the viper saw the crafty boar sprawled upon stony ground. From snout to rump, poison condensed inside him and Kungu's soul unraveled through the air above his stocky body. The misery of this vision wrenched Vidar awake.

Monstrous farmers! Vidar hadn't seen who had killed the scout, and he assumed that Kungu had been set upon by inhabitants of a Holt estaste alarmed at the news of an impending boar invasion.

Stuporous, he looked over his dim surroundings. *Kungu is dead.* The viper lowered his head. *Must I go myself and alert the legions this mountain is ripe for the taking?* The thought revolted him. A thousand stinking boars grunting and rooting in the mud! That would overwhelm his dreamcasting.

I need a new plan.

Anxiety danced in Vidar, and he decided he was hungry. Under his breath, he summoned, "Joy! Behind this door. Oh wanton joy like a bright and busy dining room seen through a frosty window. Come, buoyant soul, come and see!"

Soon, the porcelain doorknob turned, the green attic door opened, and a diminutive creature in servant's frock entered—a gerbil brimming with inexplicable curiosity. She glanced at the stillness of the tidy attic, wondering why she had detoured here.

Bewildered, she rolled her eyes at the sloping ceiling, and when she turned to go, the viper faced her, fangs poised. He swallowed her head in one gulp, letting escape not a squeak, and swiftly crammed the rest of her into his maw.

Sleepy again, Vidar decided he would think about replacing Kungu later. *Why hurry?* He had exhausted himself entrancing the squire's militia. Now, the boar lord had all the weapons. There was no need to frighten Griml immediately with this tragic news. *Who knows what panic might overtake the swine? I need time to shape a new ploy.*

The serpent curled up and gazed out a blurry window. Storm clouds gathered and the anticipation of pattering rain conveyed him to a dreamy place. There, he saw a fox carrying two small animals in crimson capes and black cowls.

The Brave Tails? Vidar dismissed this vision as a hallucination brought on by the death of Kungu, a nightmare of those hooded killers who had slain his clan so long ago. Only distantly did Griml's voice rumble, *Masked insurgents—wut the squire be callin' Brave Tails—they worshed away three o' me fine lads.*

Rumner the Swift crossed a plowed field in the storm-dark air. One rider dangled a frayed black rope, a thick eel bearded with seaweed—*No!* That rope, that eel was the blood-gummed length of a boar's severed tail.

Vidar raised up as stiff as a crowbar. "They're here!"

At that moment, the Brave Tails were actually many leagues away. Filled with adrenalin and amazed to be alive after mortal combat with Kungu, Frikee ran on the wind.

Olweena and Thrym lay low against his back, capes buffeting above them. Green clouds rolled across the sky, and fat dollops of rain thwacked the ground.

Overhead, skylarks gusted, tossed about by the mounting tempest. "The Avian Guild sees us." Through his slitted hood, Thrym raised wary eyes. "The wind is too strong for them to carry news of us—or of Kungu. They'll have to take shelter. If we hurry, we can reach Bracken Knoll before the boars know we're coming."

Frikee didn't hear a word. Wet gusts swept away Thrym's voice, as the landscape sparked with lightning, and thunder marched across the mountain skyline.

The riders paused within the thin shelter of an acacia grove and again later under a rock shelf. Resigned to those meager havens, they crouched, soaked and shivering, and nibbled silently at the few provisions remaining—some fried earthworms and soggy ant bread.

Small lights from manor houses of outlying estates looked like stars on the dark slopes of the Holt. Chewing their stale food the drenched animals mused on the warm, dry lives settled there. No one said it, yet each speculated the long odds that these lights would yet shine through the next rainy season.

Such despair drove mice and polecat back into the downpour. Frikee splashed along sunken tree lanes, and Thrym rode behind Olweena, covering her best he could against the hammering wind and rain.

Bracken Knoll glittered in the twilight's purple hour. Spent and weighed down by the wet fox pelt, Frikee dragged himself through the orchards. Workers cowering against the deluge in tool shanties watched with wonder these inhabitants of legend passing among rain-shadowed trees.

Lightning bolts looped electric chains above thrashing treetops.

Silent and sullen as specters, fox and hooded riders faded into the violet of dusk. Tattered laborers forsook their shelter and wandered into the storm gawking after.

Thrym's long sight spotted the few boar guards posted upon the fields, and the Brave Tails avoided them. In gardens near the manor house, they came upon Chisulo in the downfall. Velvet singlet and gray trousers plastered to his wet fur, the hamster looked as haggard as a tramp stalking among the lotus ponds, parting hedgerows, and stooping to search under shrubs.

A frightened cry gargled loudly from him when he confronted a demon fox bearing hooded figures out of the falling light.

"Chisulo—don't shout." Thrym doffed his cowl and slid from Frikee's back. He stamped his boots in the turf, restoring feeling to his chilled legs. His sword belt glinted with beaded diamond markings of snakeskin. "Don't be afraid, old friend. It's me—Thrym."

"Mister Seedcorn?" With a shaking paw, Chisulo fit a monocle in place and pulled back, alarmed by the desolate polecat in the sopping fox hide. "You—you—" He noted the severed boar's tail looped upon the sword belt of the cowled mouse atop the polecat, and he gasped and shrank back again.

Thrym quickly took Chisulo's arm to keep him from stepping into a lotus pond. "Yes, Chisulo, we are the Brave Tails."

"You? The guerrillas who opened the floodgates and swept away those three boars? That was you?" The hamster chittered nervously, unable to look away from the villainous orange eyes behind that fox mask. "By the Dancing Drunk Red Rodent! Lord Griml has torn apart Bracken Knoll to find and destroy you! In cruel retribution that hooligan has most miserably subjugated the squire and your sister!"

"Calm down, Chisulo. We need your help." Thrym glanced

anxiously at the flower beds and sheared hedges. "What are you doing out here?"

"Deenee is missing." He swept his monocle across the leafy darkness. "Our gerbil housemaid. She's usually so punctilious. She's been missing since forenoon."

"We will help find her. But first—" Thrym clipped on his lenses and stared up hard, trying to engage the tall hamster's dizzy eyes. "Look at me, Chisulo. Don't fret about the fox. He won't hurt you."

"That"—Chisulo could not deflect his trembling face from Frikee— "that, sir, is a polecat."

"Yes. But no one else is to know that. Nor my identity, either. Chisulo! Look at me." The stern command in Thrym's voice jerked the servant around, and Chisulo ran a distraught paw over his scalp. "We are here to kill the boars. And the squire will help us—but only if he believes we are the Brave Tails. Will you take us to him and keep our secret?"

Thrym's strong words cut through Chisulo's distraction. The hamster's twitching face calmed, and a flash of lightning illuminated a new, quivering hope deep in his eyes. "Follow me, sir! I know the manor's secret corridors. Follow me—and the Brave Tails will walk murder through this house."

CHAPTER FORTY-FOUR

Thunder and the Dead Riders

"This is dreadful!" Magdi whined, on her knees, pushing a scrub brush with both paws. Her jonquil dress, soaked with sweat and suds, hung limply on her large frame. "Those turd-rooting, canker-ridden porkers! Why must we slave for those swine? Answer me, plumpkins!"

Squire Cheevie, also bent over a scrubber, had no breath to reply. All his strength went into scouring. Lord Griml had set them to polishing the paving stones of the reception hall, where the boars had tracked mud after cavorting on the patio in the thunderstorm. If the red flagstones did not gleam ruddy as newly washed kidney beans by the time Griml returned, the boar lord had promised to bite off their heads.

Ashamed before the wife he helplessly loved, Cheevie kept his head low and his blistered paws busy. Neither could he bear to look upon the gilt-framed portraits arrayed on the high wall—his venerable ancestors: proud-whiskered Cheevoo Ground Breaker, founder of Bracken Knoll; high-tailed Choovie Hearth Builder, ingenious architect of the manor and Wright Court; clever-eyed Choovoo Arbor Ascender, vintner and innovative entrepreneur;

243

and soon—bent-whiskered, limp-tailed, vacant-eyed Cheevie Hog Slave, who lost everything.

Glazed panes in the doors that fronted the patio rattled loudly, swiped by gale winds. Both portly mice scrubbed more briskly at the stone floor, fearing the boars had already come back. They reached together for the wood bucket of soapy water beside them and caught the fright in each other's eyes. Their panic collapsed to pity, and a hapless sigh passed between them.

The patio doors banged open, and Cheevie and Magdi jumped up with alarm. They expected to confront swaggering boars. Instead, in strode a fox with abhorrent eyes, and upon its back, two caped and hooded figures rode. They pointed gold blades at the fat mice, staring agog from their sudsy puddles.

"Yaw!" A cold wash of wind and rain swept in with thunder. "Squire Cheevie, get your fighters together. Rise up against these boars!"

Cheevie dropped his scrub brush. "Who—who are you?"

"Squire!" Magdi boosted her husband off his feet in a delirious embrace. "Look! Look at the Open Claw on their capes! This frightful fox must be—"

"Rumner the Swift." Cheevie's voice tumbled out of him. "The Dead Riders. But this can't be! That's a story for tykes. The dead don't live again. Who are you?"

"Get everyone out of this house," Thrym ordered huskily, hoping to disguise his voice. "Find what weapons you can and prepare to kill the boars who flee."

"Weapons?" Cheevie tussled free of his wife's clasp. "The boars have taken all our weapons!"

"Then use rocks and farm tools!" Frikee shouted as he backed away, fading into the squall. "Do it now!"

"Kungu is dead!" Olweena waved overhead the boar's severed tail as lightning ignited the horizon. "Defend Bracken Knoll!"

The ensuing eruption of thunderclaps shook Cheevie and Magdi loose from their amazement, and they bolted into the hard rain. They peered in every direction, but the mysterious fox and riders had vanished in the night.

Hidden by darkness, the Brave Tails dismounted at the far end of the patio. Chisulo awaited them in an inconspicuous niche behind a gutter pipe.

At the back of the narrow recess, a panel of black bricks pushed open with a scraping noise—a doorway into a dark and long-unused corridor. Chisulo struck flint upon the rock wall and ignited a wax taper. Flickering light revealed side passages and forking tunnels.

"My grandfather introduced me to these passageways, of which even the squire remains unaware." Chisulo's voice advanced in echoes, and footfalls reverberated as the Brave Tails pursued the swift hamster from one tunnel to the next. "Patriarch Choovie, who designed this manse in that hostile age so long ago, intended these secret corridors for defense against your ilk, sir polecat. But then came the Brave Tails, your legendary predecessors. After they drove off the big carnivores, these hidden passages became unnecessary and fell into disuse." The servant stopped short. "Ah, we are arrived."

A small carving in the crusty rock identified a portal. Chisulo leaned his shoulder against the wall, and the stones rasped open. Into a bedchamber of tall windows, the Brave Tails beheld an extravagant crystal chandelier depending from a domed ceiling painted with scenes of naked mice in wrestling bouts and frolicking dances. On walls between high windows, ancient, mouse-sized armor gleamed: eagle-claw shields, hawk-visor helmets, snake-embossed chain mail—and Cheevie's blunderbuss.

"This is the squire's penthouse," whispered Chisulo, "now occupied by lord Griml. Though for the moment, the boar lord is away, presumably sporting in the tempest with the other boars, be wary of entering here. His movements are unpredictable."

Unbeknownst to the intruders, Griml stood directly above their heads, on the rooftop. Enthralled by violent weather, he held a grin like a mask.

"Lord Griml—" Ull's voice bounded across the rooftop. "You wants to eat? I wants to eat. All boars come to table, and they wants to eat. All we boars waitin' to eat, Lord Griml."

Griml shook himself. "Aye—food!" But he did not leave the roof. Wind flashed, and sickles of rain swept the air. The boar lord's blood smiled. Slowly he turned about. "Food be proper answer to them cloudbursts worshin' me soul. Let's eat!"

Down the stone steps of the companionway, Griml lumbered, Ull following. The boar lord paused at the entry to the penthouse, his offended snout retracting like an accordion. "Boar blood!"

Ull sniffed, and his thick hide twitched. "Kungu!"

From a holster beneath his leather armor, Griml withdrew a musket and stole forward. Two paces in, he stalled. On the regal bed in its cypress wood frame, atop sheets of yellow velvet, some evil beast had deposited the lopped, blood-crusted tail of Kungu.

Ull roared, and chandelier crystals tinkled.

Three boars rushed in through grand double doors. Two more burst out of the maid's adjoining quarters. At the sight and scent of Kungu's cutoff tail, they jarred to a halt.

A small creature in a black hood stepped from behind the cypress headboard. Wearing a magnificent red cape so oversize it trailed behind like a royal train, the figure appeared ludicrous until—from beneath that ample fabric—the squire's blunderbuss swung out, its wide muzzle leveled squarely on the boar lord.

Griml signed with his tail for tempestuous Ull and the other twitchy boars to stand down. "Assassin, thee be unnatural artful sneakin' past me guard. So cagey a soul seeks not death. Turn aside thy weapon an' thee spares thy life an' me own. Then, we be talkin' terms for thy satisfaction."

The mouse maiden tore the hood from her head. "The only satisfaction I want is your death, Griml."

"Olweena!" Heart electrified, Griml understood this was his doom. "Girl, that wonky gun ain't loaded."

Olweena smiled coldly. "If you truly believed that, you'd have killed me by now." Her aim steady, her blue stare deep and good, she dedicated her kill, "For my parents, for Blossom Vale, I slay you . . . "

Pause gloomed through her. She could not move. Griml's shadow thickened over his shoulder. She wasn't sure what she was seeing. It was black. Though she looked and looked, her eyes could not touch it.

"Vidar!" Thrym whispered from the secret corridor where he lurked with Frikee and Chisulo.

"That thing's got her hypnotized!" Rain battering against the windows muffled the raspy draw of his sword. "We've got to help her."

"Naw!" Frikee clutched Thrym's arm. "She supposed to shoot that boar and get out. We ain't taking on no sorcery snake!"

"Let go, Frikee!" Thrym twisted his arm free. The moon's prophecy catapulted through his mind: *I see the frightened Brave Tails blunder.* "We're the *Brave* Tails!"

He shot out of the hidden access. To his left, he glimpsed in soft focus the hearth from where the secret passage had opened. He also noted boars nearby, flinching at his intrusion, frantically spinning about to nab him. He ignored them. His keen sight did not waver from the large black viper entangling the boar lord.

The serpent fixed his eyes upon the running mouse.

Something like smoke but chill as sleet swirled about inside Thrym's skull. *The viper's trying to spellbind me, too!* Breathing hard as he ran, the mouse inhaled deeper the dusky fragrance of the cowl and sensed it absorb the snake's befuddling smoke. *Vidar can't penetrate the cowl!*

Griml, entwined by the serpent, struggled to bring his musket fully to bear and stared with violent frustration at the hooded mouse scampering across the suite. In a moment, Thrym dodged past the lances of the boar guards and reached Olweena.

The viper blurred forward, fangs striking.

Encircling Olweena in his arms, Thrym toppled backward. The impact of their fall discharged the blunderbuss, and an engulfing boom spewed a geyser of blue smoke and whirling sparks.

Vidar veered, nostrils scorched, and recoiled like a snapped spring, gagging and coughing.

The blunderbuss's big conical slug struck the ceiling and shattered plaster to flying chunks. With a clashing of crystal, the chandelier ripped free of its moorings and fell atop the gathering boars. Darkness pounced on the chamber, intensifying the yells of the guards, the infuriated commands from the boar lord, and Ull's frightened bellows.

Thrym dragged Olweena to her feet. She gaped about in smoky darkness.

"This way!" The mouse guided her with his arm across her shoulders, maneuvering by the flimsy red shadows from the hearth.

Racing past fallen boars snared in chandelier debris, he swung at them with his sword. The two that he scored wailed their outrage and gnawed cries as they fought to free themselves.

Thrym shoved Olweena into the passage. He and Frikee pulled at the stone door, and lightning in the tall windows floodlit a stampede of boars led by the giant Ull. Hackles upraised stiff, jaws grinding, and tusks lowered to gore, howling hog warriors shrank into darkness as the disguised door fit into place.

CHAPTER FORTY-FIVE

And Fire Tells Their Tale

What have I done? Chisulo despaired as he fled down the mansion's tunnels, paws cupping a burning wax taper. Behind him and the escaping Brave Tails, boars pounded the hidden hatch in the penthouse wall. The whole building shimmied as enraged swine rampaged throughout the mansion. *We did not walk murder through this house. We unleashed it—on us! Red Rodent, help us!*

Dim, yet piercing, shrill screams penetrated the vibrating walls. Crashes and explosions jolted loose mason blocks and chucked bits of cement. When the hamster and his companions slipped out a secret door in the foyer's coat closet, horrific destruction met them.

A caved-in ceiling's beams crisscrossed amid mounds of plaster. A staircase to the upper floors led nowhere, freestanding, its mangled banister skewed.

An earsplitting detonation ripped open the far wall, scattering jigsaw slabs of sheetrock. Ull charged into view, hurtling across the devastated room. His cannonballing hulk smashed through the opposing wall with another jarring blast, and slivers of the disintegrated wall whistled like shrapnel.

Chisulo and the Brave Tails ducked and scuttled under clouds of powdered mortar and exited past torn, gurgling pipes. Rain pelted the hamster's dazed face, and he turned about to stare up at black smoke and flames escaping from upper windows.

Through veils of rain and fumes, Thrym gazed to the cottages and bungalows crowding the base of the manor hill. "Cheevie's gathered everyone in Wright Court. The boars will attack there next."

Chisulo set his jaw. "Then, the Brave Tails must get there first."

"That's crazy stupid." Frikee glowered at the burning manse. "Them pig warriors are on a killing frenzy. They gone hog wild. We can't stand against them."

Chisulo and Olweena had already rushed into the storm, heading downhill.

Thrym took hold of the fox mask, voice raised loudly against the tempest. "You're a Brave Tail, Frikee. But nobody's brave unless they're scared. Right?"

Frikee pulled away from the fanatical mouse. *Mammy told me to stay off this crazy mountain!* He lowered his head, overwhelmed by the twists of fate that had delivered him to that night, and then lay down in the slant rain. "Awright, Squinty. Get on. Let's go get ourselves killed."

Down in Wright Court, Squire Cheevie gazed at his ancestral manor ablaze in the storm. Watching the driving rain and leaping fire dancing together, the heartsick mouse felt his whole life was some horrible dream.

"Our home!" Magdi wailed and buried her face in Squire Cheevie's ruffled blouse. He embraced her with one arm and with the other raised a rusty saber toward the conflagration.

Two armadillo smithies and a mongoose with a pitchfork knelt atop an ivy archway to Wright Court, and three chipmunks and four hares bearing makeshift lances waited nervously in the courtyard. They were the only ones that remained of Cheevie's battalion. The others had fled along with all the artisans of the hamlet and the field workers.

"We'll build a finer home," the squire consoled his wife in a numb voice. "Take refuge with the remaining females, dearest. Go quickly. I need you to show courage and see that the wives of my soldiers survive."

Magdi accepted this fateful charge, casting frequent, desponding looks over her shoulder. The curtains of rain and lowering thunder tightened her foreboding. She wanted to rush back to stand with her spouse to the death. Then, she laid eyes on the wheelwright's stable, where a wagon waited, bearing the female hares, chipmunks, armadillos, and the mongoose whose husbands had chosen to remain with their squire. Two harnessed pygmy antelopes shuffled, eager to be away. The expressions of alarm on the faces of the females squeezed her heart.

"I'm here with you, ladies. Be strong! We shall ride together to Fernholt and report this atrocity to the Council. These loathsome boars will pay with blood for what they do this day. That's what our husbands want."

"The squire ain't hired us'n to fight," one of the antelopes complained, and the wagon began to roll. "Let's git from here whilst we kin!"

"Too late!" one of the armadillo wives shrieked. "Look!"

Across the courtyard, Cheevie and his soldiers sprinted in frantic retreat. Directly behind them tumbled a landslide of flames. Griml and his boar warriors had shoved downhill huge blazing timbers from the burning manor, incinerating everything in their path. The stone wall crashed inward, and fiery debris plowed through the gate, igniting tool sheds, trellises and rooftops. A tempest from hell preceded the armored boars charging into the courtyard.

"Let's git!" an antelope yelped, and his wild-eyed partner agreed, "Through the back gate afore we git crisped!"

"Wait!" Magdi shouted at the leaping pygmy antelopes dragging behind them the wagon of wailing females. "There's another boar! I don't see the giant! Ull is missing!"

"We ain't waitin' on ye!" The antelopes broke for the open gateway at the far side of Wright Court. "Every animal fer his own self!"

Under drilling rain, the antelopes galloped. The wagon rocked violently behind them, and its blurred wheels splashed sheets of water to either side.

From the hedgerows outside the gateway, with a roar as big as the storm itself, Ull burst forth. The pygmy antelopes reared with terrified screams desperate to stop their frantic lunge. Too late they recognized their fatal error as their exposed underbellies slammed into Ull's upraised tusks.

The mighty Ull lifted both impaled antelopes into the air, their thrashing hooves pounding clumsily against his horned helmet. The bawling passengers tumbled out the tailgate and fell over one another as they fled back into the blazing hamlet.

"I eat yore brains!" Ull yelled at the scurrying animals. Shaking viciously, the immense boar toss the antelopes aside. Then, he rammed the wagon, dashing it to splinters. "Out yore roasted skulls, I eat yore brains!"

Cheevie and his soldiers ran to encircle the females, lances leveled, eyes swollen with soot and fear. Smoke and flames gushed from cottages on either side. Ull drove howling through the shattered wagon, as across the courtyard, Griml and the other warriors bore down, screaming barbarous curses and cries.

"Enough!" Cheevie shouted, lowering his saber, his voice shivering to sobs. "You boars—enough! Griml! Enough! You have destroyed all I have. No more killing!"

"Oh, plumpkins! No!" Magdi honked a loud sob, then straightened abruptly. "Give me one of those!" She reached out and snatched a lance from a chipmunk. "We will die fighting! We will not surrender to you—you monsters! You evil . . . things!"

"*Evil?*" Griml skidded to a stop and stayed his ferocious fighters with a slashing sign from his tail: *Here be sport, lads! First we mock—then we kill!* His scar-lumped snout wrinkled in a sneer at the feisty, fat mouse, and he shouted against crackling timbers, "Boars be evil? An' puny beasties be good? Aye? Them be small-minded thorts, m'lady!"

He swung forelimbs wide and raised disfigured tusks to the storm sky, hollering, "This world rolls 'pon horizons ruthless bigger than the likes o' good an' evil! Behold!" He swung his stare to either side, leering at the fires in the pounding rain.

"We boars done this! Aye! We brung fright to thee an' we drug thee down into a disasterish pit!" The boar lord cocked the hammer of his musket. "We done this not wit' evil, ye runty darters! Wit' strength! Boars be strong. 'Tis thee gnawers an' bug eaters wut be evil. Thee be weak! We live—an' thee be *killt*!"

Lightning struck across the sky in chains of blue fire. In that splendor, a fox bounded through the back gate carrying three animals. Griml's tusks, sweeping toward the fat squire and his fatter wife, jerked aside with surprise.

"By the Twelve Swollen—"

The fox leaped onto Ull's broad and bristly back, and with two white paws drove a small gold sword through a gap in the leather armor between the beast's shoulder blades.

Ull squealed and bucked wildly. The fox held fast, his hindquarters wagging in the air, white-tipped tail whipping. The three riders launched heavenward. Two capes swelled like sails, and they glided into the churning smoke of the courtyard. The third tumbled to the ground with a splat at Cheevie's boots.

Chisulo sat up, begrimed and ghastly, at the feet of his squire. "Slay boars!" he croaked defiantly and toppled over.

Out of the dense air, two hooded mice landed in a running rush in front of the boars. Their swords streaked like gold lightning, and the boar lord flinched backward grunting.

"Boars—attack!" Griml roared and fired his musket point-blank at the nearest costumed creature. The hammer clacked uselessly against the damp powder pan, and the boar flung the weapon like a mallet, cracking a hare between the eyes. "Attack!"

"Dead Riders!" the mongoose yelped at the caped mice that vanished in the spinning smoke. "Dead Riders are here!" He took a hop, hurling his pitchfork with vigor. The weapon wobbled through the rain and embedded itself upon the snout of a lunging boar, dropping him skidding to his knees. "Come on! It's Rumner and the Dead Riders!"

Squire Cheevie blinked rain and tears from his eyes and, to steady his gaze, pointed his saber at Ull, who had crashed to the ground, black blood vomiting from his snarled mouth, eyes blind. "I'll be pickled!" he bawled when Rumner the Swift jumped from the dead giant and bolted by, bloody weapon slashing at the rain.

"It's them!" Magdi gasped and clutched at the squire. "It's really the Dead Riders!" Her enormous eyes tightened suddenly. "Ladies!" She raised her lance at the females cowering alongside the shattered wagon. "Flee or fight!"

The sight of Ull dead and caped animals flitting through the ruins stymied the boars' attack. Griml jarred to a halt even as he began to move forward, and he cried out gruffly, "It be a trap! That's wut! A trap! Fall back!"

Trotters clattering over rainy cobbles, boars collided. Out of the tangled smoke, they watched fox and caped mice swiping at them with bittie swords.

Thrym, cape held wide, alighted on the pitchfork-wounded boar and gouged his gold sword through the eye slit of the beast's helmet. Thrashing and barking like a dog, the boar went down. Another boar rushed to his rescue, and hares ricocheted from out the smoky tumult and pierced his flank with two lances.

"Fall back, I says!" Griml and the remaining boars retreated into the stifling haze. Blind and choking, they rushed toward the gate.

Caped creatures pursued; tusks stabbed. Nimbly the hooded assailants dodged these panicked blows and scuffled closer. Onto Griml's flank, the fox vaulted, and the two somersaulted in a blur of hooves and paws before Frikee rolled off and disappeared again behind seething vapors.

"Run, m'lord!" a boar whimpered, hide flayed open, poison staggering his retreat. "Run!"

Vexed by not knowing what manner of beasts savaged his squad, Griml gawked about, despairing of a direction he could trust.

"This way, lord!" A powerful young scout barged through the gloom. "The path clears yon. Follow close!" He charged toward escape before battle-wise Griml, cynic of easy breaks, could restrain him.

Olweena plunged directly in the path of the proudly sprinting boar. The mouse maiden feinted a thrust and skipped aside. As her quarry twisted about in an attempt to dodge her, Thrym and Frikee sprang from the shadows, and their swords jabbed, scoring flesh in hot sprays of blood.

The brawny boar reeled, enraged and terrorized. Crouching defensively, he slashed his tusks, striking emptiness with agonized convulsions. His bleating cries pummeled Griml like blows, and the boar lord, whimpering, ducked swiftly into the darkness.

Epilog:

After the Rain

Come sunrise, the storm had passed, and clouds floated in the sky's blue enormity. The ruins of the manor house smoldered through morning mist. A charred smell mingled with damp, green scents of cypress and larch. Where Wright Court had been, the terrain looked like a charcoal sketch.

Vidar surveyed the devastation from the waterfall that concealed his slitherhole. He lay low to avoid detection by thrushes and sparrows flitting among smoky sunbeams. Hideous doubts and fears clustered in his heart, and he felt as though his fate had fractured all around him.

Perhaps the Brave Tails possessed magic stronger than his. Perhaps they could indeed return from the pit of the slain as the Dead Riders. Maybe that shrew imp who had defiled the sacred icons of the hairless apes and ruptured the viper's dreamcasting power was no mere vandal.

Of course! Vidar slid sideways, attentive to the flurrying birds. *The Dead Riders dispatched that little terror to weaken me so they could repel the boars without my interference.*

Paranoia shocked him with suspicions that the Dead Riders

had been watching him all along from the spirit world. They had murdered his family and had left him alive so they could toy with him! That freaky thought stole so much blood from his brain, his vision charred at the edges.

Terrified, he corkscrewed through the waterfall's icy tumult intent on fleeing back to the Tarn. The dousing steadied his nerves, and he paused at the cleft rock of the slitherhole. The static noise filling the chamber behind the cascade calmed him.

Griml escaped the Dead Riders. The still depths of Vidar's mind contained his telepathic bond with the boar lord. *Griml lives!* That fact quieted the last of his reckless anxiety. *The magic of the Brave Tails is not infallible. The boar lord may yet find his way back through Weasel's Pass and direct the swine legions' invasion of Riversplash Mountain. And if not—*

A plan expanded like blown glass, shaping itself around hot, breathy thoughts of revenge. He would rebuild his dream den, clean the frescoes honoring the sleek simians and ignite again the lamps of sacred dung. He would reclaim dreamspace. He would discover from where that diabolic little shrew had come and break open the secret of the Brave Tails. When Vidar next used his dreamcasting skill to summon the boars, no zombies would thwart him.

Trembling with resolve, the serpent slid into dreamspace, leaving behind defeat, leaving behind fear and doubt and all those perilous eyes in a sky full of dawn's promise.

The Avian Guild had conveyed news of the boars' defeat to most of the refugees of Bracken Knoll, and the grounds thronged with animals who had returned to rebuild the estate. A starling found Olweena and Thrym drowsing on a woodsy hillside above the high meadows of Bracken Knoll. Frikee crouched in the evergreen shrubs, guarding the equipage of the Brave Tails and keeping himself well out sight, shrinking into his infamy as a wanted criminal.

"Hey-dee thar, ye stragglin' mice!" The starling lit on a bristly branch of hemlock. "Have ye heard 'bout Bracken Knoll?" The bird relayed a breathy account of the Dead Riders' victory in fire and rain and then departed as quickly as she had arrived, eager to carry the tidings of Riversplash Mountain's ghostly heroes.

"Haw! The whole mountain's buzzing 'bout us!" Frikee's grinning head stuck out from the shrubs. "I 'spect if we showed ourselves at Fernholt, bugles and a confetti parade gone commemorate my pardon."

Bespectacled Thrym offered a weary shake of his head. "The Council's gratitude might falter some when they learn that the boar lord himself got away from us in the night."

"We better join Notty in the Tarn." Olweena exhaled a sharp, fierce sigh. "All we've accomplished is the destruction of Bracken Knoll. Nothing's changed. The boars are coming to Riversplash Mountain."

"Mercy, mousie!" Frikee stood and brushed dead leaves from his scabbed chest. "You're tougher than the average walnut."

"Frikee and I know you're right, Olweena." Thrym canceled any possible retort from the polecat with a quick, pressured stare. Then, he helped the ragged mouse maiden to stand and glanced at the black blood crusting the stump of her tail. "But before we return to the Tarn, you and I are going down to Bracken Knoll and get some proper medical attention for your wound."

"And provisions for our quest." The air around Olweena was charged and disturbed. "I'm not coming back from the Tarn until I find the white squirrels."

"Right." Thrym took her paw and led her across a ground of

fallen needles and cones. "I'll return later today, Frikee, with some food and drink for you."

"Yaw, Squinty! Make that a bacon sandwich!"

"The poison from the swords!" Thrym gasped and looked with alarm to Olweena. "If the squire barbeques those dead boars . . . "

She dismissed his concern in a bland voice. "The meat is not poisoned. When I cut off Kungu's tail, his blood got all over me. Whatever venom is on those swords breaks down almost instantly or I'd be dead."

"In that case," Frikee called after them, "throw in a side of pork rinds, too!"

The polecat sunk smiling under the shrub into feathered darkness and stifled a yawn. *Ain't mammy amazed what this loony mountain made of her little criminal.* An easy laugh drifted with him into luxurious slumber.

Thrym escorted Olweena down a mossy stairway between two slender waterfalls, and crossed the heath silently. Her eyes burned. The sight of the manor house razed to charred brick unbridled more malice than she could voice.

Beyond the parkland, the mice reached a mill converted to an infirmary. Chisulo greeted them, wearing a head bandage, his spats muddy, trousers and singlet torn. "Maiden Talkingstone! Thrym, sir!" The hamster's eyes glimmered, and he whispered with comradely pride, "Outstanding victory! The Brave Tails thrashed those filthy boars and sent lord Griml packing! Wonderful! Simply wonderful!"

"Bracken Knoll is destroyed." Olweena stared off, eyes glazed. "The boars will return. They will trample all the estates to mud. They will eat orchids while Fernholt burns."

Chisulo dropped his monocle into his paw, and his eyes went dull and flat.

"Griml escaped." Thrym flittered his whiskers. "Maiden Talkingstone isn't feeling very well. Is there anyone here competent to dress her wound?"

The hamster motioned to the mill's long threshing room. Trestle tables covered with burlap sacks served as cots upon which the wounded bled or lay stiffly with misshapen heads and plastered limbs.

"Maiden Talkingstone, I shall see that the marmot physician who so excellently treated my head injury attends to you." Chisulo edged closer to the mouse maiden, absorbed by her blue eyes and the anguish he met there. He addressed her very quietly, "Place lord Griml well out of mind, miss. Likewise, put aside all trepidation about the Boar March. You survived your tragedy on Blossom Vale and served valiantly with the Brave Tails—all this to bring us gentle animals of Riversplash Mountain that most precious and fragile treasure—hope."

Olweena took this in somberly. Ragged, filthy, and stinking like sour meat, she knew she appeared a wretch. Yet, what this hamster said made her feel possessed of a promise. She had slain boars. *Kungu—and nameless others* . . . Their blood could not atone for her losses—all the same she sensed that as soon as she had cleansed herself and bound her wound, she would have some hope to offer these animals. A peculiar patience settled over her, and with almost childlike expectation, she knew, *I belong with the Brave Tails.*

"Thank you, Chisulo." From her muddy pocket, she took her black cowl, balled up in her paw, and breathed its husky scent of summer twilight. "I almost forgot what this mountain has given me—and what I owe."

Chisulo fit his monocle in place and winked knowingly.

"Go and see your sister," Olweena spoke to Thrym in a mild

voice, all gloom gone out of her, replaced by a cool confidence. She returned the magical fabric to her pocket. "Magdi must be distraught by all this destruction."

"You don't know Magdi." Thrym nodded gratitude to Chisulo and affectionately squeezed Olweena's arm. "Take your rest here. We've a long journey ahead."

Watching the mouse maiden walk off, sullied with blood and matted dirt, her white fur now the color of wet ashes, Thrym thought he beheld an allegory of beauty and pain.

Down among the ruins of Wright Court, the squire and other combatants had stripped the dead boars and thrown their carcasses onto the embers of burnt sheds and cottages. An aroma of roasted pork rode the morning wind of the Holt, the succulent fragrance luring from hiding those that the Avian Guild had not yet alerted. Astounded animals straggled out of the woods, and Thrym joined them.

Cheevie and Magdi, the fur of their faces slick with grease, whiskers dripping bacon fat, greeted the residents returning to find their homes demolished. In yellow morning light, they feasted on crisped boars with ravens and crows and other true omnivores— gerbils, rats and lemmings—who shared their roused appetite for the flesh of beasts that would have eaten them.

Cheevie treated those creatures incapable of eating meat with pastries made from grains roasted in fire pits well away from the boar corpses. Strutting among blackened beams and rubble, the squire blustered, "We had to destroy those pigs. And—by the Dancing Drunk Red Rodent's Blessed Whiskers—my warriors and I did! Good creatures died and the manor house and our hamlet are lost, yet we fought with such valor that the Dead Riders themselves rose up and fought at our side. Yes, indeed!

Ask any who stood with us in our grim hour last night. With phantoms beside us, we fought Griml and his boar bullies—and we are victorious!"

Magdi, whiskers seared to curly black wires beaded with hog fat, sat on a cinder pile in her frazzled gown nibbling at one of Ull's uncommonly large ribs. Her admiring regard of her husband's oratory snapped when she spotted Thrym in the crowd. She dropped the charred rib, rushed over, and swept her bespectacled little brother off his feet. "Vim Thrym! You are safe!"

The squire cast a jaundiced eye on his brother-in-law. "So our cowardly Thrym crawls back. Obviously you succeeded in finding a safe hiding place elsewhere on the mountain while your betters defended our females and the honor of our ancestral estate. You never had much stomach for a fight, did you, boy?"

Before Thrym could speak, Magdi intervened, "Squire, show our brother some charity. After all, he's just a crofter of the Mere, not a mouse of arms such as you."

Cheevie continued glaring at Thrym as he mumbled, "Yes, dearest."

"Cheevie, you must dispatch messengers at once to Fernholt." Thrym did not flinch before the squire's stern, smoke-addled eyes. "Warn them that Griml has escaped. He may well be impossible to track. We should post guards at Weasel's Pass and search for him. If the boar lord gets through . . . "

Cheevie canted his head curiously. "How ever are you aware that Griml escaped?"

"Since I left here, I've been hiding in the woods above the estate," Thrym breezily lied. "At night, I visit the mills to get food. Last night, I saw everything. You and a handful of animals fought gallantly."

"Indeed!" Cheevie lifted his chin. "You observed the Dead Riders joining our defense?"

"Of course!" Thrym made his eyes big. "Why do you think I was afraid to come down until morning? They're ghosts!"

"Grim Thrym!" Magdi enclosed her brother in a robust hug. "You're safe now. And you have seen how courageously the squire defended us. So you must never be grim again. Put aside all thoughts of returning to that despicable Mere. You shall help us rebuild. And Bracken Knoll shall ever more be your home."

"I'm going to get something to eat." Thrym squirmed free and spoke to Cheevie's back as the squire returned to his victory feast, "Warn Fernholt, Cheevie. Block Weasel's Pass."

"Yes, yes, at once, of course," the squire assured, waving jubilantly without turning about. *Uppity Mere trash, presuming to instruct me, stout Cheevie, Defender of the Hearth. Pish!*

Before his sister could clutch him again, Thrym dodged into the festive crowd. He wandered out of Wright Court and up a bridle path, searching for a creek where he could bathe.

The artisans had set up tarpaulins among the giant trees, temporary canvas housing for their families. Mothers and children fetched water from a brook and tended small fires on rock shelves above. Field workers, obeying the squire's orders, distributed sacks of barley flour from the mills, and the toasted smell of griddlecakes and cockroach crunchies folded into the breezes of early morning.

Higher up the hill, the mouse came upon a brook that veered into an eddy. Bullrushes provided privacy, and he stripped and immersed himself. Lathering with a foxglove's frothy, aromatic pith, he rinsed away the grime and sweat of his adventures. He sudsed up his dingy tunic and beat it clean on a flat rock.

Wrapping the tunic about his waist, he strolled the redwoods, letting morning sun and wind dry him. At the hillcrest, he stood on a ledge and removed his lenses.

Before him sprawled all of Riversplash Mountain below the Tarn. To either side, the fog of the Cloud Forest flowed like a ghost river and ran off into the oceanic sky. Great pines clung to the cliffs of the Holt, and waterfalls poured their mists into space. The cascades crashed among headwaters of the Rill and dispersed rivers and streams across farmland into the bogs of the Mere.

"We've got to open the rock weirs," he spoke aloud, without heat. "If we don't—the boar hordes will devastate all of this." He closed his eyes. "All of it."

"Are you ready for my next prophecy?" a calm voice spoke. "Or have you seen all that you want to see?"

"Moon?" Thrym opened one eye suspiciously. "You're a new moon. Close to the sun. You're not supposed to speak."

"Oh, I still talk freely when I am with the sun—but what I have to say, he knows before I've begun."

Thrym staggered backward, face lifted to the sky, bedazzled blind. Squinty squinted through tight fingers, detecting not the slightest shadow of moon in the sun's blazing presence. "Why? Why are you talking to me now? You've never done this before."

A breezy laugh descended out of the glare. "You've rarely been this high on the mountain before. And what I have to tell you may help you endure."

"Endure?" Thrym swung his head to the side and peeked upward from the corner of one eye. "You mean—survive?"

"If you want to stay alive, you better learn to contrive."

Thrym's squint deepened to a frown. "Contrive what?"

"The boars' invasion of this mountain is your peril"—the moon's voice lowered ominously—"yet all your strategies are entirely sterile."

"Mud and garlic!" The mouse stepped right to the brink of the ledge as if summoning the whole mountain to pay attention as he pointed up at the wide crater behind him. "We're going to the Tarn to find someone to wake up the squirrel princess Hati, who . . . "

The moon clucked disapprovingly. "I'm speaking to you, Thrym, because you're doomed. Among the rocks of the Tarn you'll be entombed."

"Hey! If I'm doomed why bother prophesying?"

"What I have to say is not good news, but when it comes to fate one can't pick and choose."

"Then, why bother?" The mouse flung his arms out to either side. "Why talk to me?"

A placid chuckle flowed around him as cool as moonlight. "Because, Thrym, you can hear, and I like to watch your fear."

"My mother warned me about you." He switched his tail back and forth. "She said that anybody who listened too closely to you would go crazy."

"Well, then, Thrym, are we there, yet?" Another chuckle coursed the air. "Is your sanity at threat?"

"Yes." Thrym lowered his head and spoke meekly, "Yes, I think so, moon. You've just told me I'm doomed."

"Are you really surprised? Come on! Everything living dies."

Thrym kicked a pebble over the ledge and mumbled, "I know that."

"What's the problem, then? I didn't say when." The moon gave a casual laugh. "You jumped to an assumption. That shows some lack of gumption."

"You *are* driving me crazy, moon." Both angry and pleading, Thrym raised his voice, "So, I'm going to die someday and be buried in the Tarn. Great. Tell me about the boar invasion of Riversplash Mountain. Are we going to stop them?"

The moon's voice went cold. "Why do you act like a dunce? I've already told you once."

"Maybe I *am* a dunce." Thrym paced back and forth on the ledge. "Why do you think I've been farming the same croft for three years and still have nothing to show for it? And now I'm in love with a maiden whose life I've saved twice and she's so heartbroken she can't love me back. Yes, moon, I'm a dunce." He came to a halt. "So, tell me again—do we stop the March?"

"Chew your knuckles while the viper chuckles." The moon sounded soggy with boredom and continued in a drone, "I-see-the-frightened-Brave-Tails-blunder, and-the-mighty-boars-march-like-thunder. If-you-are-unmasked-in-the-suspense, then-all-of-your-lives-become-past-tense."

"Yeah, I remember that. Too well." Thrym twitched his whiskers pensively. "That viper—Vidar—the dreamcaster, he's behind all this somehow. He scares me. But he didn't make me blunder. I was afraid when I faced him, but I didn't blunder." His voice crackled with exasperation. "What's going to frighten the Brave Tails? What's our blunder?"

Silence floated on the sunbeams.

"Oh, don't go coy on me." He pressed a blind stare into the sky. "You're not going to leave it at that?"

The moon said with gentle ire, "I'm unhappy you made me repeat. No more till the boars end their retreat."

"Fine. Have it your way." Thrym sat on the ledge, legs dangling over the side. "Talking with you I always feel like something bad is about to happen."

The vista of bluffs, waterfalls, and the distant and lofty crags soothed him. Listening to the songs of flocking birds quieted his breath. He felt good. So the moon had told him death would bury him in the Tarn. At least, he had gotten out of the Mere—just as he had promised himself, though not as he had expected. He had become more than he had ever hoped.

A Brave Tail!

He rocked his jaw to one side and smiled at himself. Maybe he would blunder. Maybe the boar horde would tear this mountain apart. But no horror could ever deprive him of his one true pride. "I am a Brave Tail," Thyrm said aloud, arms spread to the world below him.

"Who are you talking to?" Olweena approached from among the trees. She wore fresh garments, a blue tunic and a miller's tan breeches. "You sound serious."

Thyrm jumped upright, the rims of his ears burning. "What are you doing up here?"

"You're not so hard to find. Everybody on this estate knows the squire's brother-in-*love*." She tossed an astonishingly carefree laugh his way. A bath in the mill pond and a fresh bandage on her severed tail had restored her well-being. And the physician's surprise that her wound had healed with no trace of infection put a spring in her step. "So, who are you talking to?"

"The moon." His ears crimped, awaiting her derision. "He prophesies for me."

"He did that for my auntie, too." She strolled up to him. "He likes ambiguity and riddles, so I wouldn't take too literally anything he says about dying."

"You heard all that?"

"Pretty much." She sat at the rock ledge, carefully cushioning her docked tail. "You *are* a dunce if you think I can't love you."

"What?" Thyrm sat. He fumbled his lenses onto his nose. "What are you saying?"

"Sure, I'm heartbroken." She faced him peacefully. "But what

Chisulo said is true. Surviving the tragedy of Blossom Vale and Griml's treachery is pointless unless I can bring this mountain some hope. And with hope comes love."

Thrym asked in a cracked whisper, "You—you can love *me*?"

"You're a strong mouse—and courageous. You put my life before yours. It's not hard for me to love you." She redirected her stare to the snowy horizons. "I lost everything." She looked at him again, her eyes bright, not crying yet shimmering. After a moment, she said, "I need someone to love, to stand with me against my emptiness. I need someone strong." She placed a paw on his thick forearm. "I need you."

At that moment, he became keenly aware that he was sitting half naked at the edge of the world, tunic knotted about his waist, a breeze ruffling the beige fur of his shoulders and chest.

"You look fine," she said, reading the embarrassment in his smile. "You're not very comfortable with females, are you?"

"I don't have a lot of experience." He crossed his eyes in goofy acknowledgment of his spectacles. Then, he bowed his head. "In fact, I don't have any. I'm hopeless with the mouse maidens. Who would want a suitor that can't whisker-tickle or dance in the glades without bumping snouts?"

Olweena took Thrym's head tenderly in her paws and lifted his face until their pink noses touched. She swept her whiskers forward, fluttering them against his, and in a soft breath promised, "*I* do."